Lost In The Slipstream

James Cahill

ISBN-10: 1-4810-3469-3
ISBN-13: 9781481034692

Slipstream

1. The turbulent flow of air driven backward by the propellers of an aircraft.

2. The area of reduced pressure or forward suction produced by and immediately behind a fast-moving object as it moves through air or water.

intr.v. slipstreamed, slipstreaming, slipstreams

To drive or cycle in the slipstream of a vehicle ahead.

“We fall in love, perhaps three times in a hundred years.”
The Plague
Albert Camus

“At the end of patience, you will learn, is a great anger.”
Gorky Park
Martin Cruz Smith

“In my mind, I’m probably the biggest sex maniac you ever saw.”
The Catcher in the Rye
J.D. Salinger

“You must urinate in the same spot if you wish to make foam.”
West African village proverb

Prologue

Women are magic.

Observe in silent reverence: the casual drape of a sweater over a wondrous hip as its owner shifts her weight, to the left... to the right, or the fall of a single, errant braid across a lovely face, or a graceful, rhythm-inspired move onto a dance floor. It can be no more than a giggle at a dropped frisbee, or better yet, a pair of quiet, dark eyes lingering upon us for a brief but startling extra moment, and we are gone, floating on a tsunami of affection, and she hasn't even uttered a word.

Women are magic: The classic beauty, the inadvertently sexy, the cleavage-popping sledge-hammer provocative, the sharp and articulate, the slickly sarcastic, the small and impish, the poised and elegant, the shy and mysterious - even the big, bold and brassy can weave a spell that knock us flat and leave us dead in the water.

Inner beauty?

Outer beauty?

"Whatever it is," the great Jimi Hendrix sang, "That girl's put a spell on me."

'*Whatever it is.*' This is the question! Does it emanate from the woman herself, radiating, quasar-style, in an outward direction? Or does it reside in some fascinating, receptive chemistry in the lens of the observer? And how, may I ask, can a woman simultaneously leave one man cold and put another man's jaw on the floor? This would incline toward the lens theory, but then, some rare, unbelievable creatures blithely slay us all.

As the Girl from Ipanema strolls famously to the sea, "*when she passes, each one she passes, goes 'Ahhh!'*" An American bastardized version of this transporting little tune has only 'the fellows' saying it, but in the original, Brazilian, Joao Gilberto rendition, everyone - men *and* women – releases this spontaneous gasp of enchantment. To what do we attribute this involuntary, audible and gender-neutral expulsion of breath? Well, let's not be pollyannish here. It wasn't some random haze that filled Mr. Hendrix' brain; it was a purple haze. This was no casual, indifferent selection from the color wheel.

We can pretend to shop for radials or look for the best deal on French Roast, but it's feminine magic that underpins our every moment, electrifying us, giving our lives a delicious edge, and, if we care to think about it, when unsubjugated and set free, provides the spark that uplifts entire societies.

But despite our founding fathers' decree, all are not created equal. A tiny fraction of the feminine tribe, residing at the far, torturous edge of the bell curve, possess the gift in such prodigious quantities, that they routinely body slam us - easily, mercilessly, often involuntarily - into a neighboring dimension of desire, agony, vertigo and worship, an experience perhaps best described by Mr. Hendrix himself, poetically, and backed by a screaming Stratocaster. *Purple haze all in my brain.*

Songs, poems, epics are written about such women. One of these rare creatures actually graced my simple, pedestrian life for a brief, extraordinary period. I was shocked. I am neither handsome, bad-boy dangerous, or, for that matter, even particularly confident. And I confess with some embarrassment to being pretty much broke my entire life. Thus, her sudden, inexplicable presence had the feel of a strange, impossible accident, the universe briefly, terrifyingly out of kilter. Women like that simply don't pay attention to me.

But by God, there she was.

"Lucky you!" would be an obvious response, but I'm far more compelled to wonder: Was this a blessing or a curse?

Even Jimi goes bi-polar on this formidable question, moving from, "*'Scuse me, while I kiss the sky!*" to a plea of unalloyed desperation: "*Help me!*"

The magic of women: misery or bliss?

Perhaps both; I really can't say. But the whole miraculous nightmare began with a visit to my dying father. Dad was in the hospital, and I sat at his bedside with a very difficult announcement to make.

chapter

ONE

"Timothy. Boychick. Talk to your father. What's rattling around in that keppela of yours?"

My brother Robert and I glanced quickly to the doorway of the hospital room to see if anyone was in earshot. Dad's cavalier use of Yiddish in public was always embarrassing. The hall was clear. And my sick father, amid tubes, medical gadgetry, and a strong scent of rubbing alcohol, had asked his question. Now he sat up in the hospital bed and watched as I fidgeted nervously under the gaze of his patient, blue-gray eyes.

My dad, Jerome Lewis - Levitsky, prior to Ellis Island - was in his late sixties, and though he never smoked, a black, cancerous spot had been discovered on his right lung. The lung was removed, but his illness spread and was soon diagnosed as inoperable. This was back in May, and he'd been given seven, eight months tops. I lived in Hermosa beach, and Mom tearfully broke the news over the phone, just after I returned home from another long and difficult day of teaching jr. high school English in the gang and drug-infested area known as South Central Los Angeles.

But now, while Robert and I visited on this hot, mid-July evening, despite the horrific circumstances, I had decided, after putting it off for months, it was time to come clean with my plan. I began casually, dismissively, mentioning only a need to chat. But this was family. Any attempt to bluff was transparent, even laughable. I sat uneasily at my father's bedside and wondered exactly how to explain what rattled, as he put it, around in my head. Robert, portly, balding, five years my senior, sat in a blue, vinyl chair along the far wall and was suddenly all ears. It was the absolute worst time for this, but I rallied my courage and spoke.

"I'm quitting teaching," I said, "and moving to San Francisco."

This information sat heavily in the air for a brief moment.

"Timothy," my father said, "Why are you quitting teaching?"

I cleared my throat and reached for a voice of rock-solid, phlegmless conviction. "I want to be a writer."

"A writer?"

While I did not anticipate high-fives and champagne, I was unprepared for the full and terrifying drama of my father's profound disappointment. His face wrinkled sourly. He looked down at his own liver-spotted hands, then raised his eyes heavenward and shook his head in silence.

Robert released a long, nasal exhale. He tried lamely to withhold a smirk, then pulled a small weekly planner from the breast pocket of a pressed, oxford cloth shirt. He clicked a ballpoint, opened the book and studied its contents. While this gesture was clearly a respectful attempt to allow us some kind of privacy, it was also aimed, I knew, at reminding us of his importance; his impossible schedule, his well-planned, prosperous life under complete control. My brother, a fabulously successful real estate agent, lived just over the bridge from San Francisco, in Rockridge, an upscale section of the East Bay. I hadn't actually seen or spoken to him for several years, until today in fact, when he flew down for this visit. We talked Mom into taking the night off, getting a break from her endless vigil with Dad. My brother and I then drove to the hospital in my rusting and dented yellow Honda Civic in near-complete silence.

"Timothy," my father said as he fiddled with a needle taped to the back of his hand. "How long do you plan to flounder?"

His assessment stung me. I looked down at my faded blue jeans and folded my arms over a green 10-k t-shirt. I slumped in my chair and considered the image of a large flat fish, with two, blank, befuddled eyes on one side of its head, flopping helplessly on a deck. Here it was: the symbol, chosen by my very own dad, for my life. It implied that I had accomplished nothing; that my twenty-seven years on earth had amounted to little more than self-indulgent frivolity. I had wanted this announcement made then passed over immediately in light of the bigger issue, which of course was Dad's health. I did not wish to be the main event when he was so ill. But I knew his question held another, deeper concern. Dad had already begun the little gestures of getting things in order, of seeing friends and relatives one final time; all part of an impossible effort, I imagined, to die in some kind of peace. Where his sons and wife were headed, I knew, held a sudden, consuming importance for him.

"I've *been* floundering," I said. "I can't stand teaching."

"But... *writing?*" He took a weary breath with his single, remaining lung. "I want to know my sons are set in life. Timothy. You need to earn a living."

Robert leaned forward in his chair. Then, without excusing himself, he exited. I think he mumbled 'take a leak' but I really couldn't hear him. Without my brother in the room, I felt the heat of my father's focus more directly.

Dad - paunchy, bad posture, balding on top, a gray mustache, and who frankly, never did seem particularly healthy - had now entered a level of frailty that was truly frightening. He hunched against his pillows and frowned. "Timothy. Artists... they're all... miserable alcoholics. They suffer. Is it too much to ask that I don't want my sons to suffer? I really hoped all that traveling would settle you down." He stared down at the white sheets covering his thin legs and added, "I really did."

James Cahill

Chased from Germany by Hitler, my dad, through some shrewd planning and impressive touch and go maneuvering on the part of his own father, came as a boy to New York with the rest of the Levitsky family. There, he grew up, met Mom, and continued west to California. Travel had little appeal for him, probably as his own experience of seeing the world had been fraught with watching his parents set up new lives in strange, dangerous countries, then decamping overnight to someplace safer. He wasn't pleased with my travels, which included an extended, shoestring excursion around the world, working here and there to pay for it. The whole venture struck him, I knew, as an aimless postponement of the real business of life.

Still, when I returned home after two years, I saw that Dad had thumb tacked a world map to the wall in the den. He charted my trip with a felt tip pen, jotting details: *Worked on a sheep shearing gang in New Zealand. Taught English in Thailand. Worked on a farm in Australia.* He checked out books on places I'd visited, went to museum exhibits when available - Aboriginal Art, Pacific Island Masks, African Cloth, Indian Architecture, Nepalese religion. But upon my return, he was bent on seeing me get serious. And he seemed particularly so now.

"Why not earn a living first? Get settled. You want a job at the post office? It's a good career. I can make a few calls. In your spare time you can write."

My father learned about his illness just after he retired. He was a postmaster, working his way up for thirty-five years. But *a good career?* I had watched him face postal work with boredom, then hatred, and finally a kind of numb bitterness. And I didn't wish to tell him that I had been writing. I learned quickly that nothing gets written in your spare time, you had to give it your prime time.

Each of my three years of teaching, I signed the contract, then looked down the road at nine months of depression that had me flattened by Thanksgiving. Why would a job at a post office be any different? I only knew this: I wanted to write, and a person just couldn't *do anything.* Of course, wanting to write is one thing; having talent is quite another. For this, I had only a bit of inspiration in the form of an essay entitled 'Taking the Leap', written by my current favorite writer, the rising star, Jonah Woods. Paraphrasing Goethe, Mr. Woods sagely advised: *take the leap; great forces will come to your aid.* I looked up Goethe's original quote, typed it out in large print and ceremoniously magnetized it to my fridge. I wondered about the great forces. And I desperately hoped these two men had some privy knowledge as to how the universe operated, or this could quickly become a very embarrassing enterprise.

"Stubborn," my father said. "You always take the hardest path." Then, strangely, he shook his head and smiled wearily.

He took my hand.

This was unexpected. We were not a family of hand-holders.

My brother returned, took his seat and I wished he'd taken a bit longer.

Dad's tone softened. Though I kept my eyes on him, I could feel Robert behind me, listening with all his might. "It's no secret," Dad said. "I have a few months, my God... maybe... as much as half a year." He paused, considering the unbelievable truth of this. We all did.

By the end of the year, in all likelihood, my brother and I would no longer have a father. Had our mother, an avid fan of self-help books, been in the room just then, she would have chastised Dad, thrown an exuberant fist in the air and shouted, "Think positive!" then launched into a fiery lecture on the power of such an activity. I actually didn't understand why doctors tell patients how much time they have, but Dad continually asked, and I began to see his point. If there was a countdown to be known, just tell me, and let me adjust my plans and thoughts accordingly.

"To know it's all... almost... well... it makes you think." Dad said. "Crazy thoughts." He gazed off at the windows, then smiled, his voice somewhat lighter now. "You know, when I was a young man, I wanted to sing."

"*Really?*" I was shocked. I glanced at Robert, who also appeared surprised. Dad was a competent belter of the odd Sinatra tune around the house, but I had no idea about a desire to actually sing.

He nodded. "I even took a class! Before you guys were born. I never told your mother. I gave her some cockamamie story." He shrugged. "But you know what I think about now? Aside from my sons and my wife? You know what I think about?"

I watched him.

He looked at my brother. He looked at me. "I think about how much I loved those damn singing classes. Is that crazy?"

It would have been easy to say that it wasn't crazy, but I was intrigued. Where did your thoughts go at the end of your life? After thirty-five years in a post office?

"Timothy," he said. "If you want to do this... this... *writing*... I won't stop you. Ach! How can I stop you? You're twenty-seven. You're a man. You can make decisions. How you'll survive, I don't know." He looked hard at me now. "But please, listen to your father. *Don't fool around.* You choose this... you know... if you really choose this, other choices... they disappear. Doors close. Your friends... they'll be making money, buying houses, having kids... braces, mortgages, station wagons, saving for retirement..." He trailed off, watching me, considering, possibly, that none of this had dawned on me. But he exhaled, then shook his head, in blank, fatherly capitulation. And I wondered, just then, if someday, I would also be shaking my own head in a similar manner, over a *meshuggana* son for whom I only wanted the best.

Then, he smiled. "I only ask... if you really do this, I ask one... small... favor."

I looked at him. I waited.

He said, "Write something... beautiful... for your dad."

He patted me on the back of the head.

Though his tone had a kind of joshing, pregame, score-one-for-pop quality, I took him seriously - *the man was dying for Godsake* - and said that I would.

He was silent for a moment, then added, "San Francisco? Was there once," he said with distaste. "Place is fulla kooks."

I told him I knew about the kooks, and then he added sharply to my brother and me, "And maybe it wouldn't kill either of you to visit each other once in awhile?"

Robert studied his fingernails.

But these were my dad's instructions: that I should write something beautiful, and nothing like a little pressure. With this request, the nightmare of my father's impending death, and a wondrous, guilty thrill at leaving teaching forever, I burned every lesson plan I ever made then cruised up Highway 5 to that magical city by the bay.

It was mid-August, and conservatively, I figured with gloomy calculation, I had until December to write something beautiful.

But there on Highway 5, the elation was so intense, I thought I'd try something that had tempted me since taking Physics for Non-Majors in college. Professor Emerick had explained a phenomenon called a slipstream, which, in essence, was a vacuum created behind a moving object.

In the shimmering central valley heat a Mack Truck was banging along at eighty-five in the fast lane. I let it pass, signaled, changed lanes, then accelerated to match its speed. Carefully, I brought the front bumper of my tiny Honda... up... up... behind the huge truck until I was within a mere foot of it. Then, even closer. I held my breath, removed my foot from the gas, pressed the clutch and took the stick shift out of gear.

And there I was, by God - sucked along in the slipstream, floating down the highway, with no effort at all.

chapter

TWO

With our desks arranged in a large circle, sixteen students and one professor, each with a copy of my manuscript, sat facing each other in our eternally airless classroom. Even if a previous class left a window open, Nancy Stiers - a student who dressed in black and wore a silver hoop in her left nostril - upon entering, instantly closed it. "Could you maybe leave one open a crack?" I asked a few weeks back. "Get a little fresh air?"

"I'm cold," Nancy replied as she slammed the last window shut, and each week the room was soon so stuffy it was impossible to think. During breaks, Nancy and her black-clad friends gathered in the hall where they lit cigarettes and took long, wincing, one-eye-shut drags which they then released in slow, world-weary exhales.

Our professor, Joan Birnbaum, was the mildly acclaimed author of six unpopular, mixed reviewed novels - the most recent entitled, Giving Too Much - and the instructor of Fiction Writing 404, The Art of The Short Story. She wore black. Her hair was hennaed, styled severely - almost helmet-shaped - about her large head.

Her body was solid and boxy, which perhaps contributed to my sense of her as the ballast in the classroom. Nancy sat directly across from me, up front, one seat shy of Birnbaum's desk. Class had just begun. Students took out pens, arranged manuscripts - mine and another student's - and coffee cups. Of my classmates, five were dressed in black. Otherwise, torn, faded denim was most popular, along with a gallery of tattoos: a yin-yang graced an ankle to my right, a left arm across from me was densely adorned with a peacock-tail. Both genders sported earrings. A woman to my left had short, pink hair, and bright red lipstick. Beside her was a young man, slight of build, with a shaven head and a yoga mat strapped to his backpack.

But now, every student, including Prof. Birnbaum, held at my story. We were to write two for the semester; this was my first. And it seemed, not my manuscript they held, but rather, some part of me; some delicate, sensitive bodily organ to which they could induce either tremendous pleasure or excruciating pain, depending upon their whim. All were silent. Dr. Birnbaum nodded in my direction. Beneath fluorescent tubes, with a gray, mid-day light shining weakly through the windows, I thought: *Wish me luck, Pops.* I cleared my throat, and read:

Hunger

The young academic raced up the street.

Late for a department meeting, he flew past shops; women's lingerie, furniture, books, cosmetics. But to his astonishment he paused before a restaurant - one he'd never noticed before - with a sudden, powerful hunger. Had hunger ever blindsided him like this? He couldn't say, but then he felt something else: a strange, overwhelming allure emanating from the doorway. He scratched his scalp, shrugged, poked his head inside.

His eyes adjusted to the soft, muted light as a large space opened before him. He gazed over tables of fine, expertly carved wood. A porcelain vase sat in one corner, a broad-leafed potted plant in another. A vaulted ceiling arched high overhead, held by walls of cool, whitewashed stone. And a quiet, siren-call of elegance seemed to barely whisper its welcome.

I'm late already, he reasoned as he took a seat. He'd grab a quick bite then slip into the meeting mumbling about the traffic. Department meetings! To sit through the posturing and bombast on an empty stomach would be torture beyond endurance. Of course, he was up for tenure and needed to appear eager. And punctual. But I'm here, he thought; inside and let's just make this quick.

He glanced about for a waiter.

There was none. No maitre de. No hostess. What does one shout into such exquisite emptiness? "A menu!"

A woman appeared.

Appeared? Did he miss her approach? Had he been admiring the smooth Ionic pillars at the entrance? A seascape on the far wall? He couldn't say, but she stood before him with short, brown hair, a blue dress, and an overall presentation that finally, was unremarkable. For this he was mildly grateful. Beautiful women! The impulse toward hysteria! The frenzy to be clever! Well, he was free of both. She folded her arms neatly beneath her breasts. She gazed at him skeptically.

"Nice restaurant," he said with a smile. "May I see a menu?"

"A menu?"

He looked up at her. He nodded.

"Just like that?" she said.

"Pardon?"

"You just wander about like royalty, making demands of everyone?"

"Excuse me?" he said.

"Sir." The woman took an impatient breath. "Are you not surrounded by beauty?"

"I believe I've just indicated-"

"But have you truly *noticed...*" she said, glancing about, "a harmony in the design? A subtle... poetry... informing an ideal of gentle, unassuming grace?"

He stared at her. He blinked. He checked his watch. For politeness, he took the room in once more. White candlesticks rose from silver holders; linen napkins were held neatly in pewter rings. Was there more?

"It is... exceptionally harmonious," he said.

"So why must I point these things out?" she said. "It's quite humiliating."

The man blanched. He was, of course, a gentleman. He'd read the great books, knew his taste in art and music, had visited the fine museums of Europe. Yet here was a pretty woman - *when had she become* - and he'd offended her! But what more could he say? Of course, it wasn't beauty alone, but hunger that brought him through those double oak doors a moment ago. He was hungry.

If this was a challenge, well, despite the time, he was equal to it. He narrowed his eyes to achieve a look of sophistication. He looked, once more, around the room. He nodded. "The detail *is* exquisite. The workmanship beyond compare. The place has a certain... epic quality."

"Epic?" she said, her brow raised skeptically.

"Decidedly epic," he said, pleased with his adjective. Just then, his stomach growled. "But now I really would like something to eat."

"*Something to eat?* Just like that?"

"Excuse me," he said. "This *is* a restaurant, isn't it?"

"Last I checked," she said. Her sarcasm had a sassy, exhilarating edge, and each word; each defiant toss of her short, lustrous mane seemed, oddly, to rouse the hunger in his belly. "But I'm sorry," she said. "It's the cooks. They're not... in the mood to prepare anything."

"*The cooks must be in the mood-*"

"Of course!" She flung her gaze away, and her rolling eyes seemed to flash, ever so slightly, as she blinked.

"But my stomach... it's... growling!"

"I heard it," she said. "A moment ago. It was quite obvious."

"Was it?"

"A low, rumbling baritone."

"Oh dear!"

"Difficult thing to hide even if you wanted to," she said.

For poise, he adjusted his tie. He clasped his hands and placed them gently on the table. He pressed his lips together, forced a smile. "I'd love to talk more," he said. "I really would. But the fact is, and a nuisance it seems to be-"

"You're hungry!" she said. "You announce it like we should all leap and scurry! Ach! The very words are so... vulgar!"

This stung him into silence.

As if to rally the last of her patience, she clasped her own hands at her slim waist. She closed her eyes. She opened them. "How can I explain this? Our cooks... put their very best into their work. Their artistry. Their soul." She raised her eyes reverently. "Even to cut a ripe tomato... is to... sense the shape the tomato *wants* to become. The sauces, the spices... are *intuited*. Cooking... is an achingly slow... delicate... heating. All is arranged with the care of a haiku master." Her voice rose with emotion. "A sacred gift is set before you. A single inhalation... alights you at the gateway to paradise. A taste - oh, dear God - is a blessed leap into the sublime!" She held a hand to her chest as if to steady a raging heart.

"Well," he said, his excitement gathering. "It all sounds quite exceptional! May I order?"

Her hand fell. She stared at him. "Have you not heard a word I've said?"

He touched his temples. He spoke now, in strained, measured tones. "I've heard everything! I understand completely. *But I want... something... to eat!*"

"You want to eat!" she said. "It's... disgusting the way you talk about it!"

His brow furrowed. "Now that you mention it, everything I say *does* sound disgusting." He looked at her in curiosity. "While everything you say sounds... noble. How is it possible we're talking about the same thing?"

"I assure you, sir, we are *not* talking about thc samc thing."

"I'm talking about lunch," he said. "What are you talking about?"

"Lunch."

He slapped his thighs, and the words exploded from him. "This is making me crazy! You make no sense! I'm tired of talking, and I'm late and very, very hungry! Madam. Sometimes it's nice to wait for a well-prepared, gourmet meal. To chat about art, philosophy, to share opinions. But sometimes - and I'm sorry if it sounds vulgar - sometimes, madam, *you just want to eat!* So. Please. Tell the cooks I don't need their heart, I don't need their soul, and I don't require a gift! Tell them to just... throw together a sandwich or something!"

Her eyes widened in horror. "*Throw together a sandwich? You would have them throw together a sandwich?* What kind of coarse, ill-bred - Why did we let you in here in the first place?"

"The door was open."

"And here you are."

"I'm here! And I can't decide if I'm getting hungrier or angrier by the moment." He looked at her. "It's something... about the way you flip your eyes. The way you roll them with indignation. It only makes me hungrier! If I don't get something to eat soon, I'll be forced to leave!"

"Go ahead! Make your own lunch!"

"Ach!" he said. "I hate my own cooking!"

"Well, then," she said, recrossing her arms. "Here we are."

"You know, this isn't the only restaurant in town."

"Oh, fine. Go ahead. With your attitude-"

"I assure you, Madam, there are plenty out there who don't care about my attitude."

"And I assure you, Sir, they *all* care about your attitude!"

"So?" he said. "It's better than putting up with this! It's better than starving in here! And yes, with the half-billion restaurants out there, I'll find one that's not concerned about my attitude!"

He stood. He grabbed his coat and briefcase.

"You don't know what you're getting out there," she said.

"I'll take my chances," he said curtly, and headed for the door.

"Don't go," she said gently.

"I'm going. I'm gone."

But mid-stride, he stopped.

He turned. His voice softened. "I'm sorry. You seem... sincere. And you have an admirable... passion in your convictions."

"Passion?"

"A decided passion." He observed her for a moment, considering. "And your eyes. When you get angry, it... brings out a certain... ethereal magic in your eyes."

"Ethereal... *magic?*"

"In fact," he smiled, "you remind me of a character in a novel by Tolstoy. War and Peace. Have you read it?"

She stared, canting her head ever so slightly. "You... read War and Peace?"

He nodded.

"Which character?" she asked.

"Masha."

"*Masha*?" she said. "I *loved* Masha!"

"Really?" he said. "And Pierre? What did you think of him?"

"Oh, I *adored* Pierre!" she said. "I found him to be exceptionally... Excuse me. Would you like something to nibble while we chat?"

End

A chuckle, brief and male, erupted in the back of the room, which was silenced instantly by a deadly stare from Birnbaum.

She looked us over, as if daring anyone even to smile.

I drummed a pen on a yellow legal pad, ready to take notes. Birnbaum never spoke first. Nor was it a time for me to speak. Only fools defended their stories. You sat in the circle of desks and took it, whatever it was. The room became painfully airless. Those who smoked before class now were now sipping coffee. My own desire to breathe, it seemed, set me apart.

That and my appearance. While I was medium height and in the downside of my twenties - as we pretty much all were - I had dressed for a job interview scheduled to take place after class, in khakis and a pressed, oxford powder blue shirt. In this room full of black clothing, ripped denim, piercings, tattoos and dyed and shaved hair, my attire seemed hopelessly, pathetically conventional. A trickle of sweat rolled icily down my ribs.

Nancy thrust a faded, denim arm into the air. I remembered her first story; an angry, humorless piece about the unfair treatment received by an overweight junior high school girl, at the hands of her classmates when she first got her period. Birnbaum had praised it, and her rare praise for one student always seemed to plunge the rest of us into a profound state of gloom. Conversely, it emboldened Nancy to become the strongest voice in the room.

Birnbaum nodded in Nancy's direction.

Nancy leaned forward in her desk. She pressed her lips together thoughtfully. She bobbed her head twice then exhaled through her pierced nose as if trying, tactfully, to break some very bad news. "Where this piece fails," she said, "is in its obtuse, Neanderthal sensibility stemming from a narrowness in the writer himself. The weakness of his female character is matched only by the writer's complete revulsion for women."

A group of women around Nancy nodded their heads in agreement and mumbled. Then I saw it: the nod from Birnbaum herself. This, I knew, was my death sentence.

"I don't hate women," I said quickly but weakly, breaking the rule, "and I really don't think she's all that-" Birnbaum lofted a hand, silencing me. I shouldn't have spoken. I remembered when the man with the yoga mat tried to defend an abysmal piece, telling us, "James Joyce does this kind of thing all the time," which caused much eye-rolling, mine included, and Birnbaum's final, "I assure you, Joyce never did anything like this."

Ann, the woman to Nancy's immediate left tossed the pages like so much garbage on the desk before her. "I'm sitting here thinking, 'Is this a joke?' Is this some perverse male fantasy? If the writer, *like most men*, would just stop hating women long enough to open his eyes, for Godsake... to educate himself a little-"

"*Sex is food?*" blurted Cathy, a woman to Nancy's right. "*That's* how you feel about sex?" She shook her head. "I pity *any* woman-" and though she cut herself off, a few titters erupted from her side of the room.

"I just thought," I said, breaking the rule again, "a restaurant was a good... you know... *metaphor* to illustrate-"

"*What*?" Nancy said, "*That women are edible?*"

Everyone, Birnbaum included, laughed. I reached behind my neck to rub a squadron of knots gathering there. This was the kind of slam dunk that finalized the direction of any discussion, and my hesitation to respond inspired Nancy to add, "I thought so."

Other voices chimed in now; those who hung back, silent until they knew it was a sanctioned bludgeoning. There seemed, oddly, no happiness for the success of another student, but always a malicious glee in his dismemberment. I wondered if a few men might lend me a bit of support, but the males in this class - my first in this program - seemed an oddly cowed bunch.

"It goes nowhere."

"It's not specific enough."

"Who is this guy? What's his name?"

"It's cute, maybe, but what's the point?"

"There is a tonal shift on page three," said the yoga man who thought he wrote like James Joyce. Pages rustled as everyone flipped to the offensive passage.

Our teacher smiled, nodded her head at every comment.

Then Professor Birnbaum spoke: "Cracks in the flawed persona of a writer are unavoidably laid bare in his writing. Problems like this..." She shrugged her shoulders in a gesture of hopelessness.

A small hand lofted itself in the back of the room. Heads turned. Tara Wolff, a tiny, straggle-haired, decidedly plain wisp of a woman, always in a black overcoat, was about to comment. She spoke but once a class meeting. Her contributions were brief, often cryptic. Her own stories were strange things, oddly voiced, hard to discuss, almost glimpses of madness. But when she spoke, her words never gave heed to the lay of the land. Tara existed, and no one would say happily, on a different plane, and only she and God himself knew its geography. But people listened. They had to. Her words hung in our minds like koans; enigmas to be untangled.

"Tara?" said Professor Joan Birnbaum. Our teacher blinked hard, focused on the manuscript on the table before her. Then she slowly raised her eyes to the back of the room.

"I like the use of War and Peace," Tara said, nodding her small, bespectacled head as she scrutinized my story. "Clever."

"Pretentious," said Nancy, her voice almost a whisper.

chapter

THREE

Air!

It hit me like a blessing as I exited the English Department and stepped into the cold San Francisco mist. I gazed up at a slate gray sky, then over a sea of students with backpacks and dressed much like my classmates. Except for an animated discussion among three young Asian women, all appeared grim and preoccupied. I adjusted my own backpack, zipped up my blue nylon jacket and stood for a moment in blank bewilderment over what had just occurred. I felt as if my insides had been extracted, pummeled, befouled, and the tangled, disgusting mess had been returned, autopsy-style, into my chest.

Where had I gone wrong?

I went to bed last night convinced: The story was good. My class would praise me to a point of blushing embarrassment and I would then waltz, on a rare plateau of self-esteem, into the Athletic Director's office at the university across town for a pivotal interview to occur roughly one hour from now. And I would dazzle. I would exhibit charm, wit, competence. I would be the Cross-Country Coach Father Damian had been praying for. I awoke hopeful; told myself over the course of a three-mile morning run: the plan was foolproof, and my dad's concern over how I would survive was as good as settled. But Professor Birnbaum and her wrecking crew had chewed me up, spit me out, and left me like road kill to rot in my own misery.

How could a simple dream to be a writer be so blithely trampled upon?

I only knew I felt like hell and needed a moment to regroup; to rally, if possible, some kind of upbeat mood before I faced the Athletic Director.

I crossed the street, entered the Get Up Stand Up Cafe and found a seat in the back. I placed my elbows on the table, and for a moment, held my head in my hands. This interview was far too important. Jesus, what would dad think of all this? And I felt it already; a familiar black cloud of depression blossomed inside my skull, thickening like wet cement around my eyes. On a wall before me an art deco clock showed a naked woman's bare plastic legs pointing to ten after two. This told me two things: the interview was a brief fifty minutes away, and a particular waitress - a woman of unfathomable beauty who began her shift at two - was either sick, dead, or late.

I glanced over the decor of the The Get Up Stand Up Cafe. A poster of Bob Marley was thumbtacked to one wall. An old, rusting bicycle hung in a fishnet from the ceiling. A stone statue of The Buddha sat in a corner. The clientele was coffee drinkers, several in tortured-poet black, ponytails, spectacles. A young man across the room held a latte and a gaze of ennui beneath eyebrows impaled with Lilliputian barbells. A spiral bound sat unopened before him on a graffiti covered table. Two dreadlocked white men sat in the back. Several patrons read The San Francisco Chronicle. A bespectacled man in a yellow, long-sleeved, button down shirt studied an econ. text. A Latino woman in her forties balanced her checkbook. Others leaned coolly, blandly into conversations, one hand on a coffee cup, one leg crossed over the other.

My own legs were uncrossable, I thought, looking down at them. I was a sprinter in college, but now, a distance runner bashing seventy miles a week at six minute pace; just fast enough for a brief but magical endorphin-lift out of an otherwise relentless depression.

I glanced about.

No one waited tables.

Where was my waitress?

She should have been here by now; that unforgivably beautiful creature - dark, lanky, dreadlocked - who just a few weeks ago, brought me a carrot juice, and who, in fact, inspired the very bit of scribbling which had caused my bloodletting moments ago. And I blamed her: for the story, the slaughter, and this consequent foul mood, which, in all likelihood, would destroy the upcoming interview that might have changed my life.

Of course, she never noticed me. Even if she did, what might she think? I glanced into a stretch of smoky mirrors along the wall.

"*Him?*" she might say, wrinkling her lovely nose. "*So conventional.*"

I glanced about at the cool rebels around me. My bushy hair could never be pulled back into a dashing, wind-swept ponytail, a few rakish strands falling into my eyes. She who inspires art, even bad art, would never even notice-

Was that what it was? This sophomoric bit of dreck I had actually, in a moment of giddy self-delusion, fancied a modest contribution to that thin-aired, fabulously exclusive world of letters?

I reached into my backpack and pulled out another piece I'd struggled with for months, about a summer camp I'd worked at as an undergrad. I needed to write. Besides running, writing was the only mood-lifter I knew of. I was a mess, and this was serious damage control with the clock ticking. I needed to be perky, upbeat, crackling with confidence when I stepped into the Athletic Director's office. I was about to lay the pages on the wooden table before me when I noticed a bit of graffiti. Someone had etched:

You tore my hymen
and my
heart apart.

Well, here it was: pain was everywhere and who was I to snivel? I pitied her; this poetess with an exacto, suffering a feminine angst at which I could only guess, and I covered her misery with my manuscript.

I focused now on one character, a redheaded boy named Doug; a science nerd and outcast, fast becoming a scapegoat among the other seven-year-old boys in his cabin. I checked the time, made some marginal notes and added an entire paragraph, when my attention shifted to a disturbance near the kitchen.

A tall, hardened soul with a mustache, perhaps in his fifties, was shouting. I guessed he was the manager - an unlikely character for a hip establishment like this - and he was berating two aproned Latino men. One was middle-aged, small but powerfully built, perhaps Mayan, also with a mustache. The other was a lanky, slouching adolescent who seemed to be the focus of the discussion. It appeared that the elder man spoke on behalf of the younger, who couldn't speak English, in the service of a conversation that certainly should not have taken place in front of customers.

I pulled out my spiral bound and opened it.

"Cousin, schmusin," the manager said, "Tell him he doesn't pick it up I'll boot his ass back to Cancun."

The elder spoke in hushed Spanish to his sullen, cave-chested co-worker, and I noted his excellent posture, a near-regal poise in his bearing. The youth nodded his head, then spoke quietly.

"He says he will work more fast," the elder Latino said.

"He damn well better."

This was conveyed in Spanish to the young man, who, without looking up, said, "Gracias."

"Don't grassy-ass me! Just tell him to get his lazy-" The manager halted, mid-speech.

To my left, a latte paused inches from a pierced lip. A healthy forkful of vegan cheesecake, one table over, was suspended in midair. An impassioned debate over an unfinished arm tattoo between the dreadlocked white men halted. The econ. student looked up from his text. The manager's full attention shifted from his employees to the doorway. The entire coffee shop fell into silence. Every pair of eyes – café staff and patrons alike - were fixed intently on the entryway of the Get Up Stand Up Cafe.

In what seemed a burst of heavenly radiance, she walked; nay, floated in through the double glass doors. Oh my God, she was here; this dark slip of a woman of undetermined race; some mysterious genetic alchemy that resulted in pure, unspeakable magic. Her hair was locked, reggae style - braided? Rastaed? What did I know of such things? A tiny butterfly was tattooed behind her lovely shoulder, and her slim lankiness filled a black tank top, a black calf-length skirt, ending in a pair of Greek-goddess sandals. Without breaking stride she glanced at the clock; the naked legs now pointed to twenty-five after. She smiled a flash of brilliance - surprisingly, not tinged with guilt - at her boss who had evidently forgotten the Latino workers. And it was her smile that destroyed me; a dazzling, extra-wide, klieg light affair, which her boss returned with an all-is-forgiven, obsequious grin - *the keen writer's eye misses nothing* - then she long-legged it through the swinging metal doors and disappeared into the kitchen.

Everyone in the Get Up Stand Up Cafe - bohemians, hippies, gay and straight, students, a deranged homeless man, Rastafarians - *everyone* by God, had their eyes riveted on those swinging metal doors.

I wrote every detail I could remember about the Latino workers in my Writer's Notebook - a title I had inscribed on the front to remind me of my purpose - then let my thoughts drift to a foregone destination.

Oh, my waitress!

I recalled the first time I saw her: shameless, unmentionable scenes unveiled themselves in the secret, erotic film festival of my mind; a place where women danced, unclothed and beckoning, across my brainpan with agonizing regularity. Among this pantheon my waitress appeared, outshining them all as I nibbled popcorn and worshipped her devoutly from the aisles. In the midst of this sweet daydream, I considered the cold, ugly facts. What sort of abyss existed between myself and such a creature? It wasn't only her beauty that put her light years beyond me, but also, another fathomless chasm separating all men and women.

I lifted the thought from my head, placed it gingerly on the table before me. I examined it. And I caught myself red-handed in a moment I fancied *epiphanic*, played with the idea until I got home, sat on my couch, picked up a yellow legal pad, a Papermate medium point, then settled into an outpouring of words that, far as my limited experience could tell me, felt feverish, even brilliant. Hours later I emerged from my apartment, singed, I was certain, by the fires of creative passion.

I would never trust such an impulse again.

The workshop stratification was established. I wasn't among the favored; no path lined with rainbows for me. And now I had come to the Get Up Stand Up Cafe, to gaze upon my goddess of bogus inspiration once more.

I returned to the summer camp story. I crossed out a sentence, changed a word, when my attention was diverted once again to the kitchen doors. There she emerged, aproned and stunning. An exquisite miracle she was, and just looking at her sent a sweet ache through my bloodied soul.

Dear God in Heaven, why must she be so impossible? So beyond a pedestrian, unstriking mortal as myself. All created equal? Clearly You favored this one a tad more. I caught my reflection again in the mirror. Damn these interview clothes! My hair was short, my entire head, unpierced. I glanced among the unsmiling coffee drinkers and poetic types who seemed to fill this place.

Curiously, none were actually writing.

I jotted a few marginal notes and kept one eye on my beguiling waitress as she took orders from the tables around me. Then I focused my complete attention on an early-morning scene at the summer camp, with young Douglas behaving very oddly, when I was interrupted.

"Are you writing?"

The voice was a timeless rhapsody.

She stood before me, pen in hand. I couldn't breathe.

I hoped my hair didn't look stupid.

Her tank top had some rock band logo stretched to agonizing illegibility across her fabulous, unbound breasts. In my mind, the shirt was gone and my tongue danced tiny minuets on her smooth, brown stomach.

"Trying," I said.

She smiled, her teeth a near-luminous phosphorescence that nudged me onward.

"These kids," I gestured to the page. "I'm writing about some seven-year-olds... at a summer camp I worked at. They wouldn't cooperate then and they're even worse now. It's trying to be a story."

"A *story?*" she brightened. Her dreadlocks danced.

I nodded.

She blinked once, as if to perceive this all the better. "You're a *writer?*"

"I'd like to be."

And I knew, from the sudden light in her dark-brown, near-Asian eyes, that this word held a certain cachet - was it possible? - that lifted me above the interminable rabble which, in all likelihood, had been hitting on her since puberty. Her expression held downright interest, and as I gazed at the lithe, dark shape before me, I felt a surge of something, at once, exalted and vulgar shudder wonderfully through my body.

But no. I did not need another disaster of self-delusion just now.

She glanced back toward the bar. "What can I bring you?" she said.

Dear God in Heaven, what a question.

"You have tea?" I said. "Decaf?"

"We sure do," she said, "Anything else?"

I glanced at the menu on the wall behind the counter. "Um... how's that carrot cake?"

"Oh my God," she said. I observed with fascination a metamorphosis in her lovely features, which seemed to fill with sudden, intense rapture. Her eyes closed hard in what clearly was a memory of complete, transporting, otherworldly pleasure. "It's unbelievable!"

Then all went languid and dreamy. With a look of mild tragedy, she added, "But we're all out."

It was those dark eyes - closed and now open - plus a bombed-out, nothing-to-lose recklessness left over from my recent catastrophe that fueled a brief, uncharacteristic bravado. I shocked myself when I said, "I like how you put that: *It's unbelievable, but we're all out*. Typical female. Get a guy all excited about something, then deny it from him."

As this settled in her mind, I edited: deny it *of* him, and then she stared at me, shaking her head, naughty-boy style.

"Just the tea, please," I said. And as she strode away in long, graceful steps to the counter, I was struck dead by the fabulous geometry of her ass.

Oh, how my class would crucify me for such a phrase!

But my divine waitress had smiled, and this was worth any hypothetical abuse from my Fiction Writing 404, The Art of the Short Story, seminar.

I made a few more corrections on the manuscript but had them all crossed them out when she returned, placing the tea before me.

"I'm sorry they're not cooperating," she said.

"Well, it's one boy mostly," I said. "This mad-scientist kid who likes to burn ants with a magnifying glass."

"Oh," she said. She tilted her head, her brows furrowed: *pity for ants and all living creatures*. Then, she brightened. "I like stories," she said, raising her eyebrows. "Is it *powerful?*"

My thighs tingled. My vision blurred.

She smiled.

"Well, you know, *power*," I said. I bit my lower lip in a display of deep thought. I bobbed my head twice. "To move your reader is the goal of any writer. You have to trust that once you make the leap, you'll find the power." As if of their own accord, Goethe's words flew from my lips: "*Whatever you do, or dream you can, begin it. Boldness has genius, power, and magic in it.*"

She stared at me. She blinked three times in succession. Did her pupils dilate? Perhaps a notion like the one I had just plagiarized did not waltz into the Get Up Stand Up Cafe with much regularity.

I could hardly believe my own mouth. Wasn't this a bad day? Hadn't I just been trashed, beaten, abused and reminded of the failure I was certain to become if I continued on such a path - *a writer? Who was I kidding?* - but here was this waitress, a woman of excruciating beauty staring at me with *dilating pupils*?

Before I allowed brutal reality to intrude, I spoke. "Listen. Can I, um, call you sometime?"

"I'd like that," she said. She took a napkin and a transparent plastic pen from an apron pocket, inclined slightly at her perfect hips, placed the napkin on the table and wrote. My eyes wandered quickly and with a will of their own. A solitary notion ascended gently and secretly from my thoughts, as if toward Heaven and with the sanctity of prayer: *If I could go down on this woman I would die of happiness.*

She handed me the napkin. I read it aloud: "Joy."

I finished my tea then headed for the exit, chastising myself for the crack about boldness and magic. Well, someday, I'd have my own arsenal of waitress-dazzling quips; maybe not up to the great Goethe's standard, but regardless, by God, I had it: Joy's number, written on a napkin, precious as the holy grail. I looked at it for a moment in disbelief, then tucked it safely into my pocket.

chapter

FOUR

As I was about to exit, I stopped at the door. I glanced at Joy, now waiting on other tables, and I wondered: what was all this coffee business about? As an athlete I never got near the stuff. But everyone in the Get Up Stand Up Cafe was drinking coffee. In fact, everyone in this damn city seemed to consume it by the gallon. This was Joy's world; perhaps I'd best explore it a bit.

Behind the counter was a small man in his mid-thirties, balding, but with as much of a gathered-from-the-sides ponytail as he could muster. He moved in sharp, jerky, overly formal motions. He wore black; his nametag said Fredrico.

"Excuse me," I said. "What do I need to make coffee?"

Fredrico looked me over. "You don't know how to make coffee?"

I shook my head.

The small man glanced at a woman, also behind the counter who wore short, hennaed hair and had silver studs in her ears. They shared a grin.

Did they think I didn't see them?

I looked over my shoulder to see if Joy noticed any of this. She was in the back corner, taking an order from the two dreadlocked white men who struggled mightily to appear casual in the presence of her blinding beauty. They leaned this way and that, wiggled their heads in a jokey manner, smiled lamely.

Fredrico produced a cone and some filters. I quickly saw how one fit into the other, glad I would not have to ask.

"Type of bean?"

I cleared my throat. "What do you recommend?"

Fredrico exhaled. "Depends on your taste."

"I'll trust your judgment."

As if the effort of turning was an insufferable inconvenience, he exhaled again, then twisted himself around to look over a list posted on the wall. "Try..." he wiggled his head in thought, "Mocha Java." He pronounced each syllable, emphasizing the consonants, affecting the intonation of a connoisseur.

"Pound?"

"*Pound?*" I said. "Oh, a *pound.* A pound is fine." I watched him measure the beans out from a glass bin, fill a plastic dish sitting on a scale, then pour it all into an organic-looking brown bag.

"Ground or whole bean?"

"Ground," I said, impaling him with decisiveness.

He returned momentarily with the bag. Mocha Java. One red cone. Unbleached filters. I looked the stuff over. "So," I said, "You... just pour boiling water-"

"*Not boiling!*" Fredrico shouted. "Do you want to *scald* the bean?"

The woman behind the counter giggled. Fredrico, dressed in black from head to toe, earringed, pony-tailed - even what little hair he possessed was dyed black because no hair is *that* black - rolled his eyes.

I collected my change and left.

And I'm sure they watched me exit: *the bean scalder.*

As I hit the pavement, I considered the folded napkin in my pocket, sacred as the tablets of Moses, and felt it's strange and wonderful power. I took two, nervous, pre-race, hyperventilating breaths, girding myself with oxygen for this terrifying interview about to occur. I entered my Honda and turned the key. The starter clicked twice, signaling unaffordable repairs ahead, then the engine roared to life.

chapter

FIVE

Father Damian, the Athletic Director, was a tall, graying man of the cloth, in his mid-sixties, wearing a clergy collar and a black suit. I liked him immediately. He stood, greeted me warmly and offered me a seat. The decor of his office was masculine and plush, and he sat behind a large, oak desk, in a chair of dark red leather. Behind him was a small rendering of Jesus. Otherwise, pictures of athletes and coaches of the past filled the wood-paneled walls. In their hands were basketballs, trophies and plaques, the very items that filled the glass cases of this office and those in the hall beyond. The people in the photos wore the pumped expressions of recent, thrilling victory, and it didn't take a genius to see that basketball was the main event here.

This was a basketball school.

Father Damian struck me instantly as a man of great patience and dignity. I hoped age and experience would someday bring me to a state of such self-assurance. If Father Damian was an hour hand - slow, ponderous, and steady - I was a second hand. Words left my lips quickly and long before I had chance to size them up and test them out, to see if I wished to be held accountable for them later. Father Damian's speech and behavior seemed so careful, so edited in advance, that he probably never second-guessed a single act or utterance in his life.

He asked how I planned to train my cross-country runners.

I had prepared for this. For courage, I touched the pocket that held Joy's phone number, then revealed the details of my program: long, fast runs; hill-training; speed-work. I mentioned the great New Zealand distance running coach, Arthur Lydiard, and pointed out the advantages of training at anaerobic threshold. I explained the imperative of mental preparation, and because this was a university, I tossed in the Greek ideal - perfection of mind and body.

He nodded, then leaned back in his chair.

"You must understand," Father Damian said. "Cross country is not a sport in which we have a strong tradition at this school. Much of the focus here is basketball. This is a basketball school."

"I know that," I said. "I understand."

And I did. Cross Country was a remote, inconsequential fleck of a concern; forgettably tangential to the main event here, which was basketball. How else would a division-one coaching job become available on the fly? A coaching position that paid anything substantial was impossible to find, but this one came with a tiny stipend, which, with careful economizing, would hold me together until league finals at the end of the semester, barely months away.

"Every year, it seems we only get five students to come out."

"*Five?*" This was instant bad news. In a race, it takes five runners to score. If you only enter five, and one stubs a toe and drops out, even if the other four are altitude-trained Kenyans, you forfeit. Most teams had huge numbers to choose from. You entered your seven best runners in a competition, the top five score. And of course, the odds of getting talented athletes grew with the number of bodies.

The season was just starting up; the former coach had quit or died or something. I was an emergency hire, and it would be difficult at this point to find more runners. Despite this unhappy news,

I had bigger designs here and it was time to reveal them. This move north was aimed at beginning a new life that I needed and wanted desperately. This job, appearing out of serendipitous nowhere, would keep me afloat temporarily, but I wanted to turn it into a year-long, permanent position, coaching being the one and only job I truly loved. I gathered my courage a second time and spoke. "If possible, I'd like to start a track team in the spring," I said. I explained how we'd start small, but in a few years, "Well, who knows what the focus of this school might be?"

He looked me over with amusement. "I'll give it some thought," he said. "We'll see how things go."

"So... I'm hired?"

He nodded his large, gray head, and smiled.

chapter

SIX

I thumb tacked Joy's number to the bulletin board in the kitchen of my small, one-bedroom apartment. And there it was; a plain white napkin inscribed with her beautiful, loopy handwriting. It taunted me. Getting her number was one thing; to actually call a woman like Joy was quite another. Moments of such superhuman bravado, for me, were embarrassingly rare. In a situation like this, you couldn't just *dial.* The mood had to be right. I had scared enough women away with my inescapable, oppressive gloom.

That evening, I called my mom to see how Dad was faring. She picked up on the third ring, sounding tired but happy to hear from me. Dad was about the same, she said; he had his good days and bad, we had to hope for the best.

I asked if she thought I should come home for a bit.

She said, no, that I was too busy. "Timmy? Are you writing wonderful things?"

A lump formed instantly in my throat, but I said I was writing fabulous, wonderful things, and added that I'd gotten a job.

"A job? I can't wait to tell your father. We were worried about your money holding out. What kind of job?"

"Coaching," I said.

"You don't sound so happy about it."

"I'm happy," I said, and she gave me a few medical details about Dad, and we hung up.

I lay in bed and forgave myself the lies to mom because mothers don't need to know everything. I considered the ass whipping I'd received in class today. Did I even have it in me to write anything with sufficient beauty to show to my father? And yes, the coaching job was lucky, but only *five runners*? To impress an Athletic Director who sprinkled success on his corn flakes? What if my father's warnings were dead on? *What if I couldn't pull this off?* Would I be catapulted, through some bizarre, pernicious irony, back into the classroom?

I drifted into a gloomy, fitful sleep.

Lorenzo stood grimacing before my desk. His mouth stretched to an impossible width, shouting words I could not hear or understand. From her desk, Taisha screamed unintelligibly at the top of her lungs. Eric stood atop a filing cabinet, grinning, ready to leap. A disturbance erupted in the back of my class where a crowd of students had gathered, but Lorenzo angled his head over my desk, leaning into me, shouting louder, more hysterically.

A wad of paper flew.

I noted it's graceful arc, it's touchdown on Taisha's cheek, causing her to scream more violently. Lorenzo's face seemed to broaden, his mouth expand. He shouted but I heard nothing. Eric leaned forward, swung back his arms.

Why was Taisha screaming? What in God's name was happening in the back of the room? Why the crowd? They had their assignment, an essay about their proudest moment. The classroom listed, stretched and pitched oddly. It appeared to be full of noise, but I heard nothing. Could other teachers hear it? Was my door closed?

Focus.

What did Lorenzo want?

Solve the problem of Lorenzo; the rest will follow. Concentrate. But why was Taisha red-faced, screaming, pounding her desk with her fists? Taisha, who's mother was a hooker - everyone knew she was - and who I praised so highly for her Something I'm Good At speech, which she titled: "How to Shoplift at Mervyn's," Taisha please stop screaming - but no, just Lorenzo, focus now... his mouth, his voice... "iiiiiiiiiiiiiiii..."

Eric jumped.

Taisha frisbeed her three-ring binder across the room. Unbound papers hit the air, fluttered to the ground like giant, elegant snowflakes. They drifted around my desk, about Lorenzo's head, and he was coming in now, "iiiiiiiiiiiiii" - but what was occurring in the back of the room? Why were those kids cheering?

But no... Lorenzo. Just Lorenzo! Focus on-

"iiiiiiiiiiii don't.."

"What? What, Lorenzo! I can't unders-"

"FOR THE FIFTIETH TIME, I DON'T HAVE A PENCIL!"

"Oh... a pencil," I said, and I moved slowly, as if through honey, making no progress toward the knot of youth in the back of my room, where Lilbit, the largest and toughest girl in the seventh grade held a terrified Antoine in a headlock, and was beating him viciously over the head with a closed umbrella.

I stared, strangely immobile, and everything went black.

"Oh, God," I said. I awoke, sweating and trembling in my San Francisco apartment. A dull grey light filtered through the bedroom window as I recalled that pivotal event and it's aftermath: First, the out-of-focus face of Ms. Stevens, the school nurse. I squinted about, recognized the whiteness of her office. To her left, Mr. Hickock, our tall, overweight, balding principal came into view. He was not pleased.

Ms. Stevens said something like, "... fried a few circuits," and both stared at me, she with concern, he with irritation.

"What happened?" I asked.

Mr. Hickock looked at me in disbelief. Perhaps controlling students was a snap for a man his size, and thus he couldn't fathom my ineptitude with discipline.

He said simply, "Antoine called Lilbit a heifer."

Antoine learned his lesson. I lost my job, though Mr. Hickock graciously let me finish out the year, but in truth, I might have thanked them all - a new umbrella for Lilbit, a box of Ticonderogas for Lorenzo, and I actually gave Taisha a forty-dollar gift certificate for Mervyn's. While losing my job was humiliating, quitting would have been - well, *quitting* - and certainly in my father's eyes, infinitely more demoralizing. How I envied those who could say, *just a bad fit*, and blithely move on. I had been raised on phrases like 'stick-to-it-iveness', and 'a winner never quits; a quitter never wins', and though, in retrospect, their application here seemed a reach, I thus remained in a profession I hated for three years. That I liked kids and books made teaching English seem a natural, but this logic was flawed in ways I had yet to grasp, and finally, the whole enterprise collapsed into a fat black mark in the loss column.

How long do you plan to flounder?

I lay in bed on a cold, cloudy San Francisco morning and wondered about my father's question. And I felt it; depression, creeping into my head, thick and heavy, like the fog just outside my window.

I got out of bed and put on my gray sweats.

In the hall I turned on the gas heater. It hissed, and then I listened to the click and boom of stretching metal. I stood for a moment to warm myself.

My kitchen was small; a bar on one side, the stove and fridge on the other. A calendar hung beside the bulletin board, each month revealing a different painting by Paul Gauguin, a man who chucked it all at forty-five and moved to Tahiti to become an artist. In the living room was a print of Vermeer's Head of a Girl; beside that, one of Gauguin's brightly colored renderings of Tahitian, topless native women carrying tropical fruit. On the opposite wall was a poster of the great Oregon runner, Steve Prefontaine. Beside Pre was a picture of the legendary Russian sprinter, Valery Borzov, rocketing out of the blocks in the 72 Olympics. I owned a stuffed beige couch, a chair that matched, and a plywood coffee table, all of which I'd acquired at a garage sale for a ridiculously low price.

The job, the furniture - all the pieces were in place. I had stupidly hoped this gloom wouldn't follow me north, yet it stuck, tenacious as a rash. But it wasn't *just* the gloom that I hated. That I could have handled.

A depressed person is a leper.

Humanity loves the buoyant, the upbeat. One day at lunch in the teachers lounge, everybody around me, one by one, just moved to another table. I sat alone, while another table was jammed. And what did it matter? I was a mute zombie. I wouldn't sit with myself either. Words couldn't get organized in my head, let alone, find their way to speech. Questions baffled me. A tentativeness in my voice infuriated me, left me sounding intimidated, and often inspired a strange haughtiness in people. At times, it made me ripe for slick mockery. The mean-spirited zeroed in and the lemmings followed, until entire gatherings - in living rooms or at dinner tables - were taking shots. I could only sit and stare blankly, wondering why no brilliant, eviscerating rejoinders found their way to my lips. Worst of all was to meet a lovely, interested woman at a time when the mood was crushing, hearing the hesitant sound of my own voice, and to watch her interest fade. When a teacher is depressed, students morph into piranhas. A friend, annoyed with my oppressive bleakness, said, "Just snap out of it!" and began snapping his fingers in my face.

This ambience in my head!

Wake up, greet the day with "Oh God!" because there it is.

Carry it around everywhere.

When I had time to write with some regularity the mood lifted. Oh, how it lifted! Something magic occurred in the simple act of arranging of words into paragraphs and stories. People who shunned me in my depressed state returned. How writing held the demons under lock and key, I didn't know, but I marveled at those who could go through life *not writing* and still wake up feeling wonderful. To say depression was a revolt of the soul; a soul angry that you weren't doing what you should sounds grandiose, and presumes some great flame of talent lay dormant, fighting for expression. What did the great writers mean when they said - and every last one of them said it - that they had to write? If you had to write, did this, in any way also mean that you had the slightest potential to justify the risk my father had laid out with such sobering clarity?

Anti-depressants didn't work. Each had their side effects - none sexual - but as a runner, I didn't like taking drugs, certainly over an extended period. It was simply time to face the problem as best as I understood it. Thus, the plan: turn this coaching job into something permanent, live cheaply as an air fern, and write.

And yes, that horrific question of talent.

Cracks in the flawed persona of a writer are unavoidably laid bare in his writing. Birnbaum's encouraging words.

The dream of Lorenzo and Taisha left it's residue in a foul mood that stalked me as I entered the kitchen, leaned against the sink. I needed to shake it because I was to meet my athletes in a few short hours. I glanced over a stack of bills - car insurance, PG&E, phone, still unpaid, waiting for stamps. And there it was: a small brown bag of Mocha Java, sitting on the counter top. Jesus, did I really buy all this crap? Cones, filters and *I'll scald the beans if I damn-*

Fill the pot with water... turn on the gas.

I thought about him. Mr. Mocha Java, with his dyed black hair, the silver stud in his ear. I watched tiny bubbles form at the bottom of the pot, float to the surface and *roll your eyes again and I'll remove your larynx with my bare* - Okay. Filter in the cone. Coffee in the filter. The whole ridiculous mess over the cup.

Wait for the water to boil. *But not quite.*

Pour.

So... this is it. What the world drinks every morning.

Bit of milk? *Brown sugar okay with you Miss Henna Head? Because I lay awake nights agonizing over your opinion-*

I carried the cup to the couch, placed my feet on the coffee table. A table named for this very drink: Coffee, beverage of lemmings. *Of Mr. Every-Question-Is-An-Opportunity-To-Ridicule-*

Not bad, this coffee, but in all honesty, not so great either. I could probably teach the bastard how to make the stuff. Give him a lesson in his own, nothing little corner of the univ-

I glanced into kitchen and there it was: Joy's napkin, thumb-tacked to the bulletin board where I left it last night, if I ever found the nerve...

Joy, a goddess of inconceivable beauty. I could not call now. She would sense my gloom, become repulsed by it, and I would blow my one precious chance in a lifetime. No, I would call Joy when I felt buoyant and chipper, which I hope occurred sometime in the current millennium.

I sipped coffee and wondered, if I did actually call Joy, where I might take her. A man needed to know this beforehand, because wishy-washiness was suicide, certainly with a woman like Joy. What is a date but a snapshot of the hypothetical future you offer? So. Probably someplace hip, organic, ethnic, certainly expensive. I had just moved up here and had no idea where such a place might be. Then? A gentlemanly kiss on the cheek? Or, in a wild burst of courage, on her perfect, soft lips. After three dates, a brazen wandering hand, risking the censure of a practiced arm-pin against a ribcage, and a stinging rebuff - *What do you think you're doing?*

How to answer such a question?

A beautiful woman holds the entire world in her lovely-

This Mocha Java. Not great, but... not bad either.

And Joy. So utterly, perfectly luscious, *and dear God in Heaven, who was I kidding?*

Directly across the room, in the glass-covered Gauguin, there it was, my reflection; a tad Hebraic, lamentably undashing. I searched in vain for some thrilling, irresistible element of danger.

I exhaled hopelessly, then looked instead at my mug of coffee. Guess I'll get used to the stuff - but I must confess, it's oddly... comforting. No wonder everyone slams a mug or two... a second cup? Who's stopping me?

Well, yesterday wasn't a complete disaster.

The coaching job is mine. Father Damian. Only five runners to give me, but - *this coffee's okay* - a good soul. His own brainpan - hardwood with a three-point line, infinitely more virtuous than the wanton, scandalous images that populate my own-

He asked my coaching philosophy, and by God, I gave it to him, but now, I needed to write. So the first story was a disaster. Did this signify doom? Did it mean I would never write a word to please a group of illiterates who I couldn't stand in the first place?

Do the sons of bitches think they can stop a man like me?

I shall rise, like the phoenix from the damn-

I can do this! Coach distance runners, write, and by God, *I can drink this coffee!*

I stood at my window, took a hot slug of a second cup and gazed over the tightly packed houses of the Sunset District. A few of its black-clad denizens moved about in the cold, morning mist. I addressed them: "What is a story? Ten stories? A novel?

"A bit of diligence! Hard work! Is this what scares you? Is this what sends you all shrieking? You think it's only for the select few? The gifted? The sensitive?

"*Fuck the gifted!*

"*Fuck the sensitive too!*"

"Ah! Mocha Java!

"My brew."

I took a second swig from my steaming, ceramic mug and faced the living room:

"A forthcoming novel? Most certainly! Simply pluck an idea from the sea of imagination and the miracle occurs: Art! The vision manifest!

"Was I so different, my innocent Dutch girl? Was I to be excluded, my fleet-footed Russian?

"No and no. Ten seconds flat, Olympic gold, and nothing stopped you so why should anything-

"A novel? So many pages, but... why not?

"*A stunning debut!*

"*A singular talent!*

I grabbed a book off the shelf, scanned its back cover.

"*A breathtaking achievement!*

"*Surely bodes well for a dazzling future!*

What sort of cretin utters such nonsense? He, no doubt, lounges about in an elegant bathrobe. Swirls his brandy. Takes, not walks, but constitutionals with purposeful arm action. Smokes a pipe, peers through spectacles resting on a finely tapered, aquiline - probably even talks to his wife this way:

"A lucid, diamond-like phone message!

"A vibrant, life-affirming shave!

"A lyrical cheeseburger! Opulent, eloquent French Fries!

I won't write a single word for the bastard but he'll love my book nonetheless! And my second he'll love even more - a deeper probe into the angst-filled soul of the artist.

"What dexterity!

"A master stylist at such a young age!

"More, Mr. Lewis, More!

"Ah, the burden of genius! The world a-clamor for the fruits of my intellect!"

I strode across the living room.

"The third? A major tome sweeping a vast landscape of generations. Followed by a play, dashed off in spare moments. Literary criticism? Most certainly. Honorary Ph.D.? Several, no doubt. Standing room only in my classes, based on my meteoric reputation alone. Ten novels, studied in advanced Literature courses the world over. Translated into six hundred languages.

"Another cup? Why not?"

I stood in the center of my living room. I took a long, healthy pull off a third cup of Mocha Java, and my voice was booming.

"Yes, why not, ladies and gentlemen of the Nobel Committee - why not take the risk I took at such a young and guileless age! My beginnings: humble to say the least! A common school teacher, certainly, but beneath that ludicrous facade lurked a man with a dream! Many talk, few take the plunge. Ah, your lovely Stockholm! Was it built by the cowardly? The small-minded? By God, it was built by men and women of courage and vision, just as the bricks lining the path to such a prestigious award as this, to honor the worthy, to inspire the struggling, bumbling novice to a first scribbled poem!

"Wait!

"Shall I accept? Or decline out of some obscure form of protest?

"I will, of course, graciously accept the award, the subsequent women, and watch as my works become shining beacons of hope for the lost and the weary, guiding lights for the shattered, the downtrodden. And who's to say this isn't my true purpose?

"What's this?" I faced the Tahitian women.

"My... *divine* purpose!

"Sent here, you mean, by the Almighty Himself to show blessed humanity... *the way*?

"Oh, you're far too kind.

"Well! Now that it's out there. Who's to say what form a Messiah will actually - *Messiah*? Do I dare use such a -*Christ, what do they put in this* - well, if the shoe fucking fits-"

And I saw it.

There it was, Joy's napkin - a precious, glowing bit of wonder tacked to the cork message board.

If ever there was a time-

I was instantly at the phone, one hand on the receiver. Trembling wildly, I lifted it. I dialed. One ring.

Dear God, I was calling!

Two rings.

"Hello?" The voice! Pure as newly spun silk.

"Joy. It's me. Tim."

"Tim?"

"The *writer*."

"*Tim!* How are-"

"I want to see you. *Tonight!*"

"Um, okay."

"Seven o-clock alright?"

She said it was. Oddly, she said *she* would pick *me* up.

Good. Fine. The world changes every minute and who was I to question. I gave her directions, hung up, then stared in awe at the organic-looking, light brown bag of Mocha Java, sitting, rumpled and mute on the kitchen counter.

chapter

SEVEN

"I pass out when I run."

This was how Alex Granger greeted me when I met him and my other runners that afternoon on the grassy quad in front of the ivy covered gym for our first official workout. I did not respond. The day was overcast, cool and misty. As Father Damian had predicted, only five guys showed up. We sat on the lawn in sweats as I lead them through stretches. Before me was Gary, a sandy-haired surfer from Laguna Beach; beside him, a lanky, longhaired, blond philosophy major named Steve, who had only recently taken up jogging. Two others, Nick and Peter - twins, actually - were dark haired, olive skinned and of Greek heritage. Both told me right off they were pre-med and could train, at most, two days a week. The last, Alex, had medium length brown hair, a splash of freckles across his face and the trim, hopeful physique of a runner. I grabbed an ankle and lay back to stretch a tight left quad, stare at a gray sky, and to privately consider this tiny crew and my near-impossible plan when Alex leaned over with more medical information. "I have a heart problem," he said with a grin, "and acute asthma."

I sat up, noticed a very expensive pair of Nike running shoes on his feet, and listened in silence as he recounted a tale of passing out during a run. His grin told me that he viewed his infirmities as wacky but endearing. I considered Father Damian's 'We'll see how things go,' regarding my request to make this a year-round position, and wondered with trepidation about Alex's agenda for this Cross Country season. As I listened to Alex I felt something vague and ugly rising in my stomach, but calmed myself with a term remembered from teacher-training: *Unconditional positive regard.*

A sunny, blond coed in white shorts, with a badminton racquet in her hand and Walkman on her head, just then, strode by us toward the gym, momentarily diverting our attention. We switched legs. Gary, who struck me as a consummate lady-killer, glanced at her with admirable detachment and I knew his thought: we were a team of collegiate cross-country runners, looking athletic and fabulously cool, stretching on the grass, getting ready for a workout.

"Alex," I said carefully. "People don't pass out when they run. I've never heard of a single case-"

"I do," he said, "Sometimes I even run into trees or parked cars."

I stared at him and thought: *Five runners; no more.*

We took off on a six miler, moving through the campus, to Golden Gate Park, along the Pan Handle, passed spike-haired skateboarders, roller-bladders, kids doing tricks on bicycles. We passed the Museum of Natural Science, the Planetarium, the Aquarium.

Gary was a solid, efficient runner, who moved with the easy grace of a natural athlete. Steve, I saw immediately, would be pure delight to work with. He seemed smart and serious, but a true beginner with no sense at all as to how good he could become. Once he learned to unfurl that lanky stride and make friends with pain, he might be my star. I would coax the twins to practice more than twice a week. Only Alex, who ran alongside with a bounding, spunky esprit de corps, made me nervous. Though we all - myself included - enjoyed our collegiate/athletic chic as we moved through Golden Gate Park, Alex was downright giddy.

We crested the top of Strawberry Hill - first the surfer, followed by the coach, the pre-meds and then the philosopher. Thirty yards back Alex was limping. I had been among runners for fifteen years, and Alex's was by far, the sorriest, fake-ass limp I'd ever seen. He walked the last bit, and with a grimace announced, "My knees." Even my father, an inveterate non-athlete, would shake his head over such a display. A childhood of air raids, gas masks and food shortages had left him with a low tolerance for such blatant kvetching. Robert and I certainly never got away with it.

My runners and I cruised back through the cold, gray afternoon toward the University. I had only wanted to see them on the flats and hills the first day without killing them off. On the whole, they looked fine. We had a shot at beating St. Mary's, who shared, with us, the coveted honor of perennial league doormat. But second to last would not impress Father Damian. With a miracle, we could claw our way to... fifth? Perhaps fourth? It wasn't impossible.

Only Alex worried me.

As we reached the campus, I watched my guys running tall and purposeful for the female students, and my thoughts drifted to my own sweet plans for the evening.

chapter

EIGHT

Joy and I sat kitty-corner at the edge of a sushi bar, in a restaurant in some remote, bohemian locale I would never have found on my own. The place was small, dimly lit, and seemed, for a Friday night, sparsely attended. Bamboo was arranged here and there. A mural of Japanese women in kimonos adorned one wall; a taiko drum hung from the ceiling in a corner. Two bandanaed sushi chefs moved with brisk, hygienic efficiency behind an enclosed glass counter.

Joy had picked me up as planned. Her car was a Honda Civic, almost identical to my own but a slightly newer model. When she started the engine, she turned to me and said, "I don't have any money. Are you treating?"

I said of course I would.

Joy looked effortlessly dazzling, working the clutch and stick shift as we pulled away from my apartment. She wore what appeared to be a natural dyed, black blouse with wooden buttons, a purple scarf, a black wool coat, and form-fitting, stretch black jeans.

I considered the coincidence of the Hondas. As a compulsive omen-seeker, I mentioned this, and added, "I sensed a spiritual bond immediately."

"You're such a *writer*," she said. Her voice was so feminine, so light and breathy, and her comment such a direct hit as to who I wanted to be that I felt suddenly drunken with good luck. I gazed at a tiny dream catcher dangling from her rearview and wondered: what am I doing in this car with this amazing woman?

The only other patron at the restaurant was a pony-tailed man wearing a jeans and black sport coat. He ate alone at a table by the wall, and had been sneaking glances at Joy since we entered. Before him was an intriguing dish; a bowl of rice covered with sliced, raw fish.

"Excuse me," I said.

He looked up.

"What's that called?"

He looked at me. He looked at Joy. He spoke to Joy. "Has he ever... been here before?" he said, stirring the air with his chopsticks.

Bright red exploded behind my eyes.

Joy shrugged - pure indifference, bless her lovely heart.

"It is called *donburi*," he said in an overly articulate voice.

He wore a tiny stud in one ear, but this had nothing to with my sudden desire to smash a porcelain teapot across his skull. No, he had committed the single offense that, in my brief foray into adulthood, I found unforgivable: he listened to my question, then turned to the person I was with, and answered it.

I would have strangled him with his own ponytail, had Joy not responded so wonderfully. A cool, dismissive shrug of her lovely, delicate shoulders.

Cut the bastard dead.

Ah, this Joy.

Her earrings were silver hoops and she positively sparkled. She removed her chopsticks from the paper wrapping and began a sophisticated action of rubbing them against each other. I wondered why but didn't ask. It was dangerous to ask questions in this city;

best just watch and learn. I unwrapped my own chopsticks and did the same.

"You know," Joy said, moments later, as she expertly lifted a tekka maki with her chopsticks, dipped it slowly in *shoyu* - this is what she called it - and placed it carefully into my mouth, "there's a lot you don't know about me." She licked her upper lip and appraised me with luscious dark eyes. It was true; I knew nothing about her. I only knew this: I was dizzy. For ballast, I reached for the teapot. I filled two ceramic cups.

"Tell me," I said. My own skill with chopsticks was pathetic and after an embarrassing effort, I abandoned them, and with my bare hand fed her some other kind of roll - rice on the outside and dotted with tiny orange eggs.

She fed me a fresh water eel in the same manner, and it was lovely to taste her fingertips.

"I left high school early," she said. "I wanted to experience life."

Experiencing life meant that she had come up from Los Angeles to Northern California, 'bipped and bopped' around hippie communes, then hung out in Hawaii for a while.

"The communes," she said slowly, "were very free."

Like most of her utterances, this left her lips with an airy lilt, but the final word was jettisoned from her throat a single increment loftier, calling attention to itself. And there in the sushi bar an image of Joy rose up before me; she was a wood-nymph, a fabulous water sprite, dancing with mystic, unclad deliciousness among trees and streams, fawns and butterflies. I asked what she was doing now, in San Francisco.

"My friends all say I should be an actress," Joy said absently, and added that she took an acting class on Sunday afternoons.

I was about to ask about Joy's acting aspirations, but the young man by the wall, said something to the Japanese waitress that sounded like, "*Arigato, hamatachi, yamaguchi.*" as he handed her his bill.

"Oh," she said blandly. "You speak Japanese."

He smiled, wiggled his head smugly and announced, "I lived in Japan for a year."

"That's nice," she said with a voice of pure boredom.

Hear that, fool? Who cares if you lived in Japan? Nobody in this restaurant.

I focused fully now, on Joy and this vision of her in the woods which gave me an unsettling bloodrush. "So, you mean... what? You like... romped around, naked... in the woods?"

Joy nodded lazily without taking her eyes from mine.

Where did she learn this? This super-slow, carefully patient nod of the head. It undid me. I took her hand and she played slowly with my fingers. I put an arm around her and she leaned her slim body generously against me.

I thought of Jackie, my last girlfriend. When I took Jackie's hand on our first date, she said, "Do you think I *want* you to do that?"

Joy's reaction was infinitely more hopeful. I thought again, with some uneasiness now, of Joy in the woods, and the fabulous image evaporated when the actual woman poured me a thimbleful of warm sake and brought it to my lips. "Are you writing?" she asked.

Was I writing? I stared at her for a moment, not knowing what she meant. *Writing?* Was there a keyboard before me? Were there scribbled notes everywhere, empty teacups, a sea of dishes in the sink waiting to be washed, lists of words on yellow legal pads, a guitar nearby for guilt-ridden procrastination? Was I in sweats, wool-slippers, twisting in my chair to crack my back from endless hours of sitting?

Was I writing?

"Just workin on a burp," I said.

My flippancy was a disaster.

She winced, pulled her hands, then, her entire body away, picked up a hamachi, dipped it in low-salt soy sauce and fed herself. The sushi chef watched us, and when I saw him he turned away.

I took her hand in mine. "Joy," I said, "I was... actually thinking about you... in the woods."

Jackie would have said, “Don’t lie,” but Joy said, “You *were?*” Her mystical eyes rekindled. Her brilliant smile returned. “I’m special,” she said suddenly and strangely. “God has a plan for me.”

She entwined her slender arm in mine. A light touch of her lips set my cheek aflame. Her face and voice were suddenly animated. “I want to show you this really cool place. Full of crazy artists and writers. I want you to meet my friends. You’ll like them. They’re really cool people.”

This should have felt promising - that Joy wanted to introduce me to her friends - but I didn’t like the sound of it. Cool people. It probably meant Mr. Mocha Java would be there. Mr. Don Buri, now paid and gone, whom I nearly eviscerated with his own chopsticks was probably a cool person. Most of the people in my writing class, I guessed, were cool. My history with cool people was brief but checkered.

Still, the evening was going alarmingly well. I could not risk another blunder.

chapter

NINE

The Sweet Afterburn was a yet another in Joy's repertoire of hip hangouts that I would not have found in a thousand years. The place seemed hive-like, as if this were a kind of spawning ground: Black clothes. Ponytails. Earrings. Nose rings. Eyebrow rings. Hennaed heads; hair of sixteen shades. Spectacles. Crossed legs.

Joy scanned the crowd from the doorway with gorgeous, tip-toed excitement, and I felt an instant desire to leave. I had dressed like that coach that I was, in jeans and a zippered sweat top with athletic stripes down the arms - *blue*, for Godsake.

Odd pictures hung on the walls. Most were of naked women, but with limbs, breasts and genitals twisted and distorted. I imagined some artist dressed like the patrons of this bar, overhearing the word 'edgy', nodding once, then grimly setting to work.

Joy shot an arm in the air, then took my hand and pulled me though the crowd to a remote corner where a group chatted, all similarly attired. A woman in black with thick-rimmed glasses saw Joy and screamed: "*Joy Joy Joy*!"

Joy responded, "*MARSHA MARSHA MARSHA*!"

The others looked at Joy, and regarded me, it seemed, with a brief, withering dismissal.

"This is my good friend Tim," Joy said. "He's a *writer*."

"Oh, Joy," I said, "why did you have to-"

"A writer?" said Marsha, and the others regarded me again, recalibrating their expressions to something, it seemed, slightly menacing. They looked me up and down now, taking in, I imagined, the entire unhip presentation. A lanky blond man with a ponytail, also in his late twenties, looked at me with a particular intensity.

"What do you write?" Marsha said.

The pony-tailed man appeared quite interested. He wore a black overcoat and seemed to sneer. Was it my attire? Was it because I was with this svelte, dark beauty, with whom he had some history? Or, did he simply desire some? Well, who on earth wouldn't, but I bent my thoughts hard toward a mood and expression of disarming, ingenuous humility.

"Oh, I scribble... you know... stories. And stuff."

"I *always* wanted to write," Marsha said. "Can I ask? How do you do it?"

"*Do it?*"

"How do you... you know... make yourself... *creative*?"

Joy smiled at my side, and the man with the blond ponytail attentively waited for my answer. To his left was a larger man; beefy, bearded and silent.

"Creative?" I said. "Well, I'm only a beginner, but it seems you just have to get down to work and... work hard. Then, after a few days, maybe something good happens. But, far as I can tell, basically, it's lots and lots of hard work."

Marsha frowned.

Preferring her buoyancy, I added, "But I hear long walks are good too."

She grinned instantly. "Oh! I *love* to walk!" she said, then announced to everyone, "I haven't even begun to tap my creative potential!"

No one blinked at this. I liked Marsha.

A man - or boy - appeared at her side. He seemed eight to ten years Marsha's junior, and stood with a proximity that suggested intimacy. He was either in his PJ's or some get-up from India. A medallion hung from his neck and rested on his slight chest. Spectacles perched on his small, boyish nose.

"Tim," Joy said. "This is Roshaldamonde."

I shook his hand, and he stared intensely, as if studying me. "You're a writer?"

"Oh... I try," I said, sick of the question. "What about you? Do you write?"

Without interrupting his gaze, the young man leaned his head to one side. "At the moment, no," he said. His speech was slow, considered. "But a part of me would like to."

"A... part of you?"

"On a certain level."

"A certain-"

Joy took me by the elbow, "Excuse us, I want you to meet someone." She pulled me away and whispered: "Isn't he brilliant?"

"Brilliant?" I said. "What did you say his name-"

"Roshaldamonde."

"Isn't he a bit young for your-"

"This is Jeremy," Joy said. "He's a writer too. Working on a novel."

We stood before the man with the blond ponytail. He had a slight, shoulder hunch and wore a black scarf around his neck.

"A *novel*" I said, working the humility. "That's so... long. What's it about?"

"What's it *about*?" Jeremy said, rolling his eyes. He turned to Joy. "I can't be asked a question like that."

I stared. My jaw clenched

Twice? In one evening?

Jeremy continued to look only at Joy, and completing a train of thought known only to himself, said, "I'm much too unconventional to write for Hollywood."

Did I say I wanted to write for Hollywood?

But Joy seemed oblivious, indifferent. So, I also dismissed it. Perhaps I was too sensitive - my own brother Robert had told me as much - too ready to take offense. Joy grinned. And she looked lovely, glancing around for other friends.

I felt disgustingly out of place; damn-near fluorescent among so much black clothing.

Jeremy pulled Joy aside and bantered about some World Beat band coming to Slim's. He did not look at me once, and just then, I had a vision of one of Joy's communes: beads, headbands and dope smoke. And there I was, in the middle of it all, sitting on a couch, chatting with Joy. Just struggling mightily to be casual and relaxed, unable to believe my wild good luck that this staggeringly beautiful hippie girl was actually talking to me. But my love beads were twisted and cockeyed. My jeans, rather than sporting a series of cool, frayed holes down the legs, had one embarrassing tear at the crotch. My hair, which I'd let grow to its requisite length, frizzed unhiply, perpendicular to my head. Never did it hang, relaxed and mellow, falling easily into my eyes, letting me practice that enviable, sexy gesture of pushing it back as I leaned thoughtfully into a conversation. And then Jeremy appeared behind her. He placed his arms on the back of the couch, rested his head on his forearms. His own hair fell in his face as he brooded dreamily. Then he whispered something in Joy's ear. She turned to me, excused herself, and they left together. I remained, trying to appear indifferent, bobbing my head stupidly to the music.

Though this scene fleeted hypothetically through my thoughts, I hated Jeremy for it nonetheless. I wondered if Joy had a past with him.

Just then, over Joy's shoulder a small hand waved. *To me?* Here? Who in hell would I know - *Tara?* She sat at a table with another women.

"... told my family to fuck off years ago," Jeremy said with a grin, responding to something I'd missed.

I touched Joy's hand. "Excuse me. Someone I know."

Tara smiled as I approached. She wore black, as did her friend who had hennaed hair.

"Tara!"

"Tim! This is my lover, Angela." Tara wore her genderless black overcoat. Angela was attractively boyish and gangly, with a generous smile. She wore black jeans and a black pullover sweater. Angela excused herself, and left.

"Sorry," I said. "I didn't mean to-"

"Oh... She has some other friends here."

I sat down. "It's great to see you." I looked at her for a moment. "You know, I just moved up here... all this... my *lover*... my *partner*... it's kind of-"

"From where?"

L.A., I told her. She was from Seattle.

"So... Angela..."

"Is my lover," Tara said with a smile. "What? You haven't met any-"

"Actually, you're my first."

"Well then I'm proud." Tara's grin was delightful.

"Really? Whoa! God. That's a relief." Somehow, it was also a relief seeing her. Which was odd, because I'd never actually spoken to her in class. She loved women but didn't seem to hate men. And she was warm and friendly; such a contrast from the group I had just left.

"Is it such a big deal?" Tara asked.

"Huh? Hey. No, of course not," I said, reaching for sophistication. "But... you know... I guess, I've... always, sort of... wondered-"

"About what?" Tara said with a playful smile on her face. She was a small woman; plain, with wire-rimmed glasses, but with the spark in her eyes of a very active mind.

"Well... you know-"

"I don't. What?"

"Oh, nothing," I said.

"About what we... *do?*"

"Hey! Jesus! C'mon!" I said, embarrassed. "Give me credit for a little imagination." I glanced around to gather some equanimity, then looked back at her. "More like... you *really* don't mind-"

"Ask away!"

I considered her. Tara seemed easy about this, desiring to dispense with the mystery as quickly as possible. I took a breath. "Okay. Men. We're... supposedly... *visual*. Women are more emotional... I've heard."

Tara wrinkled her nose to suggest my notion was dubious at best, but her smile was open and friendly. Her invitation to ask away felt genuine.

"When I look at a woman, I'm kind of specific." I looked at Tara in sudden apprehension. "This doesn't offend you, does it?"

"That you're *specific*?" she said, grinning, beginning to laugh.

"It's just... everyone's so *touchy* around here."

"I'm not offended."

"You sure?"

"I'm sure, for the millionth-"

"Okay," I glanced around, then said, "Ah! That waitress."

We both looked at an attractive young waitress; a woman of perhaps twenty-six wearing a tight short skirt, a low-cut blouse and bright red lipstick. "She's pretty, right?"

Tara nodded. "She's pretty."

"I look at her. I mean, to me, she's a visual delight. Does that-"

"It doesn't offend me! Will you stop?"

I turned back to the waitress. "Okay, I can't help it, but I find myself looking... at her breasts... her face... the sway of her sweet little-"

I paused.

We both looked for a moment at the waitress.

"You're a woman," I said. "You're more emotional."

"I'm so e*mo*tional," She mimicked me so good-naturedly that I laughed.

"Here's my question: What do you look at when you look at a beautiful woman?"

"Hm!" Tara said, suddenly intrigued. "I never thought about it."

"Well, look at her now," I said. "What do you see?"

We both stared intently and shamelessly at the waitress. The woman looked up from her pad and saw us. She took in each of us with bewilderment, then irritation. She came to our table and said, "Can I get you anything?"

I stammered, "We're fine."

She looked at us both now with pure annoyance. When she left, I shook my head in embarrassment. Tara laughed aloud and said, "Busted."

I looked down at the table. Among a notebook, a purse, and Angela's fanny pack, was a familiar book with a bright red cover. It was a copy of Jonah Woods' short story collection, 'Quantum Theory'. "You're a Woods fan?"

"What?"

"Jonah Woods!" I gestured to the slim volume on the table.

"Oh, Joe Woods. Sort of. He's my brother-in-law."

I stared at her. "*What?*"

"I call him my brother-in-law. He's my brother's wife's sister's husband. Is that a brother in-law?"

"*Jonah Woods is your brother-in-law?*" I said.

She nodded. "You like him?"

"*Like* him! He's my idol! He's the absolute... most incredible-"

"You can meet him if you want-"

"*Meet him?*" I was damn near trembling.

"He'll be in town in a few weeks."

"Jesus! Meet him?"

"We can... have lunch or something. Here." She produced a pen and turned her notebook toward me. "Write your number."

I took the pen and said, "I can't believe this. Jonah freaking-"

"I liked your story," she said as I wrote.

"You're a small minority," I said, handing her the pen. She wrote her own telephone number, tore it off, handed it to me, and I placed it in my wallet.

"Listen," she said. "Write something longer next time."

"Longer?" I turned and saw Joy talking with animation to her friends. "Hey, this was great. Tara. I'm so glad I got meet you. You know, outside the torture chamber. I gotta get back to my date." I thought for a moment. "Do they use that word here?"

"Never," she said. "Which one?"

"Slim... dark, dreadlocked... "

Tara stared at Joy as if suddenly enchanted. "My God, she's beautiful."

I glanced at Joy, saw how lovely she looked, then said, "I better go."

Tara nodded.

This Tara, I thought. Just listens openly and waits for the best.

Not like the group I was now approaching.

As Joy took my arm, she asked, "Who was that?"

"Someone from my class."

"Your writing class?"

Did she have to say that? I nodded.

"So what are you working on?" Marsha said.

"Just a story."

"About what?" she said. "Tell us your story."

Jeremy stared, waiting. As did Marsha, Roshaldamonde, and the big, bearded man.

I would reveal nothing to this group.

But Marsha was so sweet.

"You know," I said, "I'd love to tell you. I really would. But I have this strange fear of feeling naked when it's over." Roshaldemond canted his head quizzically. I brightened. I looked at each of them. When I spoke, I found that my voice had a surprising perkiness, fueled certainly by Tara's kindness. "Let's do this," I said. "I'll tell the story. As I talk, everyone, slowly, little by little, remove your clothes, so when I finish, you'll all be stark naked. Then I'll feel a kind of... equity. Deal?"

Jeremy rolled his eyes. "Not that interested," he said. He could have responded in some jokey way, I thought. I love people who play along, but this was not Jeremy. He looked at Joy.

So did I.

She seemed absent, grinning mysteriously, with two delicate fingers placed thoughtfully on her full, dark lips.

chapter

TEN

The night was clear and cold as Joy parked her Honda in front of my apartment. She killed the engine, fixed the parking break, undid her seat belt, and I felt the Promethean, end-of-date tension of this impossible moment.

"Beautiful night," Joy said.

"Sure is."

She smiled.

A three-quarter moon glowed silver. Distant waves crashed. A car cruised by.

I shifted nervously.

I wanted to know about this Jeremy. What was this intimacy he was trying to insinuate like a nasty wedge between myself and Joy; this woman who in fact, I had only just met? But to ask! To ask without releasing the deadly poison of jealousy seemed impossible. No, best assume a breezy disinterest. And know this: *she's with me.* By God, this miracle of a woman had fed me tekka maki by hand,

and now she was parked in front of my apartment. These were facts. And here she was, stunning in the moonlit dusk.

Can't be asked a question like that.

And why can't you be asked a question like that? Because there's no fucking novel, is there, mister too-unconventional-for-Hollywo-.

Calm thyself.

By some serendipitous, cosmic gift, she was with me now, and this must supplant my curiosity. Be silent. But a cooler voice said: *Watch out for this Jeremy.* I knew the behavior of men around a beautiful woman. Shameless self-promotion, or unrelenting mockery directed toward other men in the vicinity. If she's extremely beautiful, the idiocy increases exponentially. Among primates and rednecks, it amounts to little dick accusations and fist fights. Among Jeremy's ilk, probably a hip, nasty, sparring.

But the Sweet Afterburn was in the past, and here I was with Joy, lovely and to my left, in the driver's seat, hands on the steering wheel, marveling at the magic of the night sky. And it was time to tell her what a nice evening I'd had, and to invite her up for tea - to say anything, in fact, but the blasphemy my truest desire. I watched Joy gaze languidly at the stars, her thigh moving absently... left... then right. To affect such a noble agenda as tea seemed ludicrous.

We stared into the dark, moonlit night over San Francisco. A tiny dot of light - a satellite perhaps - moved a great distance away. A thick bluish fog crept in from the ocean, it's edge nearly upon us.

Was I really so inept? So hopelessly Prufrockian? I looked at Joy and said, "Hungry?"

"Hm?"

"I've got some, uh... bundt cake upstairs. Poppy seed. Made it myself. Old family recipe."

"Bundt cake?"

I nodded my head. I didn't know where the hell to go with this, but I put it out there. Now Joy had to decide: was she hungry or not? The mind of a woman. Such an alien intelligence as I imagined it.

"Did you say... poppy seed?"

"It came out really good."

She turned to me. "It did?"

"Mmm-hm."

I sat in silence. She looked at me blankly. What factions battled for supremacy behind those wondrous dark eyes? Good-girl saintliness? Bad girl condemnation? Pure libido, if I may delude myself? The laughably transparent invitation for bundt cake? But before Joy attended to the next wave of titanic forces that I was certain raged within her, she said, "I love poppy seed bundt cake."

The cold, enchanting fog of San Francisco enveloped us as I took her hand and lead her to my front door.

Joy sat on the couch beneath the poster of Steve Prefontaine. I placed two slices of poppy seed bundt cake on the coffee table and sat beside her. John Klemmer's 'Touch' album played quietly.

"Tea?"

She shook her head, slowly. She had removed her dark coat and tossed it on the back of the couch. Moving super-slow, she looked at me... and blinked once, as if waiting for something. My skin tingled.

"Would you like... anything else?" I asked.

She nodded. "I'd like to hear your story."

"My story?"

She sat up straight and arched her chest, slowly, lazily. "Your story," she said, and with a hint of an impish smile, she added, "I accept."

"You accept what?" As I stared at her, she stood.

"The *bargain*," She leaned into the word, as if to jog my memory.

I looked at her in confusion.

"Tell me your story, dummy," she said.

And it hit me.

She'd accepted.

She destroyed me with her enticing brown eyes, pulled at my hands, let them fall into my lap. And she kept her eyes upon me as she backed nimbly across the living room to my bookcase. There she stood before Vermeer's Head of a Girl, and I stared and wondered: *could this be happening?*

Her eyebrows raised slightly.

They signaled: *Begin.*

"Andrew," I said, clearing my throat. "A workaholic pre-med student, upon graduation, at the insistence of a cool, psychologist dad with a perm, takes a job at a summer camp. Though Andrew would prefer to study all summer to prepare for his first year of medical school, his father uses some clever financial leverage. Andrew's father's own camp counseling days meant a lot to him. A break in the wilderness from the insanity, his father said. To pull his nose out of the books *for once*, and to feel what his dad called the psychic-reorienting effect of children, prior to the huge commitment of Harvard Medical School. That's all his father asks."

Joy observed me coolly. Was she joking? Or willing to honor this half-baked bargain I concocted on the spur of the moment to avoid embarrassment. She stared, then slowly reached a lovely brown hand to a wooden button at her neck.

The fabric fell open, revealing the dark, lustrous declivity of her throat and two delicate tendons.

Her eyebrows leapt again, slightly. *Talk!*

"Andrew's dad asks if there are any women in his son's life. Connie, Andrew says. A fellow pre-med student. They study together. *And?* After a late night in the library once, they decided to grab a pizza. *And?* Andrew dropped her off at her apartment. She asked him to come up, but he said, no, he wanted to go home and study some more."

Joy winced.

"Well, Andrew's father winces too, and insists that he work at the summer camp, and tells him no medical books. But, in a scene of brilliantly rendered internal struggle, Andrew sneaks two into his suitcase."

Joy unfastened a second button, and, with a playful smile, a third, now moving gently to the soft jazz.

"The rustic camp is nestled on a thickly wooded island. Andrew is responsible for a group of seven-year-olds."

Joy's blouse was now open in front, every single button undone. Her stomach was brown and smooth; her bra, black and lacy.

"Then what?" she said.

I thought hard. Then what?

I remembered.

As if to prompt me with a threat of pure torture, Joy waited patiently until I spoke.

"One boy, as I think I named him... yes, Douglas-"

Her blouse fluttered to the floor.

Oh!

"- is an odd, mad-scientist type - perhaps a little genius, who instantly becomes an object of mockery among the other kids. They call him Poindexter."

"Aww," Joy said. She stepped out of one sandal, then the other. Though I spoke in the interests of equity, I felt a trade-deficit, growing bigger and bigger with each bit of apparel to hit the carpet. Was this story worth even a fraction of the miracle occurring before me?

"Early one morning, a young woman named Gail - a spirited, freckled, tomboy - who, in fact, had captured Andrew's attention the instant he arrived - and two other female counselors, to hearken the beginning of summer, decide to streak, at top speed, through boys camp."

Joy's eyebrows danced at this information, and she began to snake out of her jeans. Slow... liquid... side to side... past thighs... down to her knees. She paused, looked at me, smiled, and slid them to her ankles. She stepped out of them.

I took a long breath.

"Everyone in boy's camp is riveted into silence. An awed, respectful stillness pervades as the three giggling, naked young women come rocketing past. From the deck of their cabin, Douglas - ant-burner, mad-scientist - watches them pass with fascination, and when they're out of sight, he suddenly shatters the silence, shouting at the top of his lungs: '*I saw the whole boob!*'"

Joy, now wearing only two wondrous bits of lace, had a familiar look of ironic, naughty-boy disapproval.

She slowly reached behind her back. This pose - so vulnerable - hands... unclasping. The success of this venture suddenly lit her face - *delight* - and then, she pulled the black lace away from her and let it fall to the carpet.

"What happens next?" she whispered.

My pulse raced.

"*Your end of the bargain*," Joy said.

"'I saw the whole boob!' Doug shouted."

"You already said that," she sang.

"Did I? Oh." I concentrated. I remembered this particular section of the story verbatim because I'd rewritten it so many times. "As the other kids stared at Doug, Andrew read their single, shared thought: *Doug is pure dork*. But, in truth, Andrew was equally fascinated. Andrew - medical student, camp counselor - felt an overwhelming desire to sanction Doug's outburst before the others weighed in with ridicule. Or, was it simply a desire to acknowledge a boy's sudden, fabulous ascension from a *partial* boob to a *whole* boob? Andrew didn't know, but his hand was out. He shouted, *Doug!*

"And Douglas, in a moment of geeky hesitation that Andrew knew only too well, lofted his hand skyward then slapped it down on his counselor's."

"Boys," Joy whispered.

With timeless slowness, she slid her lace panties down, over her slim hips, past her thighs, to her ankles. She stepped out of them... one foot... then the other. And before me stood the most breathtaking creature to walk the earth; indeed the earth blasphemed her with every step.

In the next moment, her lithe, brown, perfect body descended lightly into my lap.

"Are you Andrew?" she asked.

"No," I said quickly.

"Good," she said. "Tell me the rest later." And as her lovely tongue singed my earlobe, I hadn't the slightest notion of the exquisite and hideous adventure upon which this amazing woman was about to take me.

chapter

ELEVEN

To be baptized in the sublime!

To emerge, sparkling, purified!

Joy left at six. Had the breakfast shift, she said. She seemed needless of sleep; in fact, I don't believe we slept at all, but once she left I checked into the land of nod until eleven. I awoke calm, rested; mind, body and spirit free.

Stay home and write?

Impossible!

I parked on Clement and paused over the memory of last night. Had lovemaking ever been steamy as this? Not in my experience.

And the heat was still with me as I damn near skipped along Clement Street.

Ah, perfect day!

A nip in the air! Lovers arm in arm.

I never knew such women existed!

My God, until now, Jackie was my only benchmark.

When I first asked Jackie to my apartment, she looked at me with an I-know-exactly-what-you-want sneer, came inside, and granted me one miserable smooch. In subsequent dates, each grudgingly bequeathed bit of her was followed by, "I hope you got what you wanted." When we finally made love, she just lay there as if benevolently relinquishing her body, as if the final pinnacle of erotic bliss was the unveiling of her, allowing me to do what I must, and I fell asleep feeling like some wretched swamp creature.

Aside from Jackie, what did I know? There was Ellie, a tall, powerfully built Nordic woman I met while backpacking in Nepal. Oh, Ellie! Her hugs were rib-cracking tests of manhood; her touch, an excruciating deep-tissue massage. She made love with a fury that left nothing of me but carnage and devastation, and she graced my fantasies still.

There was a lamentably chaste, collegiate fling with a born-again named Barbara Ann, and several fleeting dalliances; some brief, some extended, all barely worth mentioning; and that was it, from the innocence of youth until story hour last night, and no one had enlightened me that anything existed to the contrary.

Follow your heart, doors will open. This is what Mr. Woods had said, and dear God in Heaven, what magical doors they were! His essay on Taking the Leap suggested nothing like this. But now, here on Clement Street, I moved through the world, walked its streets, slipped among its people.

Ah, this city by the bay!

This snap in the air!

Breathe in!

Breathe out!

Clouds with delicate, undulating curves, hung white in a sky of stark, crystalline blue. Air so cool and crisp - breathing itself was erotic.

And lovely women were everywhere - Brown, Asian, Black, Island, White - parading up and down the street, glancing into shop windows, and by God; they had no claim on my attention today! Oh! To walk through a world of cleavage-flaunting, halter-topped beauties, with mini-skirts coquettishly a-flutter.

And to want none of them!

The sun was the only spectacle!

Just air and sunlight for me, thank you.

I had made love last night!

I was in love today!

Go ahead! Try to torment me with that errant bit of lace, as if you, Miss Innocence, didn't even know it was there. Beckon me with tantalizing decolletage!

Go naked!

You all bore me!

These clouds, this sky, that Chinese duck dripping in the window! Infinitely more fascinating!

But you other men: How you slink around, knowing if women had a glimmer of what lurked in your pathetic thoughts, you'd be condemned as the vile, unseemly creatures you are, barely up from the slime.

From that club, I hereby relinquish membership.

Oh, how that exquisite, light brown beauty was revealed, bit by torturous bit, with each slow, delicious button. Freed, as if by Thor's hammer; burst afresh from the mind of Zeus. My Joy on a half shell.

But here on Clement Street? Nothing of interest.

Mere pedestrian flesh.

Yes my homeless friend, you may certainly have a dollar. What is a dollar? What is money? A mere trifle; nay, a nuisance, a distraction, a vulgar stupidity once the heavenly vault opens for a visit. *Visit nothing!* Here I was, moving in this world yet not in this world. I hailed from a loftier domain. And what did she say at that astonishing moment, just after miraculous, tandem detonation?

"I think God brought you into my life."

I shivered at the memory.

Well, God, thank you for such sweet deliverance!

Ah! A bookstore. The Purple Plum.

Jammed.

"Excuse me. Pardon."

The magazines, the fat coffee table books, the bargain rack, and, hello! The new publications!

What have we here?

A new novel by a writer I'd never heard of. 'Cold, Cold World,' by a Mr. Ricardo Chevy. And lo! An endorsement! A blurb by the man himself.

Jonah Woods says, *"A stunning, invigorating bit of magic, by a writer at the height of his powers."*

Good enough! Twelve dollars, and within minutes, I was in my office, yes, the office of a Division One, Head Men's Cross Country Coach. I was to meet my runners for a Saturday afternoon workout and had about thirty minutes until they arrived. The women's volleyball coach who shared the office was off today and I had the place to myself.

I removed the book from the bag and read more of Jonah Woods' glowing blurb.

"A scintillating work of prose, riveting, full of warmth and elegance, and one approaches the final pages with sadness, for many reasons, not the least of which is that this miracle of a book has come to a close."

Jonah Woods!

The man was actually living it: The artist's life! Write brilliantly, blurb in your spare time because, of course, the world craves your opinion. I had watched his meteoric career since his first published story in The New Yorker, a marvel entitled, "Inhale, Exhale," only a suggestion of what was to come from his wildly talented hand.

Well, the Woodsman had a good ten years on me, was now a lecturer at some hot college in the south - one of those literary merit positions that didn't require a Ph.D., which, of course, was a secret hope for my own, hypothetical future.

Ph.D. in English?

Feh!

What is a doctorate but a neon sign of chronic low self-esteem?

Let the fools blather about symbols and images! Let them obsess over genres and influences! Let them squabble over who is major or minor! Was it fun to stare at your students and boom at the top of your lungs, as did Dr. Evans, my bearded, pot-bellied Existential Lit. professor, in what certainly was his finest moment: "But don't you see?" he shouted, "Gregor Samsa has always *been* a bug!"

I shouted this into the emptiness of my office.

Wasn't fun in the slightest.

Woods had the right idea. Literary merit, by God. Inhale, Exhale!

Joy and I had made plans to meet that evening at some cafe called The Owl and Monkey on 9th and Irving. Her last words before she left my apartment this morning?

"Tim?"

"Joy?"

"I look forward to seeing you."

This scant bit of information, even now, was nothing short of thrilling.

Sitting at my desk I was suddenly enraptured by yet another unbelievable memory of last night: Joy lying naked on her side. I glided my fingertips over the rise of her spellbinding hip; chocolate brown, smooth as silk, discovering an exquisite miracle at the confluence of her perfect thighs.

My Joy, as she walks among mortals, there it is: glowing like magelight; a beckoning call to a land of enchantment. This, she takes with her to buy toothpaste, detergent. This, she carries over sidewalks, mingling with mere pedestrians. This, she travels with in her Honda, waiting for a light to change.

Among the dreck of humanity my Goddess walks, like some secret angel, a double agent of Heaven. An alien of some far away galaxy, hailing from an infinitely superior race. She walks among us, not knowing who she is or why she's here, at the mercy of forces she's powerless to ignore, but here, perhaps to show us we could all do better to conspire with such forces rather than struggle against them.

How is it that she sparkles and crackles with sensuality, while all others move through the world like dim, extinguished bulbs?

My Joy.

I brought my runners on a warm-up jog to the base of Strawberry Hill, where we would soon launch into ten hill repetitions. My mood still soared, and if ever there was a time for a coach's pep talk, it was today.

My small team sat before me beneath some oak trees. On the nearby lake a few romantic souls floated about in paddle boats.

I looked at my runners; sweaty, breathing moderately. I waited. When I had their attention, I began.

"We train for one specific moment," I said. I made eye contact with each of them. I was precisely twenty-seven, which I knew sounded ancient to these twenty-year-olds. Still, I tried to infuse my words with the gravity of someone at least twice my age. Perhaps like Father Damian. Or like my father - Christ, could that man hold court at a dinner table. And I wanted it now; the bearing of age and maturity, of some wise mentor who'd been around, knew about the world. "In each race... in training... by God, in life itself, there comes a moment where we're tired, where it hurts. Maybe you get passed; don't panic- *Alex, are you-*"

"I hear you, coach."

Alex's gaze was dreamy, off among the boaters. He seemed lost in the labyrinth of his own thoughts and reluctant to leave. But they all listened now.

"This is the crucial moment," I continued, "and every runner has one of two thoughts: I will push through this, or, I will start inventing excuses for my bad performance. It happens to you, and it happens to the runner next to you and to every runner in the race. The moment will arrive as pure pain. But I want to tell you something about pain: *it won't kill you*. It comes and there it is. Notice it. Make friends, shake hands, get acquainted. But choose to *push through it*. Push through it today, in practice, and when the race comes, the moment will arrive as nothing but a trifle. A nuisance, easily dispensed with. That's what today is about. Okay?"

They nodded.

Gary and Steve seemed to listen. Nick and Peter, consummate students, blinked attentively, and seemed to make detailed mental notations, later to be typed, collated and filed. Alex had mostly watched the boats.

"Ten Hills," I said. "Let's go."

I dragged a toe through the dirt.

We lined up.

We ran.

Gary and I took off, the others behind us. Gary had a feisty love of running; the harder the workout, the better. He bounded easily up Strawberry Hill, challenging me to sprint over the last hundred meters. On the second interval, I gestured for Steve to pull up alongside of us. He accelerated with an easy, lanky fluidity and caught us. The faster pace was new to him, but he adjusted with no trouble. Before we began the third blast up the hill, Gary stepped up beside me at the starting line. He flicked his sandy blond hair out of his eyes and said, "You're lookin at a guy who got laid *twice* last summer!"

Breathing hard, sweating, I took my fictional camp counselor's cue, and we slapped hands. Standing at the line while the runners gathered, I had two thoughts. One: In light of Gary's comment, I wondered if my reach for wise-elder gravitas was laughable. Two: While Gary's summer accomplishment was commendable, certainly for an undergrad, I considered my own shift in erotic fortunes, my state of dizzy exhaustion, and these congratulatory high-fives. And I wondered: love and sex - the entire magical package - or even sex alone! - were they celebrated simply because of their lamentable and terrifying rarity?

I pushed this notion from my thoughts, put a toe on the line and said, "Runners... set... and... go!"

Steve and Gary, to my utter delight, burned the third hill, and in fact, ran together and ahead of me for the next seven intervals. Peter and Nick were behind, out of shape, and though they dragged the last few hills, both valiantly completed the entire workout. Only running and more running would cure the situation, but they seemed up to it.

Alex quit after five hills.

"Shin splints, coach," he said.

He was my fifth runner. There wasn't a thing I could do about it.

chapter

TWELVE

An hour later, I was showered, dressed, and sitting at a wooden table in The Owl and Monkey Cafe. The place was populated by bohemians, hippies, students, the pierced, the tattooed. Against a far wall, a young curly-haired man poured over science text. By the front window, an elderly woman in gray sweats worked a crossword puzzle. Two female, overweight, middle-aged teachers behind me graded stacks of essays. Though tired from the workout, I had roughly half an hour before Joy arrived and thought I'd try to write something. The second story was due in a few short weeks. My father's health was plummeting. I needed something beautiful. Not the summer camp story. I would not bring three streaking female camp counselors into Birnbaum's class.

So.

Pick up this pen, open this writer's notebook, and begin. Just some bit of truth to make the world laugh or weep without widening the cracks in the flaws of my persona. Put pen to paper and-

A tiny, explosive sound caught my attention. A woman, perhaps thirty years of age, sat three tables over, wearing crystals, black clothes. She was Caucasian, and beside her sat an African American, a Rastafarian. He wore a Haile Selassie medallion over a green and red sweatshirt with the word Ganga printed across the front. His dreadlocks were stuffed into large, colorful knit cap.

But the tiny sound came from a small boy who sat on the floor, beneath their table. He was white, therefore, barring some genetic anomaly, hers, and was quite busy, playing with army men, toy tanks, and jeeps. And he was making those depressing, only-child, play-by-yourself car-crashing noises. "*puchhhh... puchhhh!*"

This place wasn't particularly clean - earthy, Joy might say - and I wondered about this mother who would consign her child to such filth beneath the table. She looked up; caught me watching. I turned back to my notebook.

From the corner of my eye, I caught her staring at me. She leaned against the Rastafarian and after a moment, said, "He can't accept us."

What? I thought, without looking up.

I let the meaning of this settle, then allowed myself one, brief glance.

Both stared at me openly. She smiled sadly; the Rastaman grinned outright.

"The world can't accept us," she said, her tone bittersweet. She inclined her head onto his shoulder. "We're always shocking people."

I blinked hard. And they watched me, in my short hair, my collegiate sweat top.

Where was Joy?

Determined to write one worthwhile sentence, I gripped up my pen, but just then, an earringed young man a table over announced to a pretty Asian woman across from him, "I was born into a Jewish family. But my ideas are my own." He sat back, nodded his head a few times and added, "Been getting into Native American stuff lately. And a little Zen. I think you'll find I'm pretty unconventional."

He's Jewish, I wrote, *but his ideas are his own.* I glanced among the other patrons. At a corner table a young man sat a trench coat, a scarf, and a beret. On the small table before him was a cup of coffee, a pen and a notebook. And he jotted... what? *A thought?*

I felt breathless, dizzy. Why was this feeling of doom upon me? I needed to calm down, to focus, and write something decent, but this suddenly felt impossible. The summer camp story was stuck, going nowhere, and I wondered if, in some strange way, it had served its purpose already. *What if I couldn't write anything else?* And what if, for lack of anything better, I *did* bring it to class?

The insipid prose only serves to underscore severe limitations in the writer himself-

My thoughts were interrupted by a woman sitting near the front window, who announced with some volume, "I *mute* the commercials!"

She sat with two other women. All three were middle-aged, dressed in black, with hennaed hair. The tallest had spoken. Her mouth and jaw were set what-do-I-care-what-people-think style, and her friends must have been impressed because she felt that the information deserved repetition: "*I mute the commercials!*" I noticed a cigar box on the table before her.

"Does this have meat in it?" A female voice sung out across the room. By the far wall two pretty women sat at a table. Rather, one was pretty. Both wore headscarves, many bracelets and crystals. The prettier and lankier of the two pointed at something on a menu to a waiter - a bored, paunchy young man with an untucked white shirt and a heavy ring in the septum his nose.

He said no, it didn't it didn't have meat. Everything they served was vegan.

The woman who asked had long hair and she seemed to hold her eyes open, effortfully wider than necessary. When the waiter left, I tried to write, but she spoke again. She told her friend she was thinking of going on a liver cleanse. Further bits of her conversation became vaguely audible: *homeopathy... goldenseal... arnica... body work... macrobiotic... a juice fast to purge...* while the plainer woman nodded her head, pressed her lips, listening intently. Their clothes were earth toned natural cotton, and loose enough to do a yoga stretch right there in the chair - which the prettier one did - some leg wrap-around number. Then she produced a tiny vial, pulled out a dropper and placed ten drops under her tongue, as I counted. She had swum with dolphins, she said, then nodded slowly, "It was a very... healing... experience."

I wrote: *Joy, where do you find these places?*

Just then, conversation ceased.

The unconventional Jew whose ideas were his own swiveled his head and stared. The woman who swum with dolphins and was soon to go on a liver cleanse was transfixed, her dropper hovering inches from her tiny bottle. The mom with a son beneath the table lifted her head from her Rastaman's shoulder. The three hennaheads turned in silent unison.

Joy stood in the doorway.

She wore a flowing skirt graced with the muted hues of an untouched rain forest. Her perfect torso was held smoothly by a black, Danskin top. Every innocuous word was held in check, in order for each patron and employee of the Owl and Monkey Cafe to gaze without distraction. And all, I imagined, pondered one primary, shared question: Who was the lucky bastard this gorgeous woman was craning her lovely neck to find?

Joy was radiant. Was it her clothing? No, you could put her in deep sea diving gear and she'd still silence any conversation.

Conversation?

Breathing itself had ceased!

I waited. Briefly.

And she saw me.

Oh, sweet, perfect moment!

Her brilliant smile! Her lighter-than-air float to my table!

I glanced one brief, lingering moment at the boy under the table, wondered how my milk-chocolate beauty figured into his mother's world view, felt the piquant envy of her dreadlocked partner, and then, the air of The Owl and Monkey was enkindled by the melody of my lover's voice.

"Sorry I'm late."

"You look beautiful."

"Everyone's been telling me," Joy said.

I hated that response but dismissed it because she looked so beautiful.

"There's a cool Japanese place around the corner," she said. "I'm starving."

I looked at her. I was no math wiz, but my calculations were quick. Sushi last night, tempura tonight - I'd be homeless in a matter of weeks. I cleared my throat and said, "I was thinking, maybe... burritos."

Joy's magical smile vanished.

I felt a million eyes upon us. I said Japanese food sounded fine, gathered my things and took her arm.

"I don't have any money," Joy said as we exited the cafe. "Are you treating?"

She buttoned up her sweater and stunned me with an incapacitating smile. And I thought of Albert Camus, who said, somewhere in The Plague: *We fall in love, perhaps three times in a hundred years.* Rent was due soon: five hundred and fifty. I had it in the bank, and a bit more for food and whatnot. The first check for coaching would not arrive for several weeks. My father would, of course, advise prudence, and my plan, accordingly, was to avoid restaurants, sell some used books and this would zero me out for the month. But here was Joy waiting expectantly, wanting to be treated to Japanese food, easily a set back of fifty big ones. And there was Albert Camus, standing on the sidewalk behind her. He wore a dark overcoat with an upturned collar, held a burning cigarette, and his piercing, nihilistic gaze told me: *This is it, mon ami; the real deal. Blow it, and you'll wait a long time for anything even remotely-*

"Of course," I smiled. "I'd be happy to treat."

I zipped my sweat top against the cold, misty air. We passed a begging, homeless man crouched on cardboard in a doorway. Joy pulled at my hand, stopping us. "Give him something," she said.

"Joy, I really can't afford-"

"But you have so much," she said with surprising solemnity. She pressed her lips together as if in silent prayer. She closed her eyes devoutly. She opened them. "… and they have so little. Why, to him, you are rich."

You are rich?

Why the sudden loss of contractions?

"Joy, I'm sorry. Not today, okay." We continued, and as we were about to pass a small corner market I remembered that I needed postage stamps. Behind the counter was a Middle Eastern man wearing a turban. I handed him a ten. He produced a small book of twenty stamps and held out my change. In a move so quick it stunned me, Joy placed her hand, cup-style, in mine, intercepted just over four dollars, and was out the door. When I reached the sidewalk, I saw her, down the street, handing my change to the homeless man.

Joy smiled as she approached. I stood mutely, blinking back my anger, as Joy took my arm and lead me to the Japanese restaurant.

We sat in The Laughing Lotus stuffed on tempura, sashimi, and miso soup. I ate mostly in silence. And I struggled to understand the owner of this lovely but impertinent hand that had plucked four dollars of the small stash that remained from three unhappy years as a teacher, earmarked to stave off poverty and see me through the beginning of a writer's apprenticeship that, with an impossible amount of luck, would end sometime before my own death. Cash kept me writing - the dream alive - and a bit of it was just disposed of, given to a homeless man, and a more significant amount would soon finance this medium-priced feast we had just completed. When the miso had arrived, as if reading my thoughts, Joy said philosophically, "I believe money is a nuisance. If you have it, get rid of it."

So here it was. Her cosmological underpinnings.

And the ugly implication: I was too attached to material things. I considered this through the tempura, the sashimi, and three glasses of plum wine. But something uglier was afoot. She was the lovely, free-spirited bohemian; I, the penny-pinching miser. Her role, as she saw it, was to edify. It *was* only a few dollars, and I was fabulously in love. I tried to embrace this point of view, knew how easily she would roll her beautiful eyes at my pettiness if I broached a discussion of money. And I was gone, on my ass in love. How often was I in love? Almost never. Lust-crazed always, but never in love. I was in the midst of something miraculous - I knew this - and I needed to be careful. The prospect of three scant, precious occurrences of love in a hundred years - as Camus had warned - allowed for some extra expense. And certainly, Joy wasn't just any woman. I had to proceed carefully, work myself out of this mood, and move the conversation to less jagged shoals.

When I felt my voice could achieve a convincing, upbeat tone, I spoke.

"So," I said. "What are you looking for... in a man?"

"Oh..." she mused. "Someone... tall."

"Tall?" I said. I bobbed a chopstick thoughtfully. "What if... he's not exactly tall? What if he's... I don't know... an intellectual giant instead?"

"I'd consider it," she said, her impishness returning. "And you?"

"Me?" I sat up. "What am I looking for? In a woman?"

She nodded. I thought about her question.

"Well... she's smart... She loves sex more than life itself. And..." I considered this briefly, "she can bake."

Joy broke into a half-smile, then stared off. She looked at me. She laughed, then took my hand in hers, moved her third finger slowly around my palm. I quivered. What magic was in this woman's touch? Jackie's hands were Siberiesque compared to-

"I can't bake," she said slowly.

"Bummer," I said.

"Let's go." She leaned across the small table and touched a mystical wet tongue lightly to my lips.

I paid. The bill was forty-eight even and she made no move to contribute even a tip. Edifying as this might be, it couldn't continue. But as I carefully stood, more immediate hungers silenced me.

chapter

THIRTEEN

Joy tossed her sweater onto the couch and headed to the bathroom. I flipped through the bills I'd left on the kitchen counter. My car insurance was late. I thought I had a few days. The check was written; it just needed a stamp. I fished them from my pocket as Joy entered the living room and settled herself on the couch. I looked at her and she smiled as if reading my mind, as if loving my appreciation of her. What was it like to be the owner such physical perfection? I had no idea, but I opened the book of stamps, tore one off, licked it, then said absently, "Joy? Who's your insurance company?"

She thumbed a Track and Field News she found on my coffee table.

"Hmm?"

"Car insurance," I said without looking up. "Who do you-"

"I don't have any."

I looked over at her. "You don't *have* any?"

She shook her head.

"Joy, everyone has to-"

"God would never let me get in an accident," she said, flipping a page.

I affixed the stamp and slowly stole a look at Joy. She glanced at a few pictures, tossed the magazine back on the coffee table, then picked up a New Yorker.

I repeated this startling information to myself:

She has no car insurance.

Why?

Because God would never let her get in an accident.

I licked the envelope, sealed it slowly, placed it on the counter, near the door where I'd see it tomorrow. I looked at her again. There she was, flipping through the New Yorker. Not even pausing for the cartoons.

God would never let her get in an accident.

She said this so easily, implying a certain chumminess. Behind her was Valery Borzov; to his left, Steve Prefontaine. A threesome of supremely physically gifted individuals.

I watched her, tried to arrange all of this in my head. Her friends, her expectation to be treated, our encounter with the homeless man, her divine exemption from car insurance. They seemed to congeal sourly in my stomach.

"What about Jeremy?" I said.

"What about him?"

I stared at her. "I don't know. Does *he* have car insurance?"

"Jeremy?" She shrugged absently.

I moved around the bar without taking my eyes from her. "How's his novel coming?"

"He's very private about his writing."

Leave it there, a voice told me. Shut up now. Clamp your fucking lips-

"I bet he's private," I said. "How well do you know him?"

"He's just a friend."

Shut the hell-

"A friend?"

She looked at me for a moment, nodded, and I said, "I don't know. I just got the feeling, at one time, you were... *dating* him or something."

"*Dating*," she said.

How I hated the little trick of repeating one unfortunately uttered uncool term for the sake of mockery. And I hated the direction my brain was irrevocably shoving me.

"You were then?"

"For awhile." Then she added, simply, "He's a genius."

I forced a laugh.

"Tim," she said softly, flipping a page. "Let's not talk about past lovers."

This stinger, dropped lightly as a silk handkerchief, staggered me to the roots of my toes. I mastered it enough to do nothing but blink, and to place an elbow on the bar for equilibrium in a suddenly tilting apartment. A genius, she said. Not a critical, judgmental molecule in that perfect body. Of course, this was precisely the cancer that metastasized exponentially, within me this very moment.

Joy gave up on the New Yorker, then picked up a science magazine filled with Hubble Telescope pictures of the universe.

"Tim."

"What?"

"What's wrong? You look... I don't know, strange."

I sat beside her, put an arm around her, felt the blessing of her slender, miraculous proximity. How I only wanted to touch her again, just as I had the previous night, when she lowered herself, a stark naked blessing, into my lap. And who could say? Maybe God did protect her in traffic, and the rest of us had to fend for ourselves. It wasn't all that far-fetched. If God existed, if he played favorites, wouldn't Joy be one of them?

"Joy," I laughed. "You wouldn't believe these people at that cafe tonight."

She pulled her head back. "What about them?"

"What about them? They purge their livers! They brag about muting commercials! They swim with Dolphins, ignore their kids and put drops of God knows what under their tongues." I shook my head. "They remind me of your friends. Jesus, where did you find that crew? *Can't be asked a question like that.* May I tell you *why* he can't be asked a question like that? Because there's no book! Mr. Genius doesn't even write. And that guy in his PJ's? What's his name?"

"Roshaldemond?"

"*Roshaldemond.*" I repeated sarcastically.

"Why are you so cynical?"

"Marcia, she was nice. But that big guy. No love from him. My God, who are these people?"

She smiled. "They're just.... free spirits."

"*Free spirits?* Joy, please. They're anything but-"

She pulled away from me. "I had no idea you were so critical."

"*Critical?*"

"What do you... just... hate everyone?"

I considered Joy's assessment; that I hated everyone. And the terrifying fact that woman I loved had just pulled away from me, her face filled with distaste.

"You do," she said irritably. She grabbed the science magazine on her lap and said, "You probably even hate... *astronauts!*"

"Astronauts?" I looked at the magazine. I looked at her.

She stared at me. "*You hate astronauts?*"

"Joy, relax," I said. "I like astronauts... mostly."

"Mostly?"

I shrugged.

"*What?*" she said.

I looked at her. "Okay. Why do they to always have to go up in space, look down at the earth, and say: '*It looks so... fragile.*'? Every damn astronaut says the same, exact-"

She tossed the book onto the coffee table.

She looked at me for a long, open-mouthed moment, with a barely perceptible headshake. When she spoke, her words came in slow, pious disbelief: "You don't think the earth is fragile?"

How was this happening?

"Of course! God! Of course I do! I'm sure it is! The earth is terribly, horribly fragile!" I fought to calm my voice: "I just don't think it *looks* fragile! It just sounds like something they planned on saying when they filled out the *damn astronaut job applica-*"

"You don't think the earth is fragile?" she repeated, her voice soft as a zephyr.

"Joy." I stared at her. "Why are we talking about this?"

But I saw the delineation in her mind clearly: The cool, laid-back hippie vs. the clear-cutting, toxic waste dumping, meat eating Republican.

"Joy, you don't have the slightest idea what I'm-"

"Why are you shouting at me?"

"I'm not shouting! Joy. In Calcutta they give bus rides for rich tourists to gawk at starving Indians. Would you like to know why? So they can fly home, work up a soulful voice over a ten course dinner and tell their friends: '*I saw a baby, so weak, it couldn't even cry.*'

Joy looked at me. "You are so callous."

"Callous? *I'm much too unconventional to be-*"

"Would you please stop talking about-"

"Christ! I haven't even started-"

"Stop cursing at me."

I stopped. I couldn't believe what was leaving my lips. I took a breath, tried to think of exactly what it was I wanted to say. I wasn't even sure. The evening was descending into hell. I had no idea why.

"I'm sorry," I said. I took her hand in both of mine. "In fact, please forget everything I just... they're all free spirits. Your friends, okay? Joy, all I really want from anyone is kindness. That's it. And, well... frankly-"

"They're nice to me," she said, implying, clearly, that if there was a problem it was mine alone.

Of course they're nice to you, I thought, finally biting my lip. The world queues up to kiss your gorgeous-

"You wear me out," she said suddenly. She dropped my hands and exited to the bedroom.

What could this mean? That I wore her out? But there I was: shorthaired, tragically unhip, sitting alone in my living room. Why couldn't I simply close my mouth? I was damn near shaking.

In a moment, I stood in the doorway of my bedroom. Joy was on her side, beneath the covers, facing the wall. I tried not to look at the feminine curve of her hip. I tried not to imagine those smooth dark legs beneath the sheets. Leo Tolstoy used to play a game with his brothers: Stand in a corner and try not to think of a white bear.

Good luck.

My God, I loved her. What prompted me go off on astronauts? About her friends? Jesus, I needed to calm down.

I saw some movement, some mumbling or something.

"Are you praying," I asked.

She nodded. "And so should you."

Don't answer.

"How exactly does one pray?" I said. "Do we ask for what we want? Money, love, and success? Won't God find that a bit selfish? Or do we pray for world peace and the end of hunger? Then he'll reward our thoughtfulness and give us the crap we wanted in the first place. Isn't He clever enough to see through that one?"

Joy said nothing.

"Okay, God, let's have a little world peace!" I waited a moment. "What do you know! No world peace! And guess what else? No Beamer!"

"Will you *please stop!*"

I stopped.

I was shaking. My God, what was happening? Should I touch her? No... not now. Don't try to fix this now. Christ, I needed to calm down. This was only our second night together! Here I was, caught in the horrific, smoochless dead end of an inane discussion I shouldn't have begun in the first place. I was lucky she didn't leave.

Well, she couldn't; we'd taken my car tonight.

Before my mouth could betray me again, I backed away, returning to the living room. There was Borzov. There was Steve.

So competitive, Joy would say. The decor of my living room was a disaster. I should get few posters of the Buddha, a coffee table book on Zen, a zafu, a meditation bowl. A few goddam dream catchers.

Relax. Breathe.

Reading is relaxing, I thought. And there was Ricardo Chevy, sitting on the coffee table. Cold, Cold World.

One of our best....

yes, yes...

... A singularly rich and abundant work. Luminous... compelling.

Mr. Woods' endorsement. I opened the book. I read a page. I read two. I read them both over a second time. It all seemed so... dull. I forced my way through ten pages. I tortured myself for twenty-five, when the boredom, the sheer wincing at lame, wordy, overwritten sentences became so painful I was ready to rip the book to pieces and fling them at the wall.

Was it me?

Was I missing something?

Either way: twelve bucks, gone.

I put the book down, sat for a moment. When I felt calmer, I entered the bedroom, got into a pair of boxers and a t-shirt and climbed into bed.

I ought to be more accepting. I ought to embrace them, Joy's friends, magnanimously, each on their own path to selfhood. Creating themselves, Joy would say. Fine. I thought; just be nice about it. That's all I really-

What did I care about any of them?

I cared only for this love, this beauty at my side. I would make coffee in the morning as a peace offering. I would lay the Sunday Chronicle at her feet. We'd spend the day in bed. Reading. Drinking coffee.

I would make it perfectly.

I would not scald the beans.

chapter

FOURTEEN

We awoke.

Or rather, I awoke. The cloudy morning illuminated the cream-colored curtains, brightening the room with a soft, gray light. Joy was still here, and for this I was grateful. She could have demanded a ride, and I wondered why she stayed. I went to the front door, picked up the newspaper, tossed it on the bed with enough violence to jolt anyone from the land of nod.

Joy did not stir.

In the kitchen, wearing gray sweats and wool socks, I prepared my peace offering. Coffee, brewed to perfection.

Yes, I ought to be less judgmental. Yes, Joy, they're creating themselves, but consider: is a self created? Or discovered?

Never mind.

I cared only for this beauty, this miracle, now a-snooze in my bed.

I lifted the pot of water away from the flame just prior to boiling. This morning was far too important. The Sunday Chronicle would soon be spread out on the blankets. We would drink, read, chat amicably. Coffee for Joy, decaf tea for me. A bit of toast - whole wheat - spread lightly with butter and honey. I arranged it all on a tray, and when I entered the bedroom, she had a pillow propped up and was reading the pink section. She did not acknowledge my entrance. This was instant bad news: Joy was a tenacious grudge-holder, even through eight hours of sleep.

"Ah," I said holding the tray at the doorway, "Each day, a fresh start, a new beginning. The mistakes of the past are forgiven, forgotten, and we take our place, once again, at the starting line." I placed the tray on the nightstand, handed her a cup and said, "Forgive me?"

She looked at the cup, took it, neither thanked nor forgave, and continued to read. I opened the curtains and the morning sun mildly lit the room. Joy wore one of my UC Santa Barbara track t-shirts. I didn't know if she wore anything else.

Whereas a night of sleep transformed me into some misshapen mollusk, when Joy awoke, even angry, she looked fabulous. She brought the cup to her full, dark lips, each small sip defining her perfect cheekbones.

I got into bed beside her. I looked at the headlines but thought: What did I care about the news? I had my own catastrophes. My fate hung on a knife edge. I hadn't planned beyond coffee.

"You know," I said. "When handed a cup of coffee, some people might say - I don't know - the words mean nothing, but... take the word *gratitude*. Do we feel it? Is there a corresponding emotion for the word gratitude? Perhaps not. Just the same, people say silly things - like, when handed a cup of very carefully brewed coffee - they might say... *thank you*. Of course, it's meaningless. Perhaps even hypocritical, but it's kind of nice-"

Joy said nothing.

I bit down on my lower lip.

"Some might think - that's Mocha Java by the way - that to say absolutely nothing... is downright rude. So... *please... thank you...* make this rough, harsh world a tiny bit-"

"Thank you." It was grudging and sarcastic, but despite her tone, still had a disarming childish quality.

She did not look up.

I took a breath. Was her plan to sip coffee, read the paper, then ask for a ride home?

Don't panic.

Breathe.

Focus.

Here she was, in my bedroom. I loved her, and if she goes, according to Albert, I won't feel such love again for a long, long time.

Outside, the morning was clouding up and getting darker. Soon, a light mist would fall. Joy continued to read the movie section. I took a sip of tea, thought hard, planned my next move. I put the cup on the nightstand, then slid down under the covers. With the barely perceptible touch of my left hand, I made a fabulous discovery; she wore only a t-shirt and nothing more. I continued my delicate exploration. Her knees were propped up, and she continued to read. Her indifference frightened me, but still, I touched her lovely thigh. It was smooth, warm, perfect. I slid my fingertips slowly over her exquisite, brown stomach. I discovered a perfect hip.

She said nothing.

I inched my hand, cautious but courageous, back along the smooth contours of her soft thigh...

I moved it slowly, lightly, down, to her beautiful bottom. I played there for a bit. She didn't move.

A silent treatment.

A lesson.

Voiceless vengeance.

She read.

She sipped Mocha Java.

Slowly, carefully, my intrepid fingers danced, feather-like over her miraculous skin, alighting gently upon creation's most exquisite mystery.

She flipped a page, unmoved.

I dallied; a maestro of lightness I was, in a netherworld of enchantment.

She read.

And she read.

I performed a maneuver I invented myself, coined: The Athenian Rhapsody, executed brilliantly, but now with a subtle, extemporaneous flourish on the follow-through.

How she feigned indifference I could not fathom, but Joy flipped through the pink pages, perusing now, the horoscopes.

She didn't speak, didn't flinch, but, thank God, did not push me away.

And here I was in this domain of endless mystery.

Such beckoning softness.

Quietly, secretly, though my brain was torqued in frustrated madness, I continued to play; my touch delicate, patient.

She didn't move.

"Joy?" I said.

"Hmm."

"You gonna keep reading that?"

"Yep."

My fingertips graced her, weightless as air.

She neither encouraged me, prevented me, nor cared.

I took a breath. And I lay beside her in resignation, my hand camped out where it was, not about to relinquish terrain already captured.

"Well, you know what they say," I said.

She flipped a page, and without looking at me, spoke for the fourth time that morning, "What?"

I grinned. "Each to his own pink section."

It took a moment for Joy to sort through this, but in the next instant, sections of the Sunday Chronicle - Sports, Bay Area, Real Estate - were smashing me over the head, and my lovely girlfriend of nearly three days was laughing. She was up on her knees, in nothing but a t-shirt, battering me with a Macy's catalog in one hand, classifieds in the other.

"You are sooo... *disgusting*!" she shouted, pulverizing me as I laughed loud and wickedly, and just then, light as a summer breeze, Joy passed gas.

"Ahh!" I shouted. "Such a sound from one so beautiful!"

"You heard that?"

"Most of San Francisco heard it!"

"Shut up!"

She pummeled me with the food section and I tackled her sweet and thrilling 120 pounds of pure magic onto my bed.

"I love you so much I can hardly breathe," I said, in disbelief at what had just left my lips. I had never uttered such words to anyone else. And I would not, according to Albert, for another thirty-three point three years.

"Let's get some breakfast," Joy said with sudden delight on her face. "Let's go out."

Fair enough. It was Sunday. My runners had a day off, and I could give up a day of writing. And I would not rush this sea change, and this woman, who I was barely beginning to understand.

chapter

FIFTEEN

Though we parked as near as possible, we were still a good quarter-mile from Sweet Nothings. The morning was overcast and chilly. A cable car rumbled up Church Street. I put my arm around Joy's waist and pulled her close as we headed toward Market, then up through the Castro where well-groomed men in tight jeans moved around us, parted for us.

"Here I am, on this crisp, foggy San Francisco morning, with my wondrous girl, exquisitely breasted, mystically tushed, the desire of all men, the envy of all women. Gaze if you must. Crave these lips but dismiss the thought; *they're mine!* Perfection, from the top of her head to the tips of her toes! Marvel these long, elegant legs. What wizardry inflames these eyes?"

I stopped, faced a store window. I stood behind her as we observed her reflection. I placed my hands lightly on her hips, my mouth just beside her ear. "Such breasts! Perfect. Soft. And... you can even feed babies with them! What a package is my Joy!"

She looked at each of them, left, then right. I held out her arms, as if, for the world to ponder, then slowly glided my hands over her ribs, her waist. "Caress with your eyes, such fabulous, feminine contours. Fathom the rapture of such enticing declivities."

Joy hit me gently on the arm - a wholesome girl's disapproval - but not hard enough to make me stop. It signaled, in fact, quite the opposite. I returned my hands to her ribs. "But steal a glance, if you dare, upon such round, erotic symmetry, a slight agonizing bounce with each delicate footfall. Orbs of magic - ah, what sorcery lies in such shapely wonder?"

The corners of Joy's mouth rose slightly. And I could see it. A slight, puckish look. Again, her feigned censure, which in fact, made her more wholesome and lent me, I hoped and prayed, an element of rakish, erotic danger.

Men. We are bad, and bad we must be.

Pity the fool who makes noble speeches about a woman's inner beauty, and stares into the sanctimonious misty-blue as ladies in earshot nod in righteous, bland approval.

Upon this man the curse of friendship descends.

He goes home alone.

He jacks off.

The fool can have his friendship.

Here, today on Castro Street, the inoculation of that pestilence was evident in my lover's sweet dimples.

Continuing along the sidewalk she turned around, held both my hands, and walked backward, smiling at me; a cool, sideways bob to her gait.

I was toppled, undone.

Grinning with embarrassment.

How did she manage this?

Who knew, but I was dead in the water. I surrendered happily.

A homeless man crouched by a brick wall, probably where he slept on newspapers the night before. His clothes were filthy, in tatters. He held out a hand. I tried to look away, but Joy said, "Give him something."

What did I care?

I reached in my pocket, handed him a dollar.

Soon, we faced each other in a booth at Sweet Nothings eating carrot cake, far and away her favorite breakfast. We warmed our hands around lattes. Sweet Nothings, yet another in her endless repertoire of hip hangouts. The clientele was adorned with earrings, black clothes, cornrows, ponytails. A young, pierced woman ordering at the counter wore tight black jeans and a black, metal-studded belt. Hippies, rebels, bohemians - *I loved them all!*

The menu had something called the Tofu Scramble. Beneath that, The Vegan.

My woman was home.

We shared a carrot cake, sipped lattes. Decaf and soy for me.

Joy's beauty was so natural she required no prep time. She wore my sweatpants, my t-shirt, a sweater - not a stitch more - and we were out of the apartment. Had I known such early morning impulsiveness in any woman?

If I said to Jackie, "Let's go out for breakfast," she would say, "You didn't tell me we were going out for breakfast."

"I just thought of it."

She would exhale in exasperation, look out the window, decide on her attire.

I would pick up a novel, sit on the couch, and wait.

After a bath, a make-up and hair session, a few touch-ups with an iron, roughly three hours later, when I was no longer in the mood for breakfast, we would leave. I used to ask her to hurry, but this caused fights that would last all day, and I finally understood that she was only comfortable in the world if she was prepared for it.

Joy was born prepared. If she wasn't, the world would probably recalibrate just to suit her. Today, she was ready before I was, bless her soul.

I placed a bit of carrot cake in Joy's mouth and watched the miracle of pleasure consume her. She threw her head back, closed her eyes and said, "*Mmm....*" I had seen this look on her face before: sushi, lovemaking. Ah, the things she enjoyed. I mused over this, about Jackie, measuring the polarities of these two women. I raised a bit of carrot cake on a fork to her lips, and readied myself to observe a second wave of bliss.

It was like the last, only more audible.

Then, her large, slow brown eyes, locked unflinching onto mine. I stared back, met her gaze in loving retaliation, but the power emanating from her crushed me, dissolved me, left me weightless and floating. Adrift with no ballast.

Disarmed, speechless, tingling.

Gone.

How could I desire a woman so much?

Elbows on the table, she bobbed her fork in mid-air, appraised me coquettishly, and said, "There's a lot you don't know about me."

I took her free hand across the tabletop. With the other she carefully impaled her carrot cake.

"You were a hippie," I said. "So... I guess... what? Communes?"

She nodded slowly.

"Drugs?" I said.

She nodded, and did miraculous things with her lips as she stared at me.

"People walking around... naked in the forest?"

She nodded again.

I considered this briefly. A glimmer of a notion banged at a door I wasn't quite ready to open. I glanced around at the people in other booths. Two hippies smooched in the corner. A black-clad woman with hennaed hair pronounced, articulately as possible, "I will have thee... Tofu Scramble," to a tattooed and earringed waiter. A homeless man mumbled over a cup of coffee. A somber, multi-pierced woman stood behind the counter at an espresso machine.

"Tim," Joy said, calling me from my reverie. "Are you writing?"

I looked at her, startled.

I considered her question. I would not make the same mistake twice.

"Why yes, Joy. I'm writing."

She brightened.

"You're quite... perceptive," I said. I looked into her eyes. I tried for all I was worth to make my gaze penetrating. "You know, Joy, it's uncanny... what the artist perceives beyond the... ken of pedestrian sensibility." I glanced around. I took it in, all of it, nodding with gravity at the miracle of creation.

A leaf had blown onto the floor beside me. I picked it up, turned it slowly in my fingers. I looked at my lovely woman. "You know," I said. "It's all... so... amazing... when you shine the light of art onto the world. Even a leaf -" My voice trailed off, letting silence speak volumes her imagination would complete. Joy watched me and listened, I hoped, musing over the intricate, fathomless depths of my creative soul.

She sipped her latte and watched me. She shifted in her seat. Dear God, I nearly lost her last night, but she was with me now. Her gaze sent an intoxicating ache through my chest. Again, I looked into her eyes. "Joy," I said. "Let's go home."

"Not yet."

"Not yet?"

"Tell me what you're writing."

I would not blow this twice. I thought hard. I pushed my poor little brain beyond the red line. I tried to guess the bent of her desire.

"Well, actually, it's about you."

Her dark pupils widened ever so slightly.

"Joy... you inspire me. I'm writing a story about you."

Her eyebrows rose, barely.

"Forgive me. It's a bit of a... fantasy."

The homeless man in the corner stood, then staggered out the door. A young couple, both in black trench coats entered and settled in a booth.

"About me?"

"May I?"

She waited. I held both her hands. She never took her eyes from mine, and I'm certain that in my twenty-seven years, I've never had a woman's attention the way I had Joy's at this moment.

I watch you from a vast distance.

On a warm, tropical beach... Hawaii, Tahiti, perhaps the rugged west coast of Australia, and you walk lazily toward me. A soft breeze rises -

"Wait," Joy said. "What am I wearing?"

I thought hard, then -

You wear a bikini top. A brightly colored flowered wrap is tied at your hip. As you walk, a smooth, dark thigh appears... then disappears. You hold a book in one hand. The breeze blows your skirt lovingly around your long, brown legs.

From behind some trees, I watch you.

You glance about, quite sure you're alone, that this endless beach is yours. The waves rise... then fall... one, then another, slow and languid. The water is warm, deep blue. And I watch you. As you approach I can make out your graceful features. Large, lazy brown eyes. Slender arms. Your smooth, brown stomach.

You stop.

A breath of wind tosses your hair, your skirt.

"What's my hair like?" She stared at me.

"Um... loose... flowy."

"Flowy?" Joy considered this. "Okay."

You gaze about to all horizons... but you're satisfied.

Not a soul for miles.

A Chekhovian sadness envelopes me.

I don't know how or why I'm there. But as I watch, I discover, I'm not wearing a stitch! Who knows why? But the sight of your slim, brown figure, alone on the sand has my blood racing.

I looked at Joy to see how she fared with this euphemism.

She blinked in comprehension.

You glance around, one last time, and then -

I paused. She waited.

- you remove your wrap. Joy. You're wearing absolutely nothing beneath. You lay it down slowly, tossing it out with the breeze - it flutters, then settles gently on the warm sand. You reach both hands behind your back. In the next instant, your top is undone and dropped carelessly onto the cloth.

I tremble before the most sacred vision I've ever been blessed to gaze upon. But you look so natural, so at ease amid the sand, the breeze, the waves. You belong here, naked and lovely, on this beach.

The breeze caresses you. I am that breeze. I embrace your smooth, dark skin; kiss your legs, your arms, your perfect chest. You jog down to the water, enter carefully. Slowly, you immerse your legs, your hips. The warm sea envelopes you, loves you. You splash in the swells. You duck beneath a breaker, rise like a graceful mermaid, then return to the sand, dripping, sparkling like some bejeweled goddess as you lay upon the cloth. You pick up your book, read a line, then turn it face down beside you.

You feel sleepy. You close your eyes.

Some force, possibly the most powerful in the universe, impels me. I'm by your side, kneeling, perhaps in worship, with a desire I've never known possible. Your legs. Your smooth hips. Your silken, ebony skin. Dear God in Heaven, what a divine sight you are!

The breeze lifts, gently.

Your eyes open.

You're not startled.

You're neither afraid nor embarrassed.

You look me over with a calm and poise that is yours alone.

I'm embarrassed yet I can't stop admiring you. My hand reaches, but - do I dare touch a vision so rare it may disappear on contact?

With only your eyes you grant me tacit consent.

Slowly, lightly, I touch your warm thigh. I lightly trace the delicate outline of each rib, scale the summit of one breast.

I look up. Down the beach, far away, where you first emerged onto the sand, several people appear. They are mere dots now, but they move slowly in our direction.

My breath catches.

"What's wrong?" you ask. Your words are comforting.

You follow my gaze.

"I don't want them to see me..."

You look me over now, as if for the first time. You touch me, so lightly.

My entire body ignites at the fire in your fingertips.

You glance again at the intruders, far, far off down the beach.

You look at me with beguiling brown eyes and say slowly, "I know a perfect place..."

"Let's go!" Joy said, suddenly on her feet and gripping my hand.

"What?"

"Pay! Now!"

I caught the gentle scent of a sea breeze, took a deep, intoxicating inhalation. I removed my wallet and as I became lost in the depths of her dark irises, she spoke with an urgency that shocked me, "Let's *go!*"

She ripped the wallet from my hand, threw a ten on the table, then pulled me out of booth, out of the coffee shop.

"C'mon!"

We exited into the cool San Francisco morning. The world seemed oddly tinged; passionate, feverish, inflamed with some single-minded trajectory, and Joy pulled me. We slipped among gay lovers. Men and more men, who saw little to notice in Joy, who might have wondered, as I did, at our haste. A thirtyish man in a tight black shirt looked me up and down. He grinned. We passed a Thai restaurant, an upscale clothing store. Joy pulled me away from the morning crowd and up a side road where the pedestrians thinned then disappeared. She knew every little, curious turn and path in this strange, magical city, and soon we were heading up a steep incline. Suddenly, Joy left my side, and she tried the front door of an apartment. *"Joy, what are you -"* It was locked. She retrieved my arm again and we took a path that became stairs, up and up, over a hill, down steps on the other side, to a small, almost porch size area on a grassy hillside. No one was around. Trees. An apartment building in the distance.

I trembled.

Joy smiled, laughed, and stared at me.

"Love me," she said.

"What?"

Her breath came hard and fast. In one unbelievable motion, her clothing - sweater, t-shirt and sweat pants were on the ground beside her. And here it was - her spellbinding, slender form in the San Francisco mist.

I stared in wonder. What sort of creature was this? I looked around.

"What if someone-"

"I don't care."

I fought my belt, and in a moment, my clothes were also in a heap on the ground.

"*Love me*," she said again, her breath coming wildly now.

My consciousness seemed to narrow; to drop down from my head and rise up from my feet, converging powerfully in one agonizing focus - the center of space, of time; a sweet, burning apex yearning mindlessly toward one otherworldly dimension - mild resistance, then sweet, delicious immersion - a cliff dive from a thousand feet, slipping into a warm tropical ocean, a mythic place beckoning with such urgency, deep, deep, lost and gone, engulfed in darkness, swallowed in blissful warmth, ascending and falling across a universe time-twisted, snow boarding comet trails, past Andromeda, Cassiopeia, galaxies unnamed, sweet mystic nubbles above, an insane volcano below, luscious valleys, peaks, delicate ridges, oh, to be graced with such soft, loving surroundings, surely a presentiment of Heaven, surely a hearkening to the garden itself, then *rain*, fiery, tempestuous, a flood of warm honey, engulfed in sweet, wet witchcraft as I reach, extend, expand a thousand times to fill this electrified firmament, yes, oh baby yes; I am splayed, splattered across the cosmos, a kidney bulleting past Mars, a spleen careening through the Pleadies, and my soul supernovas in a blinding cacophony of color, of light, and of Joy, moaning then grinning, breathless, clutching me and staring with her impossibly delicious dark eyes.

"*Hold me!*" she said, and I held her as she quaked powerfully in my arms, then laughed and laughed, my perfect angel.

Oh, my God, I loved this woman.

She settled into a series of quiet shudders as I held her. Her breath slowed as she nuzzled her face onto my shoulder.

After a moment, she asked, "What's that thing you said?"

"What?"

"Check... checkovary something."

"Chekhovian?"

"Uh-huh."

"A Russian writer," I said, catching my breath. "Anton Chekhov. He once wrote: *Great beauty has the effect of making you sad, because you can never possess it.*"

This struck Joy as so achingly romantic that she sighed deeply and tragically into my neck.

I embraced her, regained some composure. I looked around quickly - no one.

Trees. Concrete steps. Mist. One bird.

No one.

She held me. She kissed me, then gazed at me, her dark eyes languid and dreamy.

We laughed, jumped into our clothes, dashed back over the hill and down the last flights of stairs. Soon, we were back in the Castro, among people who had just been shopping, looking for a parking space, eating a croissant; and the world seemed ludicrous. We burst into giggles every few steps, contained ourselves, giggled again. Would anything in my life compare remotely to this? Was this the peak and the rest mere filler between now and death?

"Joy, that was the wildest, most amazing - I mean, my God, were you ever so, unbelievably-"

"It was neat," she said.

"Neat? Just *neat?*" We walked. We walked and I considered this adjective: *neat.* We passed a policeman on a bike, an elderly woman walking a large, white dog, but there it was: *neat.* Why should I let this bother me? It was, admittedly, a small thing. A minor nuisance, like underwear that creeps. On a continuum from dull to miraculous, she placed our last few minutes somewhere in the middle. Pedestrian, ordinary. A pathetic five. My peak experience was, for her, a pleasant moment, trifling at best.

In a word: *neat.*

Well, what really, did a choice of adjectives matter? Why belabor it? Why create problems? Hadn't my own brother told me a thousand times, I create my own misery? I never knew what he meant, but perhaps this was one of those times. Perhaps this was a prime example of my neurosis, as he called it.

Still, there it was: *neat.*

Don't make a big thing out of it. It's immaterial. Paltry. Inconsequential, meaningless, picayune, unimportant, nothing.

Less than nothing.

But it stayed with me.

Why be such a fool as to ruin a mood like this?

I shook myself free of it as we walked along Castro Street.

"Ah, to be in the wake of making love to my Joy. Body, mind and spirit eases into sweet communion with the world. A wish only to hear the sound of laughing children, to pet animals, and should someone cast an insult my way? Well, *I once had self-esteem issues too.* I float on a sea of bliss, a smile of beatitude plays upon my lips; for a small girl jumping rope, a businessman, a gas attendant. All, blessed wonders of creation."

But... *neat.*

"So," Joy said, "If it makes you feel so good, why don't you just-"

"What are you suggesting?"

"You know," she said.

I spoke before any shock at such ignorance could uglify this rare condition of serenity.

"Hardly compares," I said. "Not even in the same universe."

"What do you mean?" she asked.

"I mean it just doesn't feel... like *this.* Instead, you walk through the world, an unwholesome, rodent-like creature; twisted and bent, headachey, a mind rushing and irritable. Children are malicious, pick-pocketing vermin; women, unsavory whores wanting only brief, vulgar pleasure and your wallet. You trust no one and why should you? All humanity is but spiders and roaches, ready to ridicule and jeer and laugh while you seethe in murderous, shifty-eyed anger. Nothing of any worth can be accomplished; your mind can barely function. The world casts you aside like the debris that you are. Your joints ache. You neck is an anarchy of knots and you twist your head from side to side for relief that never comes. Your skin is afire with itches as if you'd rolled in poison ivy for a week. If addressed, you snap at humanity; a race so horrific and vile, it's a wonder you don't slit your own miserable throat to terminate such impossible, undeserved misery. If ever we were offered a glimpse of hell, this, my love is - why?" I looked at her. "Isn't that how you feel?"

She shook her head.

"How *do* you feel?" I asked.

"If I -"

"Uh-huh."

"Great," she said, and she pulled me, just then, into a women's cosmetics store. The walls were mirrored; hair products were to the left, bottles of lotion and exfoliants were to the right. Three sales ladies chatted at the counter. Each had multiple rings in their ears and noses. One had blue hair, two were hennaed. Joy brought me to a mirrored table covered with lipstick. There were nearly forty types, many of shades I'd never even imagined on lips before this moment.

"Which one do you like?" she asked.

I looked them over. I pointed to one called China, a color in the distant, fluorescent, outer reaches of red. She picked it up.

"Will you buy it for me?"

I blinked several times at the price. I'd never known lipstick could cost twenty-five dollars.

"As a memento of today," she said.

"Why do women wear lipstick?" I mused as we exited. "Why do they want glistening lips?"

She glanced at me.

"*Glistening lips. Glistening lips. Glistening lips.*" I said. "Your lips are glistening. What do you suppose a woman might hope to-"

"I don't know," Joy said.

"C'mon," I said. "Take a single, solitary stab-"

Joy suddenly stopped, a grin of expectation alighting her face. "Let's celebrate! Let's go out for sushi!"

I blinked hard. "Sushi?" The word had a crippling effect on me, like a bar of glowing, green kryptonite proffered to Superman. "Joy," I said, "don't you have your acting class this afternoon?"

"They're every week. You can miss a few. Listen. I know a great place in Japan Town," she said. "You'll like it. Everything floats by on little boats."

"Japan Town?" I said. "Isn't that a bit-"

"What?" she said sharply. "*Expensive?*"

Okay, I thought. Just this once. A final splurge, then bite the freaking bullet. This *was* a special day. I would eat nothing but brown rice for the rest of the month. I would sell used books. This city was lousy with used book stores. And didn't people indulge once in awhile? Didn't they paint towns red; or dash, in bursts of romantic impulse, off to the Caribbean? Was I to be denied? This was my first chance at love - the real thing! Good God, I thought she might leave me after last night. And this little episode in the Castro was flat-out, the most unbelievable moment in my life.

A bit of sushi, the price of this roller coaster? A bargain by any stretch.

"Of course it isn't," I said, and I added with as much disdain as I could muster, "Money. Pfft!" We would float from one metaphysical plane to the next. How could I give credence to such terrestrial concerns, I thought, as her lovely grin flashed in a surprise of brilliant noontime San Francisco sunlight.

chapter SIXTEEN

After a return home and a quick tandem shower, we sat at the counter of Yokima's in Japantown. Before us was a tiny river. Toy boats were linked together, floating in an endless circle around three, very clean, knife-wielding Japanese chefs.

I watched my woman, with blank sophistication, once again, enjoy the ritual of breaking her chopsticks apart and rubbing them together. An Asian waitress with long, glossy black hair poured hot saki into two tiny porcelain cups. We toasted and sipped. My body still hummed quietly from the morning. Joy looked at me and said, "Talk to me."

"Huh?"

She stared, waiting.

Did she want another story?

And I wondered: how many billions of similar fantasies were inspired by my Joy? How often had she inflamed the thoughts of those in her electrified vicinity?

"You want to hear more?"

She nodded.

And I had an odd notion, just then, sitting there at the sushi bar.

"Joy, what if there was, you know, something like... a viewing room. A celestial viewing room. And in this room, you had the opportunity to see *every sexual fantasy* that anyone ever had about you. Would you?"

"Would I what?"

"Would you want to see them?"

She stared at me, then burst out laughing. "Only Tim. Only you would come up with something so... you're nuts. You're certifiable."

"I know. So?"

"So what?"

"So... *would you?*"

She shook her head in a reach for exasperation. "What's in that skull of yours? What did you get for a brain? Nobody I know thinks about... or talks about... I mean, I think maybe that's what I like about you. *A celestial viewing room*? For what? Masturbation fantasies?"

"*Sexual* fantasies."

"What's the dif-"

"Would you?"

She raised her eyebrows, moved the top of her head from side to side abstractedly, shrugged and said, "Why not?"

I stared at her. "You would? Are you sure?"

She nodded. *Tim I don't think this is such a good idea.*

Why? It's just for fun. Don't be so-

We are suddenly sitting alone in a darkened movie theater, floating through the blackness of space with only the twinkling heavens above. We share a bag of popcorn. Blank screens are everywhere, then, all around us are images of Joy, in various stages of undress, attitudes of seduction. She is alluring, on beaches, in bedrooms, in an airplane, on a boat, on a desk.

And men arrive.

"Oh my God!" Joy says, "There's my high school math teacher! There's Joe Sperling, my next door... And, oh! That shy little guy in English ten,

who kind of stared a lot... my God, these are so graphic! Who are all these people? There's... Jeremy? Greg? I had no idea..."

"And Roshal... Joy," I said. "There's... my God, there's so many of these. Lights! Lights!"

"Wait!" Joy said.

"Wait for what? This is pure, horrible- "

"Let's do you."

"Me?"

Joy shouts, "Masturbation fantasies of Tim!"

"I said sexual!"

"No difference!"

"There's a big dif-. Who is that?"

"She looks... older"

"My God! Aunt... Gladys?"

"And that?"

"Freida Feldman? From my eleventh grade science class? She gave me that birthday card but never said another word-"

"You must have been nice to her.

"Nice? I teased her mercilessly. And... everyone... has their clothes on. These are so-

"Boring!" shout several disembodied voices behind us. "Bring back Joy!"

Chants of 'Bring back Joy' erupt.

The scenes shift. Joy's image appears endlessly around us.

"My God!" Joy says.

"Joy!" I said. "I can't believe this... there's... thousands! Millions!"

"I never met any of these -"

"Stop this!" I shouted. "Stop this at once-"

Barely a second had elapsed.

I looked at Joy, sitting at the sushi bar.

"Those communes," I said, staring at her. "You said they were... what? Very... free?"

Joy nodded slowly.

"I guess there was a lot of... nudity?"

She nodded again. I let my imagination embrace the scene now; Joy and her unadorned, svelte self, scampering among redwoods. Then, the thought intruded, the one I'd been avoiding. It arrived, ugly and painful, and though I tried to push it back, it coerced itself from my throat with a belligerence all its own.

"And a lot of that, what... free love... sort of thing?"

She nodded again.

I watched her for a moment, aching with terrified curiosity but equally fearful of sounding naive and uncool. "Joy?" I glanced around, at a middle-aged couple across the tiny fake river, at the waterfalls and mountains of an Asian landscape on the wall beyond.

I looked at her. The words choked out of my mouth.

"Did you participate in... orgies?"

She nodded, slowly.

I swallowed. My next question came in careful, measured breaths. "Joy. How many... men... have you..." Though I nearly gagged on them, I forced the words out. "... had sex with?"

She looked at me with her slow, hypnotic eyes.

She blinked once and said, "Lots."

The tiny word escaped her lips with a light, erotic, delicacy that eviscerated me.

"Lots? *Lots?*" I was damn near shaking. "What is 'lots'? A hundred? A thousand?"

"Tim."

"*Two thousand?*"

"Tim," she said.

"*How many is 'lots'?*"

I sat in silence for a moment, and watched a single, tiny boat float by, covered with rice and bright red fish roe. And I saw them. I was there, in my mind, uninvolved, but there. A smoke filled room - dope? incense? hash? who knew? - a gaggle of entangled humanity, and there was Joy, naked as a jaybird, moving casually among them. Choosing this one, now that one, now two or three simultaneously. She'd been roaming the woods in the buff all day, stoking fires in all she passed, but was now stoned, giving herself willingly, blithely, in what tomorrow all would refer to as 'a beautiful experience'.

How was I to take to this? And here we sat, me with my lovely free-spirit. My wood nymph. My water sprite. Favored by the Gods to such a degree that she didn't even need car insurance which the rest of us - rabble that we were - had to pay for.

"Excuse me," I said.

I needed a moment and I headed for the men's room, desiring only a sanctuary where sanity still reigned. Someone had filled the urinals with tiny ice cubes. I forced my mind toward grandness, tolerance. It was a big world, I thought, unzipping philosophically. What is *lots*? What is *neat?* Why get hung up on simple, semantic - *die, sons of bitches!* - nonsense? And while I was at it, what is this; this *dating*? An opportunity for a woman to assess a potential mate's skill as a provider, as measured through the cold lens of a discriminating nesting instinct? Was this what Joy was doing? If so, how did I measure up? And suddenly, standing in that immaculate restroom it all came rushing at me: my father's death sentence, my vanishing money, this ache in my heart for a perplexing, promiscuous beauty, Camus' terrifying warning, nothing on the horizon that even resembled a story - to present to my class or my father - and the painful truth of an untalented group of runners on whom I'd hung every hope for salvation, and now, this staggering, casually dropped revelation: *Lots.*

I returned to the barstool and sat beside Joy, who welcomed me with her wondrous smile.

The sushi chef bowed and greeted me. "*Hai!*"

I pulled a plate from a boat. In a gesture of gastronomic bravado, I chose the most brazenly strange item I could find. Some orange, eggy, spiny blob of yuck wrapped in seaweed. I dipped it in soy sauce and downed it in a single, reckless mouthful. It had a sharp, unpleasant swampy tang. "This tastes.... interesting."

"Here," Joy said. Her grin was brilliant as she poured me a cup of tea from a pot she had ordered - at what cost I did not know - while I was gone.

"Ah. Green tea," I said, raising the porcelain cup. "Very healing."

chapter

SEVENTEEN

The bill was sixty-one dollars and then some. I brought Joy home - she had a few errands to run before the evening shift. Back at my apartment that night, I collapsed onto my bed, stared up at the ceiling, and thought about Joy. It struck me that she was in possession of a unique code of conduct incorporating this single tenet: Let no steamy kilocalorie go unrequited. Of all the women I'd known, none were like Joy.

Everyone I knew would call her a slut, and, well... I had to wonder: wasn't sex something a woman gave sparingly, a precious gift to a special person? This was how I understood the female of the species. An indiscriminate, cavalier attitude was the male domain, and any women who attempted it ended up feeling like some vile swamp creature. Thus, prostitutes baffled me, yet even they possessed a dignity that arrived in the form of a stipend.

Sex for money. I had to think about this.

One time I reached amorously for Jackie, and she said, "Oh, no you don't!" because earlier in the day I'd committed some baffling romantic oversight: "There was a perfect time during that movie for you to lean over and tell me you loved me... but you didn't." Wasn't she also using sex as a bargaining chip?

"They're *all* prostitutes!" I declared aloud, in a passing, dubious moment of epiphany.

But where did this leave Joy?

I had no idea, but the phrase, 'unconditional positive regard' resurrected itself yet again. And I would have to leave it there: No idea. I would count my blessings, I decided, and then, my imagination drifted...

Laying there in the dark, I saw them once again: that tangle of naked bodies - wearing nothing but love beads, loopy grins, an affectation of transcendence - on floors, couches, tossed-out mattresses - skin of all shades, pipes, bongs, powders and pills passed here and there. I saw it all. A whole movement, galvanized by a few noble souls in protest of a far away war in Asia, while the vast majority focused instead on getting young women to drop their panties.

And here was my Joy, wending her naked way among them; men screaming silently to her with their minds, men already with women - average, pedestrian woman, but wishing to exchange them for a goddess - men squeezing their eyelids together tight enough to pretend the women in their arms *was* Joy. And there was Joy, moving through a mystical haze of smoke and music, choosing which engorged lucky bastard on whom to bestow her celestial gifts. Prayers flew heavenward: *Choose me! I won't break another commandment if only You grant me this one, tiny -*

And Joy maneuvers her slender perfection to some fortunate soul who promises: *I shall never sin again.*

But what sort of cranial wiring allows a woman to be promiscuous, given the guilt most women would feel? What to make of this, "*Lots*," tossed off so casually for my miserable contemplation? Did she look back, shake her head and grin over a wild, reckless, ill-spent youth? She wasn't old enough for such easy nostalgia.

Joy stood somewhere beyond the realm of my understanding, and though I hated to admit, it scared me. Getting my hands shoved away, awful as it was, was familiar territory.

Drifting toward sleep, another image arose. Joy was spinning. She whirled her lithe body out of a dressing room, a new skirt perpendicular to her hips, her panties white and brief, and she spun into the arms of Jeremy. He wore a black, bohemian sport coat, and had a plastic credit card extended from his fingertips. And Joy was spinning and spinning, into his arms and into my dreams, until she was nauseated and I was nauseated watching.

I bolted from the bed, headed to the bathroom and puked my guts out.

The following morning, I awoke feeling somewhat better, still light-headed, dizzy as I stood. I put on my thick, cotton sweats, headed to the living room and pulled back the curtains. It was the beginning of a damp, foggy day and I turned up the thermostat. I stood by the heater, contemplating my next move. I had no contingency plan for the miraculous, impossible presence of Joy. But here she was, contorting my universe in ways I'd never dreamed possible. I knew Camus was probably right and I'd best heed his warning. After I'd warmed up, I placed a hand on the telephone and held it there for a good minute. I hated what I was about to do, but saw no alternative.

I dialed.

chapter

EIGHTEEN

"So," my brother Robert said, "Written anything?"

We sat at a table at the Get Up Stand Up Cafe, and before answering, I looked him over. Robert's paunch had grown a bit since I'd last seen him at the hospital in Los Angeles. He wore khaki pants, a dark green pullover sweater and sported a tiny silver hoop in one ear. I knew he arrived purely in deference to Dad's *other* request, that the two of us visit once in awhile. We could tell Dad later, that yes, we met for lunch. My brother's question was perfunctory in tone, and seemed directed at me from a downward angle, from the loftier place of a man of affluence. In addition to a substantial two-story home, his universe consisted of a lucrative job in real estate, an attractive and demanding shiksa wife, two kids, a Lexus, and a smugness over a life that frankly, made me gag. Though I tried to isolate a particular moment, it was truthfully without any clear demarcation that Robert and I had had as little contact as possible in the past several years. And he appeared somewhat ill at ease here at the Get Up Stand Up, like some obsessive hand washer who was suddenly shoved into a cesspool.

I had arranged this lunch date in a true spirit of congeniality, of shelving a history of animosity. But already, his tone tweaked me. It had, not only a sneer, but the nasal exhale of superiority, even mockery. I felt my mouth, throat, and tongue - the entire speech apparatus - of it's own accord, bare it's fangs and morph in a direction I could not control. I was suddenly glad he was uncomfortable here.

Joy, chronically late, had yet to arrive for the lunch shift. In fact, only one waitress was on duty; a young, somber, pasty-faced woman in black with bits of metal impaling her lips, nose, ears, eyebrows, and, I believe, her tongue. She was overextended and had brought us only water. I knew it would be awhile before she returned, so I grabbed a few menus from the cashier and laid them before us.

"Written anything?" I said. "Are you *serious*? My God, in my Fiction Writing Seminar, you wouldn't believe the *praise* - I mean, I can't even begin - honestly, it's damn near embarrassing. It's like... *reluctant* praise, you know, like everyone's jealous. I don't care. I'm on my way to a novel. I'm nearly done with it, if you must know."

"A novel?" my brother said, an eyebrow raised. "So soon?"

I nodded, glancing around, bored.

Robert flipped open a menu dismissively. He scrutinized it. "A novel about what?"

I released a disdainful exhale; disdain and impatience for a world view so prosaic. "I can't be asked a question like that," I said.

This stung him in the most perfect way possible. I knew his job bored him to oblivion. I would bet any amount he'd been cheating on his wife, or was dying to. His wife, Leona, with her bright red fake fingernails and her endless hours at the gym exuded such an Icelandic frost toward him the few times I visited that I could easily guess the sort of love life my brother had. In fact, at odd moments when we were more communicative, he'd told me as much, but now, he knew nothing about my life. One sweet phrase - unfortunately borrowed, yet again - suddenly imbued my existence with his most miraculous fantasies. I lived in San Francisco. The City. The name alone - even the snooty nickname - conjured a wild, subliminal envy he failed miserably to contain, even when I mentioned where I lived, one week ago, over the phone.

"Tell Dad?" he asked, tentatively.

"What?"

"About the novel?"

I shook my head. Whether he saw through me or not, I didn't know, but he returned instantly to his true advantage.

"So you need money."

I looked him in the eye. I leaned forward, conspiratorially, earnest now, brother to brother. "I met a woman," I said, watching his reaction. "An amazing, incredible woman. Robert. Imagine your most impossible fantasy. Slim and dark, kind of a hippie... vegetarian... organic yoga-babe... free-spirit. And these eyes that send you half-way across-"

"And what," he said with a chuckle, "You can't afford her?"

"I can afford her," I lied. "That's not the problem," I said, already sick of this game, of myself for playing it, and that this was the state of my relationship with my brother. "She just... likes sushi," I added with a shrug.

"Then she's not a vegetarian."

"Okay," I said, "Christ. She's a fucking *fish eating* vegetarian."

"There's no such thing as a *fish eating vegetarian*. She's simply not a veg-"

"Fine," I said. "It's true. She's not. I just want to... you know... treat her well."

Robert leaned back, looked over the menu, trying, I knew, to figure out what he could eat in such a place without revealing any unhip ineptitude. Now that the preliminary sparring was over and he had seized the high ground, I took a moment to think about him. The rift began, maybe in high school - my god, this sounds silly now - when he removed the baffles from the tailpipe of his Volkswagen, he said, because it sounded better.

Everyone with a car in high school was doing it: removing the baffles in their tailpipes. It sounded annoyingly loud and I told him so. He insisted that it sounded better, and he cruised around the neighborhood, roaring like a 747 until a policeman pulled him over and hit him with a fix-it ticket.

I didn't gloat.

In college, Robert joined a fraternity that was into expensive clothes and restaurants. My brother spent a small fortune on both, and when the family went out to dinner, he looked down his nose, affected the accent of a connoisseur and said, "I don't like the service here." Robert then counseled our parents on how to adjust the tip accordingly.

Later, he went to therapy and brought our mother to tears.

He shouted at her:

"Why are you so afraid of your feelings!"

"You never held me!"

"You have no boundaries!"

"Fuck you!"

He pronounced this person needy, that person controlling, that woman provocative. A married couple we knew was enmeshed, symbiotic and dysfunctional. If he liked someone, they were nurturing, soulful.

I was moving once, and he offered to help. He never showed up.

"Met with my men's group," Robert said, when I called to find out where he was.

I held back my disappointment and asked what he spent the day doing.

"Made masks," he said. "Danced around. Cried."

"Cried?" I said. "About what?"

"Family stuff. Loss of connection with my family."

He took a breathing workshop.

He took ecstasy.

He took yoga, primal scream therapy, a class in meditation.

He attended EST, was Rolfed.

He studied Buddhism.

In truth, I minded none of this: the baffles, the restaurants, the Buddhism, the earring, although the shouting at our mother still rankled. What bothered me was his smug condescension at every obnoxious phase. As if I didn't get it, as if I was hopelessly conventional while he was cutting edge, and any challenge or question elicited a patronizing a roll of his eyes and a dismissive puff of breath.

This was the rift.

This was why I had almost no desire to call my brother.

My brother, the Buddhist Real Estate man, sat across from me in the Get Up Stand Up Cafe, studied the menu, and released a barely audible private laugh, aimed either at my cluelessness or my need for money - I couldn't tell which. But I had bigger problems. Certainly, I wanted something better with my brother, but I also wanted Joy and I needed a loan. This was family. The bills were about to arrive and the check from coaching not for another few weeks. In times like this, one turned to family. I looked around for Joy. She either hadn't arrived yet or had entered through the back of the restaurant.

There was actually a time when my brother and I talked - often about women - and I wondered if such a connection could be tactfully resurrected. Robert loved women, and in this regard, he possessed an odd and somewhat endearing quirk. My brother maintained a particular and poignant regret over opportunities for sex that had come his way, but for some reason, he'd taken a pass. He told me about three such women - two in college, one on a trip to Europe.

"Jesus!" he said once over a beer. "What in hell was I thinking?"

I suggested then, sympathetically, that a slice of poppy seed bundt cake - Robert loved bundt cake - eaten ten years ago would not make him any less hungry now. He nodded thoughtfully and said, "But still." I understood his, 'but still', and now, I wanted this - some commiserating wavelength from the past. Simply put, I wanted to talk about women, as I had some perplexities of my own in this regard, and sadly, no one else to sort them out with.

I began from a safe distance.

"You remember a Hemingway character named Brett Ashley?"

"Wait," he said. "Refresh my...

"Hemingway. The Sun Also-"

"Barely," he said. "Jesus, that's what? Eleventh grade? Vaguely... she's gorgeous... and a bit... slutty, if I recall?"

"But that's the thing," I said, suddenly animated. "Why *slut*? I mean, why is she a slut? Can't she just be, you know... erotically generous?"

Robert appraised me in silence, then said, "You obsess about the strangest-"

"I'm not obsessing!" I took a breath. Talking to Robert was exasperating. "Just try... *consider*, for one moment, without dragging all your therapy-"

"What have you got against therapy?" Robert said, with the tiniest bit of anger.

"Not a thing. I love therapy."

"It's nothing more than-"

"I know. Reparenting. You've told me a thousand-"

"So why do you insist on-"

"But what about *my* needs?" I said with a grin.

Robert rolled his eyes. "That's got nothing to do with-"

"That's not *my* shit!" I said, my voice rising. "That's *your* shit! You've got to *own your own-*"

"*Will you be quiet?*" he said, glancing around.

"Hey, Robert, remember that thing you used to do? What did you call it? '*Active listening*'? I'd say something, and you'd go, '*What I'm hearing you say*,' then repeat exactly what I just-"

"I didn't repeat *exactly* -"

"You did too!" I said, "Word for fucking-"

"I did not!"

"God, it drove me crazy."

"You're delusional."

"Fine," I said. "I'm delusional. Now will you please-"

"I'm *listening*."

"But not *actively*."

"Fuck you."

We were silent.

I couldn't resist this, but God, he was maddening. He glanced about, arms folded, trying to achieve a demeanor of impatience, of superiority, but I saw the pout behind it. I both enjoyed and regretted it. Was this goddam sparring unavoidable? He tossed out a hand, the-stage-is-yours style.

After a moment, I said, "Brett Ashley. She's in love with Jake, but it's not Jake she finally wants."

"Why not?"

"Well, he can't get a… you know."

"You can't say hard-on?" The supercilious grin returned.

"*Hard-on.* I said it. But just listen. You never listen. You always gotta correct me. I can't finish a damn-"

"I'm listening," he said, and he had it now: the high ground of sexual sophistication. Why in hell couldn't I just say hard-on?

For a display of exasperation and a reach for serenity, I closed my eyes then opened them. "Do you think… is it possible… that a woman could love sex… *more than the man she's making love to?*"

Robert seemed here now - present, as he would say - and the smugness was gone. A thoughtful crease deepened between his eyebrows.

"In fact," I added, "maybe he's just… *incidental?*"

Robert considered this. "I don't know," he said. "I guess it's… but what are you so concerned about?"

"I told you," I said. "I'm dating a woman."

"And?"

At last, I had his full attention.

"Well," I said. "I've never known a woman who liked… sex… so much."

He stared at me, then said, "You're complaining?"

"No… God no. I'm not complaining," I said. "I'm just… I don't know… *tired.* I should be getting more sleep, but Joy… she wants to make love all night. Night after night." I looked my brother in the eye. "She wants to *fuck all night.*" I was dying to say it: *Fuck all night*, with its offhanded, dashing implication. "I mean, I'd always dreamed about this, but I've never actually… Robert. It's exhausting."

"So?" my brother said, looking at me. "What's the problem?"

I certainly had his attention.

"What if... what if it's not *me*?" I said. "What if it's *just sex*?"

"Is that such a-"

"And the other thing; I'm crazy about her! I'm absolutely out of my mind over this woman. What if this whole relationship, to her, is *only about sex*? What if I'm... *dispensable*."

Despite the obvious danger of risking such an insecurity, it was a chance I felt willing to take. Of course he could use this to skewer me, and he might, but I had to trust this as a neutral zone; this effort to comprehend that baffling opposite sex who we both desired to distraction. I watched him, waited for his reaction.

Robert looked away, then shook his head in what seemed a sudden and surprising moment of profound sadness.

"Only sex!" Robert said, leaning in now, his posture softening. "Listen. Every guy I know is dying for a woman like that! *Dying!* Do you know what I go through to get *anything* from Leona?"

I looked at him.

"I thought you guys were doing okay," I lied.

"*Okay*. Sure. Jesus. Of course, yes, she's a wonderful - but my God, do you know what a battle it is; how I have to *demean* myself, how I plead like a goddam - Tim! Just sex. *Just sex!* I swear, every guy I know - listen; you got it made, buddy. Take my word. This is every man's-"

"Every man's?"

"My brother," he said. "Baby brother. Trust me. If this is your situation, trust me. Enjoy it! Don't question it. Do whatever you can, whatever it takes to keep it going. Because when it ends, let me tell you, buddy; when it ends, you will look back on this as the one, single, bright moment in a lifetime of complete and utter misery. And when it's gone - trust me on this, little brother - it's gone for a long, long-"

"Robert," I said. I hesitated. "There's more."

"What?"

Almost ashamed at what I was about to say, as if betraying an unspoken confidence, I leaned in toward my brother and nearly whispered, "She's been to *orgies*."

The word had a percussive effect, and Robert's head jolted a tiny bit backwards. I waited as this astonishing information found footing in his mind. A slight, intrigued smile played on his lips. "Really?"

And I knew that it lifted his fantasy of my Joy into some fabulous realm of erotic mystery. "Really?" he said again, blinking several times.

I nodded.

He sat back now, recalibrating his demeanor to something less shocked, more casual and sophisticated, and said, "Hey, not that it matters, but... what does she look like?"

"What does she *look* like?"

"I mean, I don't want to sound, you know, shallow, but... is she... attractive?"

I glanced toward the kitchen. "You tell me. Here she comes."

He followed my gaze, and then my brother stared. I had seen this look in Robert before, but never so violently as now. Whereas most men in the Get Up Stand Up seemed comical in their overdone efforts to appear relaxed before the incredible wattage of Joy's beauty, my brother Robert appeared as if his very skin began to rumble and quake with desire.

"*That's your girlfriend?*"

Robert looked at me, then back at Joy. I know, hard to believe. Well, life is one mystery to the next and here was mine. Joy looked particularly striking this afternoon. It was my second favorite look: she wore jeans and tight black t-shirt. Nothing special, but any attire on her was spellbinding. Her dreadlocks bounced and she smiled her wide, radiant smile as she moved, light as air toward our table.

I introduced them and they shook hands.

I saw my brother's wrist ignite, a flame roar up his forearm, whoosh across his chest and down the center of his torso. For this meeting, I had intended no malice, but what could any man feel but an ache to possess Joy commingled with a desire to slit my throat. Anything less would cast him into the profoundest of depressions.

Certainly she was mine, but I had no idea on what slippery basis such a blessing existed.

"It's so nice to meet you," she said in a bland, waitressy way. Cold yet polite. I wondered if this was the unconscious reflex of a beautiful woman in the presence of a man who wore desire all over his face. I wondered if she would remember this moment in two minutes. I took her hand, pulled her close and gave her a proprietary peck on the cheek.

"What can I bring you?" she asked.

"I'll have the mystic burger," I said.

"You and that meat," Robert said.

"*What?*" I said, half-smiling.

He looked at Joy. "Tim's been stuffing himself with meat since I've known him. I'll have thee..." Robert looked at the menu and wiggled his head, "tofu and tabuli salad."

"Coming up," Joy said, and we watched her float back to the kitchen.

I looked at Robert. "*Me and that meat?* You've been gorging yourself on meat since God knows-"

"No I haven't."

"Robert! All those summer barbecues. Chunks of tri-tip hanging out of your mouth, and you announcing to the world: 'I love red meat!'" I laughed.

He shrugged. He glanced around, leaned back, looked at me for a moment, then said casually, "I had an affair."

"You *what?*"

"Best thing I ever did."

"You had an *affair*? I thought you and Leona were doing-"

"We are, I guess. But doing fine... that's got nothing to do with this."

I looked at him, let him enjoy his moment.

"But... this... affair," I said. "Did it... you know... effect your marriage in any way?"

He shook his head.

"Really?" I asked.

"Not in the slightest," he said.

"Why not?"

My brother shrugged, then smiled.

"Because," he said. "I've compartmentalized it."

We stood in the gravel parking lot, just beside his Lexus. It was early afternoon, and the day was overcast and cool. A truck passed. Out of the range of Joy's charm, my brother was settled, calmer. I had watched him struggle through a tofu and tabuli salad as we chatted about various gloomy topics: Dad's plummeting health, mom's future. I should have known better than to bring him to the Get Up Stand Up Cafe. Even though Joy ignored him, cut him dead with a face of pure boredom when he tried to be jokey with her, Robert would not say she was nasty, unfriendly, or cold. I knew him. Instead, he'd see his inability to generate her interest as his own failure, and his esteem for her would rise accordingly.

"Where's your car?" he asked.

I pointed to my Honda.

"With that dent in the door?"

I nodded.

He gave it a brief, professional appraisal. "Get that dent fixed," he said. "That's your car. That's your self-esteem!"

"My what?"

He unlocked the door of his burnished silver Lexus, thought for a moment, then turned to me, "We're having a little barbecue in a few weeks. Anniversary. Give me a call." Then he added, "You've got potential, Tim. You're problem is, you've got no ambition."

Despite his ungainly size, Robert managed a cool body-swing into his Lexus. I had initially considered a request for a loan of three hundred dollars, but the idea faded through lunch and died instantly when his surround-sound stereo blasted some spineless New Age music. I saw a cd cover on the passenger seat - 'Love Song of the Lotus'.

As he drove off, I thought: I have ambitions that would terrify the bastard. And it would be a cold day in hell before I attended a barbecue at his house. Still, I felt sad for the state of my relationship with my brother.

But now I had other concerns.

Joy would grace my apartment that evening. I had barely enough cash to pay rent if I ate nothing but potatoes for the rest of the month. And I had cross country practice in one hour and a problem there I hadn't begun to figure out. I stood at the door of my yellow Honda and pulled out my wallet. I had no credit card, no hope of qualifying for one. Almost nothing in the bank. I counted out my money. My severely compromised budget might grant me an embarrassingly cheap evening with Joy, and, if I was very careful, a few gallons of low lead for my rusting and dented self-esteem.

chapter

NINETEEN

I sat in my coach's office, checked the clock, waited for Alex. Practice began in half-an-hour and this wouldn't take long. The women's volleyball coach was down in the gym, bumping and setting with her team. On her desk was a wooden duck, and behind it on the wall, a calendar. This month had a picture of hands splayed over a net, blocking a powerful spike. Because my job was tentative after the league meet, the walls on my half of the office were bare. "You want the job?" My mother would say, "Put some pictures on the wall! Put some *tchockies* on your desk! *Visualize it!* "

Well, I was, sort of. In tiny ways, my team was beginning to gel. We placed sixth out of eight teams the previous weekend at a meet down on the peninsula. Steve was seventh, Gary thirteenth. Nick and Peter ran together for twenty-sixth and twenty-seventh, while Alex trailed at the back of the pack at thirty-ninth.

"Improving," Father Damian said, passing me in the hall that next Monday. He wore his clergy collar and a black coat. He was positive, upbeat as always. Though his encouragement was warm and avuncular, his compliment was mild at best. Here was a man who had two actual NCAA trophies in his office. They were not recent, but certainly, he had tasted the rapture of fabulous athletic success. Though my runners, I knew, were a distant afterthought in the March Madness of his passion, Father Damian was fair-minded. A sixth-place finish was an improvement; a step in the right direction.

In cross-country, a spectator sees only the beginning and end of a race. When the gun went off last weekend, Alex blasted the first hundred meters and, for the unschooled fan, performed a dazzling display of grit for the sparse crowd. Then he eased into a jog, plodded for six miles until he had about three hundred meters to go, at which point, back in view, he threw back his head and burst into a terrifying kick. With a look of agonizing determination, he passed two straggling, out-of-shape runners, cheered on by the polite but clueless.

Still, the team as a whole was improving. We had possibilities. Keeping everyone healthy, getting Alex up to the middle of the pack, and the others to push just a bit harder could make us a surprising mid-pack finish in the league meet. It was a remote possibility. Of course, I had additional, more personal designs. A mid-pack finish would certainly support my case for a full-time job, but only Alex, as I doped this out, stood between me and my dream. The scheme was a long shot. The stakes were high, if not frightening. Though I did not know the alchemy of conjuring a story from my fingertips, improving a runner, mercifully, was decidedly less mysterious. But athletic and physiological expertise would not help me with Alex. Alex Granger, in the precise, therapeutic language of coaches, was a head case.

As I waited for him, I thought over what I might say. I was tired. The few hours I crashed in the early mornings were hardly enough to make up for night after night of erotic mayhem. I was exhausted, on the brink of a cold, not quite sure of the logic of my thinking. But Alex seemed beyond logic. His workouts were comical, if not irritating. The other day we ran intervals on the track at the west end of the Polo Fields in Golden Gate Park. Steve, with his lanky muscular stride, instantly took the lead. Gary ran off his shoulder. Nick and Peter were five, then ten yards back. Alex slowly jogged the entire workout in dead last until the final, four hundred meters. Then he sprinted full-speed, passing everyone, sporting a heroic, I'll-show-them grimace on his face which he maintained for several minutes after he crossed the finish line. Gary and Steve cruised in after him, openly annoyed.

"Alex," I said, pulling him aside after a recovery jog. "What happened? You plodded almost the whole workout."

"My thigh, coach. Felt a twinge."

"Your thigh? Alex. You sprinted the last four-hundred."

"It loosened up," he said with a slight grin, "so I thought I'd show my stuff."

Alex arrived in my office wearing purple racing shorts, a yellow singlet, and sat in the chair across from me. I asked him what he thought of his race last weekend.

"It was okay," he said, "Except for my knee." He shook his brown hair from his face.

I sat back, looked him in the eye. "Alex. I want you to think about running with consistency. No more bursting off the line like a maniac. No more wild, closing kicks. Find a good, strong rhythm; one you can manage for six point two miles. Then, hold it. You've done it... I've seen you... a few times in practice."

"That's how I run, coach. That's how I ran in high school."

I repeated silently to myself: *That's how he ran in high school.* I picked up a pencil, tapped it a few times on the blotter to give me a moment. This was a blithe dismissal. I waited for the shudder in my chest to subside. "Well, Alex. This is college."

It sounded lame even as it left my lips.

This is college? Why, come to think of it, I had noted a decided paucity of hall passes. Thank you, coach, for that incisive gem. The fog has lifted; my path is clear. I shall now, no doubt, run like the wind!

I was spent. How to cross the line between the blank expression before me, to some place of understanding?

"That all, coach?" Alex said, getting up.

"No," I said. He sat down, looked at me, and waited.

The idea landed in my head with no time to scrutinize it. My brain was mush, certainly, but erotic mush. I took a breath, cast better judgment aside, and spoke.

"When I ran in college," I said, "we had a guy on the team named Eugene. Full scholarship guy from Texas." I leaned back, shook my head in awe at the memory. "Big, strong sprinter; so smooth, I swear, he seemed to take flight when he ran. Try as I might, I couldn't keep up with him. He kicked my butt every single workout." Alex appeared puzzled but interested. "I dated a girl named Barbara Ann at the time." I smiled. "A real cutie, and, well, a serious Christian, and I never got anywhere with her, if you know what I mean."

A grin lit Alex's face.

"Date after date, nothing. Nada. Endless frustration. Alex. I was terribly shy in college, but finally, we talked. I asked why she was always so, well; frosty with me. Barbara Ann told me she was saving herself for marriage."

Alex looked at me with a silent, odd fascination, as if he was being allowed into a world about which he knew absolutely nothing. Had Gary been privy to this, he would certainly have shaken his head in man to man commiseration. Alex's look suggested, that aside from an errant game of spin the bottle, his nexus with the fairer sex was at best, hypothetical. I knew this was probably some breach of professionalism, but I was rolling now, and desperate.

"So I asked her, 'Tell me. What happens in the heat of passion? What do you do when things get to the point of no return?' You know what she said?"

He looked at me blankly.

"She gave me most amazing answer."

I paused dramatically. Alex blinked three times, and waited.

"She said, 'Nothing happens. Nothing happens because I've made a decision. So nothing *can* happen.'"

Alex continued to stare.

"Well, I went home, frustrated," I said, and Alex grinned. "But the next day I went to my track workout. And there was Eugene.

Tall, lanky and powerful. And like Barbara Ann, I made a decision. I thought, today, Mr. Full Scholarship, I'm going to run with you. No matter how fast you go, I'll be right there, on your shoulder. I will die before you pull away from me."

I had Alex's attention.

"It was early in the season. We had to run five, half-mile loops on the grass. Eleven of us began. After two loops, three guys fell back, forming a second group. After four, the second group had grown to six. Then one runner dropped out and walked. On the fifth, a 400 meter runner, also on a full-scholarship, cut the corner to shorten the distance. Three of us finished the workout with Eugene. Alex, it was painful, but you know what? I didn't die. And as we began to jog our warm-down, Eugene - who would be league champ that year and an All-American his senior year - looked over the guys who dropped back, shook his head and said, 'I can tell those guys ain't gonna be shit.'

"Alex, I gotta tell you, he wasn't even talking about me, but it was the most flattering compliment I'd ever received. Of course, I never beat him in a race. That was my freshman year and I usually got pummeled. But... little by little... my times improved."

He pushed his hair out of his eyes. I leaned forward and revealed my desperation: "Alex. We only have five guys out here. Everyone's important. If you run like I know you can, we have a shot for a decent finish in the league meet." He waited, and I added, "Now I'm finished."

As he was leaving, I said, "Alex."

He turned at the doorway.

"Probably best to keep this conversation under your hat."

He looked me, puzzled, and I added, "Just between us, okay?"

He nodded and left.

It looked like rain and I wanted to get this over with quickly. We took the van down to the vast grassy stretch of the Polo Fields and did a short warm-up. Not many people were about. Two guys in sweats tossed a football, and three others, a rugby ball. A very talented dog bolted full speed across the grass, and in a brief, gravity defying moment, leapt, hung in the air and caught a well-chewed frisbee in its teeth.

My five runners were all here today, and I sent them off on a moderately long run, up through the park, then down to the ocean, along the Great Highway, up to lake Merced, then a straight shot on Sunset back to Golden Gate Park. The course had some hills and usually took me about an hour and two minutes. I paced around among the trees. Because of the drizzle, I wore a blue, nylon athletic department raincoat. I looked like a coach, and if anyone had doubts, I held a clipboard and checked my stopwatch every few minutes. A pair of sweethearts paused for a smooch by their Saab, then entered and drove off. A group of brightly clad bikers buzzed down the hill, their shouted conversation rising then diminishing as they passed. Two squirrels played tag in a pine tree. A woman on roller blades cruised by in a crouch, her rubber-tipped ski poles tucked beneath her arms.

I looked for my runners. I waited.

At just under an hour, I heard an odd, rhythmic chanting. And then, at one hour and twelve seconds, Gary, then Steve, and then, yes yes yes, Alex, in the flesh, all three, dripping sweat and breathing hard, exploded through the trees, clapping, grinning, and chanting: *"Ba ba baaaaaa, ba Barberannn!"*

chapter

TWENTY

I parked diagonally in front of Compadre's, a Mexican Restaurant in the Mission District. The rain poured hard now. A young couple exited the double glass doors. Three Latino cooks worked quickly behind a steamy window. The time was eight-fifteen. I had picked up Joy from work, and she promptly told me she'd had only a salad for lunch and was famished. "I don't have any money," she had said, her smile ablaze, "Are you treating?" I expected this but didn't respond. I was tired of hearing it, and sick of it now as we sat in the Honda, watching pedestrians maneuver quickly though the deluge. Some hunched their shoulders, gritted their teeth. Others strolled, relaxed and easy, appearing to enjoy the onslaught.

I sat nervously. I had insisted on burritos because they were cheap, much cheaper than Joy's preferences. Actual cooking was next, and my plan was to go step by step. But from Joy's posture, I could see that I had entered a minefield. She did not look pleased about burritos. In planning my escape from the classroom and embarking upon this insane dream to be a writer, I did not budget for a woman like Joy. My state of gaga was not only unexpected, but, as Albert had warned, not to taken lightly. Fabulous, frequent sex, as my own brother had pointed out, was a rare blessing in this brief, terrestrial stint, the loss of which would have me cursing my stupidity for a lifetime. Joy was a puzzle and I had to be careful. She sat beside me now, poised and beautiful, her profile so wondrous that every atom in my body inclined toward acquiescence. Just pay. Just pay and continue this hiatus in heaven.

But I was broke.

Well, I'd had a mild coaching coup this afternoon. Alex had stepped up, and with this and little else to buoy me, I turned to Joy. "What's wrong?" I said. "You don't like burritos?"

She shrugged.

Casual as possible, I added, "And you can pay for yourself tonight."

She released a sharp, unsmiling laugh. I understood this to mean: *Who do you think you're dealing with?* It was a good question, and while I knew this moment was inevitable, in my tired, frazzled condition, I felt consumed by a sudden rush of fear.

Joy was silent.

Rain poured. Neither of us left the car.

"And please, Joy, never, ever ask me to treat again. If I want to treat, I'll treat. But don't ask."

She didn't respond. A silence, monstrous and ugly, hung in the small interior of my Honda. And there it was. I had spoken.

On the sidewalk, a young Latino mother pushed her baby along in a stroller that enclosed the child in a clear, plastic window.

We watched them pass.

"Joy," I said. "I can't afford this. Going out all the time. If you want to go out, you can pay for yourself sometimes. You have a job."

She stared out the window and exhaled. She wore a black wool coat. And I watched with no small amount of dread, as her jaw muscles clenched around her cheekbones. She's just a woman, I told myself, no better than anyone.

She turned toward me. "*I... deserve... to be treated.*" She pronounced each word with a strained, get-it-through-your-head quality.

This struck me as a very odd reply. I wondered if she was parroting some *Self-Esteem on a Date* article, but Joy didn't read magazines, far as I knew. I'd never actually seen her read anything. I turned to her, and repeated with astonishment, "*You deserve-*"

"My men pay for me."

I let these two astonishing comments hang in the air for a moment. I considered these men - *her* men. Perhaps handsomer. Taller. Owners of newer cars. What little effort it would take her to find a man who outflanked me in so many ways. Were these comments really so surprising?

"What's the big deal?" she said. "It's one little thing! One little problem. You won't let it go."

I felt instantly petty. And unmanly.

Of course a man should pay for his woman.

"A friend called me from Boston," she said. "He wanted me to visit. I said I didn't have any money for a ticket. He called back a moment later and said a ticket was being Fed Exed." This she delivered so-there style, I imagined, to illustrate the standard I was being held to.

Then she shook her head. And for the second time in our brief relationship, she said, "You wear me out."

What could this mean? I considered the horrible consequences of wearing her out. Sitting there in the Honda, I attempted a bold leap of empathy, to see this through her eyes. I read her mind: *I'm gorgeous and everyone wants me. You're not, so you have to pay extra. Understand and appreciate your good fortune.*

An odd logic, but my God, why be naive? Wasn't this how the world worked? Wasn't this how people treated her? Get any of those fawning, ingratiating patrons at the Get Up Stand Up privately over a beer and they'd say, "Beauty doesn't impress me. It's what's inside that matters." Then watch them humbled into puddles of drool as Joy took their order. Why pretend it was any different? Why get upset about it? Technically, it wasn't even her fault! If I didn't like the system I could take it up with God someday, but this did me little good now. At the moment, only two things seemed to matter: Joy *was* lovely and I was damn lucky.

Her men. They fly her to Boston. I didn't care to consider why.

I had to be careful here. Arguing was pointless. But any display of weakness, I knew, was suicide - instant and irrevocable. I willed indifference to my limbs, though a pure, rattling panic now seemed to overwhelm those weary, uncooperative appendages.

Then, strangely, Joy's posture slackened. She glanced out the window, exhaled and said, "I was always daddy's little girl, okay?"

What?

Here was something.

This was called a concession. I knew this because, as a student teacher, I had taught the argumentative essay. You propped up your case by giving in to your opponent in some inconsequential manner. This made your listener feel honored and respected even as you proceeded to eviscerate him. But here it was. Daddy spoiled her, now the world.

You thought it, wimp, now say it.

"So... what?" I said. "You're a spoiled brat?"

"Ooooo!" she said, looking directly at me, her face the unprettiest and scariest I'd ever seen it. I instantly regretted my bravado. Why couldn't I simply have taken this olive branch and worked with it? I began to tremble. If she noticed I would blame the weather.

We now sat for an extended silence in front of the Mexican restaurant. The rain pounded heavily. Through the fogged windows of Compadre's, I could see that the place was crowded. A young couple exited, clutching each other beneath an umbrella. A bent, elderly Asian man strode by holding a folded newspaper over his head. Two boys moved quickly through the rain in hooded, nylon windbreakers.

"I don't think we should make love anymore," Joy said suddenly.

This hit me like a solid shot to the solar plexus.

I was breathless, silent.

A strange coldness blossomed in the hollow of my chest; like the blood-gush of some bizarre, internal amputation. She was taking this single step back, a step away from me. A preliminary move aimed at distancing herself forever.

It was her trump card and it was a doozy.

I was so tired. And suddenly, inexplicably, on the verge of tears.

Tears.

I fought them back manfully.

I gathered myself, forced my voice into a rugged lower register where it wouldn't crack embarrassingly, and said, "Why?"

"I just think we should stop," she said. Her voice was cold, waitressy.

I played nervously with a steering wheel cover that was coming apart. I had been awake for nearly five nights straight. Joy didn't seem to need sleep and was unaffected. That I ran seventy miles a week didn't help. My eyes were rimmed with red. I was no match for Joy's scorched-earth approach to lovemaking. If I slept, she said, "No! Don't go to sleep!" And we made love again. And again.

I was exhausted, and smitten to near-delirium.

And now she was taking this step away from me.

No more lovemaking.

Tears, despite my most valiant efforts, loosened from my eyes. I tried to conceal them, the shift in my breathing, and a sudden, uncontrollable shivering.

I swallowed hard, trying to master my mood.

The period I wept was brief, silent, and private.

I cleared my throat. I leaned back. I watched a foursome in black clothing exit the restaurant, unfurl their umbrellas. Tired as I was, the brief escape into weepiness calmed me. I glanced at Joy as she stared gorgeously out the window and I felt hopelessly outgunned. A group of African American teenagers, looking endearingly badass in low-slung baggy pants and hooded Raiders coats half-danced by, upper-bodies and arms moving to rhythmic rap, either sung or on headphones. Hard to tell which from the car, but they reminded me of my former students, just happy to be together and out on the town. I had enjoyed them so much, even though I struggled with them, even after the episode with Antoine and Lilbit that finished me off.

I looked to my right at the woman I loved. A rich man would capitulate. A truly strong man would start the engine and drop her off at her apartment for the last time. I was too poor for the former, too drunk on her for the latter. I thought of Camus, of the terrifying rarity of love. Yes, I was hopelessly outgunned. Why couldn't dealing with Joy be as logical as dealing with athletes? I remembered my very own pep talk: *Maybe you get passed; don't panic.* Okay, Swami, I'll try not to pan- And just then, with a peaceful calm that followed my tears, with the rain pounding on the roof, a wild, impossible notion formed in my head. It was desperate, laughable; a ridiculous long shot. If I had any weapon at all with Joy, this one was pathetically low-caliber.

So aim, by God, was everything.

"Joy," I said, forcing an ease into my words. "Of course you don't mean that. My beautiful Joy."

She looked away from me, down the rainy street.

"Of course you don't." The terror was briefly gone, and I stared straight ahead, afraid to look at her now for the palpable fear I'd lose my nerve. I gazed out at the rain, which seemed to suddenly kick into a higher gear. My voice became languid. "Because tonight, my sweet woman, I will kiss your beautiful, soft lips. Once... twice. I kiss them a third time. A long, long time... I will touch your perfect tongue with mine. In that wondrous moment of contact we will be transported to a place of palm trees, of coconuts, and a light, cool breeze. I shall unbutton your blouse, remove it slowly. Your blouse, your bra. I will kiss each breast. I will unbutton your skirt."

I would not look over at her. She sat in silence.

"Your skirt is gone Joy. Gone. Your shoes, gone. Nothing covers you now but a fragment of lace... brief... and white. I gaze into the dark night of your eyes. With two fingers I delicately slide the last bit from your luscious hips, over your smooth brown thighs, to the warm sand.

"Joy. You are completely... perfectly naked."

She was still silent. I took a long, audible breath; released an exhale of appreciation.

"I will kiss you again and we stand now, magically, in the center of my bedroom."

"I grace my fingers over your ribs, your stomach. Your back. Your beautiful legs."

I took another slow breath.

"Dear God in Heaven, what a sight. I lay you down on soft flannel sheets. They're cold... and we climb under the comforter to keep warm. I touch you, Joy - your back, your shoulders, tracing your silky curves. I touch you in your most secret, feminine places. And now I'm about to tell you what has been in my mind since the moment I met you. Forgive me this thought, my love. But, in fact, every moment with you... every thought of you... every touch of you feels sacred. I grace my lips over your slim, dark stomach. I lightly kiss you, lower... and lower... until slowly... I'm kissing the loveliest miracle in this vast, mysterious universe, and... my sweet woman, my beautiful woman, my perfect, wondrous woman, I kiss you now where you're wetter and saltier than the deep blue-"

She jolted suddenly. She stared straight ahead, blinked several times in succession.

She swallowed.

"That's not fair," Joy said.

What, I wondered. What's not fair?

Then, in the sealed off space of my Honda, I caught the delicious scent of a warm island sea breeze.

"Let's go home," she said.

chapter

TWENTY-ONE

When the Red Sea parted for Moses and he received his first, miraculous beckoning call to the promised land, I'm certain that it spoke to him: *Commune with this and you will never suffer again until the end of time. You will, in fact, forget suffering completely, until even the harshest of your memories become nothing but pure Joy.*

Her stomach; dark, satiny; a pillow from heaven. To the north, the soft pyramids of Egypt. To the south, a place bewitching and perfumed with the delicate scents of Persia.

I gazed upon my Joy; tangible, terrestrial proof of a benevolent deity. I tasted of her and thought: God truly loves us.

I looked up. The terrain, bristly, then smooth and brown with a lovely mole to my immediate left, then mountainous, dark-brown tipped, and finally, a full-lipped mouth in wonder, as if, for the first time, *in pure surrender.* Joy watched me, oddly fascinated. Why? Were her divine bequeathings - all ten billion of them - only of the pedestrian, homerun variety?

I couldn't begin to guess, but oh, my Joy.

How her lovely back arched down, past those two sweet dimples, then curving, curving, round and graceful.

To hold those perfect spheres!

To worship at the alter of madness!

I drank deeply until her eyes closed tightly and her luscious hundred and twenty pounds of svelte magic trembled in delicious silence.

"No one ever..."

"Did that before?" I said, moments later. "Really?"

She shook her head. "What... what's it like?"

Ah, this woman. I pulled her toward me.

"May I now describe this rare privilege?"

A silent smile of assent.

"A plunge into a cool ocean.

"Floating on a raft through the steamy, primordial jungles of the Amazon.

"An early morning walk on a negative ionic day, during that brisk and perfect stretch between Halloween and Superbowl.

"Showering naked beneath a Hawaiian waterfall.

"Boarding Lufthansa for Stockholm to accept a Nobel Peace Prize.

"A glimpse of Heaven.

"A private... conversation... with God."

"With God?" Joy said.

I nodded.

"And what did God say?"

Her question was rhetorical. I looked into the mystery of her beautiful dark eyes as she awaited my answer. And I thought, this is it. This is what it's like to truly be in love. "He said: *'Oh, my son... welcome to Paradise.'*"

A tiny smile played on Joy's divine features. With a sleepy voice, she mumbled, "Welcome to paradise." She placed a tiny kiss on my cheek, and then fell into a deep and peaceful eight-hour slumber.

chapter

TWENTY-TWO

In the morning, she rubbed the sleep from her eyes and turned toward me. "I just remembered. There's a potluck at Jeremy's in a few weeks? It's his birthday. Will you come?"

She told me the date. It was the very evening after league finals, the event upon which my fate hinged.

"I'd love to," I lied. "A pot luck. What should I bring?"

"Anything," she said. Then, "I'm hungry. Got anything to eat?"

I said that I did, and for a moment she looked at me strangely - probably remembering exactly *why* she was so hungry - and I said quickly and buoyantly as possible, "I make the best omelets in the world."

I opened the fridge, removed a carton of eggs laid by vegetarian chickens, organic cheddar, and one organic purple onion. Joy stepped into the shower.

The phone rang. It was Tara.

"He's here," she said.

"Jonah Woods?"

"One and the same. Flies out this evening. Meet us for lunch?"

"My God," I said, gazing at the bathroom. The door was open and Joy's dark, muted figure was visible behind the opaque glass of the shower. "Bring your friend if you want," Tara said as if reading my thoughts. She told me where and when as I watched Joy scrub her legs. We hung up.

I considered whether or not to bring Joy.

I fried the onions, grated some cheddar. I cracked the eggs into a bowl, stirred them up. I removed the onions, poured the eggs into the hot pan, added the cheddar, then the onions. I smiled at Joy as she exited the bathroom wrapped in a towel and returned to the warmth of the bed. The omelette was perfect - a work of art if you must know - and I slid it onto a plate. In a moment I was in bed on a cold Saturday morning with my lovely woman. We fed each other in silence.

Perhaps this would impress her, I thought. Her man knows a famous writer. Of course, she'd never heard of him. *Tim Lewis*, she might tell a friend, *Hob nobs with the literary set. Why just the other day, we sat down to lunch with the great Jonah Woods.*

Might even smooth over the near-disaster of last night.

And the great Mr. Woods.

Well, he'd see the beauty of my woman. Certainly this would lend me a certain cachet. *This guy must be something if he's with her*, he would no doubt conclude. Perhaps he'd take an interest in me. Place me under his wing. Nurture me along as a benevolent mentor.

Such things happened.

The morning was cold and gray. Waves crashed faintly in the distance. As we finished I told Joy about Jonah Woods.

"I actually think his style is a bit too careful... over-edited, subdued and tempered; no wild bursts of passion. He lacks the little thrills of a dazzling wordsmith, but he always seems to pack a knockout punch in the end. One story in particular killed me, 'Inhale, Exhale,' about a young man in college and a women he loved - an impish, delightful young lady. He was educated and she wasn't. She worked at a fast-food place, and though he loved her and they even slept together several times, his own snobbery made him keep her at a cool distance. In fact, he loved her his entire life, but married one wrong woman after another, divorcing each, finally settling on a woman who was equally educated, but an annoying social climber. Purely by accident, he sees his former sweetheart twenty-five years later. She's married now and he still loves her and he realizes his mistake and that's where the story ends, and it's an honest, human tale about having your head up your ass, about letting the world do your thinking for you, about missing the best thing that comes your way in this brief, impossible stint on earth. Would you like to join us for lunch?"

Joy shrugged indifferently and took the plate from me. But I felt something odd and unsettling as I watched her slender shape, in nothing but one of my 10-K t-shirts, exit my bedroom and head for the kitchen.

chapter

TWENTY-THREE

The four of us sat at a raised wooden table at O'Shay's on Geary. Smoked mirrors lined the walls around us. An aproned, balding bartender served drinks behind a long, oaken bar along the far wall. A soccer game played silently on a TV suspended from the ceiling in the back corner. The place was about half full with suited business types and students, eating burgers, drinking pints, and laughing loud and spasmodically, as if trying to convince themselves they were having a wild time. When we entered moments ago, heads turned and conversation fell as everyone seemed to treat themselves to an extended, shameless eyeful of the woman at my side. I realized with mild surprise that I was getting acclimated to this - I didn't want to murder a single person - and the chatter revved up again when we took our seats. Joy sat to my right, Tara across from us, and there, at the head of the table was the master himself, in the flesh, eating a Stetson Burger with blue cheese, drinking an India Pale Ale.

We all ate burgers, except Joy, who had a salad. Joy was slumming it today, wearing a black linen sport coat that looked somewhat second hand, with the sleeves pushed above her elbows. Though her look was decidedly bohemian, her beaded dreadlocks seemed exceptionally elegant as she listened silently, alternately eating, then resting her chin on her hand. It was a look of mystery, silent and pure.

Tara wore a black sweater and black jeans, and had pulled her hair back into a bun. She also sat quietly; not the screaming silence of Joy, but instead, appeared thoughtful, subdued, almost invisible, and this didn't seem to bother her.

And there was the Woodsman! Besides Professor Birnbaum who no one ever heard of, Jonah Woods was my first actual writer! *Published*, and descending now from that lofty place to grace our table. His clothes were not black! No earring! No ponytail! He sported a blue polo shirt, corduroy pants, brown leather oxfords. In fact, he wore not a single accessory suggesting an inner or outer universe that was eccentric, tortured, or quirky.

I could barely contain my happiness.

He was balding and looked like he might have been an athlete at one time - a baseball player, maybe. He did not speak rapidly like some darting intellect; but rather, in a slow, considered manner. He might have been in his mid-forties, and he seemed relaxed; at home in his body, his life. Well, Jesus Christ, who wouldn't be? Published! To obtain sweet residence in that enchanted realm! Only one thing about him irked me. He hadn't stopped talking since we sat down. Was I being petty? It seemed, clearly, if a guest-of-honor status was to be had here, well, he had claimed it. I'd hoped for a bit of conversation. Or, at the very least, to be noticed.

No, I hadn't quite entered his viewfinder, but someone certainly had.

Joy listened with a detached, enigmatic silence. Whereas my own attempts at mysterious detachment always left me utterly ignored, Joy's silent moments provoked everyone's fascination. Jonah Woods appeared downright inspired. He talked and he talked. Was this loquaciousness the result of Joy's proximity, or was it something else? Though I wanted to be a writer more than anything else in the world, for the first time, I wondered: What exactly were the liabilities of sitting alone in a room all day?

He spoke of his broken home with sadness, then told of his reckless youth. "I was wild!" he said, then nodded thoughtfully and smiled to himself. "Damn lucky to be alive."

I muscled in, "Where did you get the idea for 'Inhale, Exhale'?"

To my utter shock, he committed it; the sin I hated above all others. Jonah Woods looked at me for the duration of my question, then turned to Joy and said, "Now there's a story!" He began an extended monologue about an upper class friend and a pretty girl they both liked. "I was crazy about her!" He threw back his head in a display of disarming boyishness.

Joy smiled.

He continued.

Of course, he was married with two kids. Of course, I wasn't so naive as to think such a status caused a man to barf in the presence of an attractive woman, but my God! Must every word be directed to the woman at my side? And with such animation? I had wanted to like him. And truthfully, much as I hated to admit it, I wanted him to like *me*.

When he seemed to be winding up, because of my frustration with the summer camp story, I asked, "What do you when you get stuck?"

He looked at me briefly, then turned to Joy. "I don't get stuck," he said. This launched him into extended monologue of his process - making stacks of notes, which, he said never even looked at when he began to write.

He grinned, shook his head in self-effacing bewilderment, then said to Joy, "Sometimes it takes me *four months* to write a story!"

As if the rhythm of his speech demanded it, we gave him the response he angled for: "*Really?*" And we pressed our lips together and shook our heads: *Imagine, even-a-guy-like-you.*

He took a slug of India Pale Ale while a group of young men in baseball caps burst into laughter behind us. Bits of their conversation reached us:

"What say to a little garlic-fries action?"

"Stomach-ache city, dude. I'm like so feelin a pizza."

"Shroomsters?"

"Shroomsters!" they all repeated in unison.

"What're we talkin on the beer front?"

"Two pitchers of Sierra and where's a waitress when you - oh, there you are."

When they were quiet Tara asked, "How do you know when a story's going well?"

I spoke. "I think... I don't know... when it feels like you're... having fun-"

"I wouldn't say '*fun*'." Jonah Woods spat the word with such distaste that I felt my ears burn. I had meant to add, like blasting a ten miler, but he turned to Joy and explained how he knew a story was going well. I couldn't pay attention. Then, he gazed off abstractedly, pressed his lips together, and with sudden richness said, "It's really.... quite spiritual. I think of it as... a communion with the eternal." As if in agreement with himself, he bobbed his head twice.

"Mmm," Joy said.

I looked at her, then back at Jonah Woods.

I asked him what his perfect day of writing looked like.

He told Joy: "I wake up, read for awhile, then get to work." Then, as if he'd just noticed me, he turned only his head and said, "What's your routine."

I tried to think.

What was my routine?

"About the same," I said, annoyed with my sudden blankness. I asked what books he might recommend. He noted several, and this lead to extended tales of famous writers he knew personally, actually hung out with. He shared the story of his own beginnings. His voice softened. "I cried when my first story appeared in The New Yorker."

I looked over at Tara. She stared, silent and shameless, at Joy.

I felt invisible, but for the small, inconsequential noises I made when I asked questions. I took a long draught of pale ale, and suddenly, there I was, back in the The Celestial Viewing Room. I sat alone in that dreadful theater, and before me, on screen, was Tara, rubbing Joy's smooth, naked back. A chaste, pious back rub. Then, to my horror, I saw that Joy was being fucked by Jonah Woods.

I shuddered.

I had hoped, perhaps like a fool, for some kind of great conversation, but when called upon to speak, I felt out of the rhythm, like playing doubles tennis with a ball-hogging partner. And what could I say? When the ball came my way, I'd bumbled it, proven my ineptitude. At any rate, no mentoring wings were offered and I felt embarrassed that I had even secretly considered this.

Joy checked her watch and said, "Nice meeting you." She placed a hand on my arm. "Gotta get to work."

"Oh?" Mr. Woods said, his face full of concern. "Where do you work?"

"Across town," she said.

"Need a ride?" He raised his eyebrows, blinked a look of helpful innocence. "I'd be happy to run you over."

I had already mentioned that I had to go to cross country practice, just a few blocks from O'Shay's. I had meant to drive Joy to the Get Up Stand Up Cafe, but this generous offer from Jonah Woods would clearly save me time. I could not turn down the great writer's favor with a transparent and pathetic display of possessiveness.

Joy shrugged her assent.

To her credit, she showed some class. She had done nothing to encourage the man's attention. I could do little but sit there. I would have to trust her. But what, I wondered with some trepidation, was her notion of loyalty?

Then, as if to plunge a red-hot dagger into my skull, the great one, with his professor's salary, a benefits package, and royalties from a well-reviewed short story collection, reached casually for his wallet and tossed down a credit card. I pulled out my wallet, but he waved me off.

I had one more question. "What do you think of that writer, Ricardo Chevy?"

"Met him once."

"You know," I said. "I read - or tried to read his novel, 'Cold, Cold World'. Had a hard time with it."

"Couldn't stand that book," Jonah Woods said. "Big problem with the main character."

I stared at him for a moment. I was about to ask: *then why the glowing blurb*, but stopped myself.

In a moment, we stood before his rent-a-car - a brown Volvo, parked in front of O'Shay's. The sky was gray, the traffic on Geary was light. Jonah Woods opened the passenger door, and Joy settled herself into the front seat. Then I witnessed a scene of such utter ghastliness, I could hardly believe my eyes. A flower box hung below a window of O'Shay's. Before closing the door, Jonah Woods smiled thoughtfully, went to the flower box and plucked a pink rose. With a sudden lightness in his feet, he took two near-balletic steps toward the car, then gallantly handed the flower to Joy.

She smiled.

She took the flower.

She said thank-you.

I said good-bye, told Joy I'd see her tonight. He closed the door.

Tara and I stood at the curb as they pulled into the traffic on Geary. She's my girl, I told myself. And this was Joy's life. Been fending them off since puberty.

A day at the office; nothing more.

chapter

TWENTY-FOUR

"Your bother-in-law," I said to Tara, "Nice guy."

Tara and I sat in a coffee shop around the corner from O'Shay's as I had a little time before cross-country practice, now that I wasn't driving Joy to work. I tried to mask my gloom, to infuse my voice with enthusiasm. Rather than reply, Tara pressed her lips together, nodded, then excused herself to use the bathroom.

The clientele was sparse. An older, disheveled man wearing a black beret sat in a corner, sketching on a large pad. A young couple, easily in their teens, with black clothing, blue hair, various piercings and faces white as paste chatted along the wall. To divert my thoughts - which at this moment, were cruising across the city in the backseat of a rented Volvo - I forced myself to eavesdrop.

The boy smirked, and spoke in a slow, deep voice. "I went to Mexico..." he dragged out the last letter. "an I like... had these reallyweird clothes on.... and these dudes are all, 'Hey man, are you from Cali*for*nia?'" He leaned back, grinned, held up his hands defensively, and said, "... an I'm all, *whoa!...*"

The girl was clearly impressed. She smiled and spoke in an equally slow and drawn out voice, "*Whoa!...*"

I repeated his cryptic tale in my head, tried to make sense of it. I guessed the boy stayed at some resort with his parents, then had this encounter, maybe in a brunch line. The 'dudes' might have been kids from Iowa, who had little experience with someone dressed like him. They asked their innocent question about California. The boy - suddenly, *all whoa!* - grinned, held up his hands defensively and took a step backward.

I wondered how the Iowans felt about this.

I sipped a decaf.

Well, that was the famous Jonah Woods. Tara's brother-in-law. This gathering over burgers, arranged for my benefit, that I'd both anticipated and fretted over, had come and gone. And the love of my life was now, I hoped and prayed, riding with him, flower in hand, to be politely, respectfully, and chastely dropped off at The Get Up Stand Up Cafe. Tara had done me a favor in arranging this. I would show nothing but gratitude.

She returned and sat before me in her black sweater. She'd brushed out her hair, and had it splashed over her shoulders. It shone in various shades of brown. I'd never noticed Tara's hair before. It was beautiful, and I told her so.

She looked slightly embarrassed, pushed a swatch of it off her shoulder, and thanked me.

"Funny," I said.

"What?"

"I couldn't believe it. That book, Cold, Cold World! He said he didn't like it! But his endorsement was right there on the cover. *A stunning, invigorating bit of magic, by a writer at the height of his powers.* Now he says he had a problem with the main character. I tried to read it."

"What did you think?"

"It was... I don't know... sort of-"

"Boring!" Tara said. "I tried too."

"Really?" I said. "*Really*? You thought so, too? Jesus, I thought it was just over my head or something. So why did he-"

"They're friends," Tara said. She glanced off, laughed to herself, shook her head. "They're not friends. I think they actually hate each other. *Problem with the main character.* I doubt if he read half of it."

"No kidding?" I said. "Then why the glowing-"

"That's how it works," Tara said almost to herself. "And people will read it, hate it, and tell everyone they loved it."

"Why?"

She looked at me. "Because Joe Woods said, right there on the cover, that he liked it. Please, don't get me started."

I considered her words for a moment, and I wondered: Why did some women prefer women? But I said, "What a deal. To know a famous writer and get to call him by his nickname."

"His nickname?"

"Joe."

"I call him Joe because that *is* his name," Tara said.

"*What?*"

"He changed it to Jonah. Thought it sounded more literary."

"*More literary?*"

I had a sudden impulse to skip cross-country practice and bolt to the Get Up Stand Up Cafe. But this was impossible. The league meet was fast approaching; my runners had to be ready. And what would I do? If Joy was there, waitressing, I'd feel like an idiot. If she wasn't I'd go out of my fucking mind. Indifference - and trust - was the only approach. My God, this was a normal day when I woke up.

"So, how's it going?" Tara said, taking a sip of her latte. I wondered if she sensed my distress.

"What?" I said. "My writing?"

She smiled, "Your Joy."

"Ah, my Joy," I said, as if the subject had only just entered my thoughts. I considered Tara. Aside from being, by far, the brightest light in my writing class, I hardly knew her. Could I trust her? Truth be told, I was desperate for a confidant. "What did you think?" I said evasively.

"Joy?" Tara said. "She didn't say much."

Well who could get a damn word in, I thought. Then I slumped in my chair. I told her about Joy's endless, expensive requests.

"And if you say 'no'?"

I held up my hands like I didn't want to think about it.

Tara nodded once in silence, then, without looking at me, she asked in a voice light as raindrops, "And sex with her is amazing?"

I nearly sprayed her with decaf. "How did you know?"

Tara shrugged. "She's beautiful... but it's more than that. She just... radiates something."

"You noticed it?"

"Hard not to," Tara said, and then, for an extended moment, she seemed to appraise me.

"What?" I said self-consciously. "You think I'm dating above my weight class?"

"Huh?" She said with surprise. "Don't be ridic-" She grinned. "Did you just make that up?"

"What?"

"Dating above-"

"-my weight class?" I said. "I don't know. I guess. I wrestled one year in high school-"

"It's good," Tara said. "Use it."

"Really?" I said. "Wow. It just sort of... came to me. Just popped into my head. Jesus, maybe there's hope for even a wretch like-"

"I wouldn't go that far," she said, impishly.

"And you?" I said.

"Me?"

"You, smartass."

"What about me?"

"Your Angela."

"My Angela," Tara said, "We're great, except she's starting a masters program up in Portland. In January. We'll be long-distancing it for awhile."

"Sorry," I said. "And the writing?"

"I think something's nearly done," she said. "Haven't left the apartment for days."

"I'm jealous," I said. "Can't wait to see it."

She asked about my own writing.

"Oh, God, I don't know. That's a nightmare of a question. Several false starts. But something should break soon. I'm sort of preoccupied."

"I can tell," Tara said.

I nodded. Then I thought, what the hell; I mentioned Camus, and the line about love that I found in The Plague.

"Three times in a hundred years?" she said skeptically.

"Maybe Joy will change."

Tara glanced out the window and tightened a corner of her mouth. I read her expression to mean: *and maybe God will join us for a latte.*

The next few weeks passed in a precarious holding pattern.

My father's condition worsened. My mother dissuaded me from coming down for any reason. When Dad was well enough to speak to me, he also insisted.

I had several ideas for stories but they went nowhere. Nothing left my pen with sufficient beauty to turn in to my writing class or to show to my sick father.

Despite my dad's illness, and against all logic regarding what should properly be consuming my attention, a strange, sensual magic had enveloped me. I was dizzy with desire for Joy, and exhausted from sleepless, passion-filled nights. Joy toured me through her enchanting haunts: The Haight, Noe Valley, The Mission, Clement Street, Golden Gate Park. Off we went on moony, dippy, lovesick walks through fairy tale neighborhoods, my hands unable to leave her lovely waist, her back, her arms. And everywhere was the spellbinding fog; the mist filling my head, intoxicating me, though I was already drunken with Joy at my side, and we returned to cold flannel sheets and laughed, touched, merged and sighed until late into the night.

The depression was kept at bay. Running, writing, coaching, and insane, other-worldly lovemaking - these seemed to be the prescription.

I received my first of two paychecks from coaching and watched it evaporate instantly in haze of maguro and saki. Any argument for prudence and my sensually benevolent wonder turned glacial. But when I didn't argue, oh, dear God in Heaven! To climb under the sheets with Joy! Hallucinatory events each, all preceded now by steamy, requested narrations. Difficult at first, I began to enjoy these preludes, particularly given such fabulous motivation. She was a winsome wood nymph of the forest. An exotic Massai maiden bathing in an ancient Rift Valley stream. A bewitching mermaid in a kingdom beneath the sea. I was a lost hiker. A bush pilot, parachuted from a burning plane. A deep-sea diver. "Do the beach one," Joy said, and I altered details, every shift aimed at lifting my sweet lover to a more ragged edge of passion.

I did not ask about her ride to work with Jonah Woods. I mastered my curiosity; compartmentalized it, as Robert would say.

The cross-country league meet was almost upon us. And my team was improving. Alex ran more consistently, not nearly as well he could, but his feigned ailments and appeals for pity had subsided. Steve was gaining confidence, getting stronger than I could have dreamed. In two races, he actually challenged the lead runners of opposing teams and placed in the top five. As a team, we had three mid-pack finishes; not great, certainly, but a tremendous improvement over previous years. I would need something very special from my runners in the league meet, this last race of the season, to impress Father Damian, to make a solid case for a year-round job, and for my life to take the turn I desired more than anything.

The weekend prior to the league meet, Steve and Gary told me they were eating at a pizza place called Georgio's on Clement Street and they saw Joy and I as we walked past.

"Who was *that*?" Gary asked at practice on Monday.

"Girlfriend," I said.

"*My God!*" Steve said. "You've been seriously holding out on us coach."

Gary asked me to bring her to the league meet. I instantly said no.

That Wednesday before the big race, on the jog back to campus after a brief speed workout, my runners, who had embraced a new habit of chanting on runs, erupted: "*Bring her, Bring her!*"

"Not a chance," I said.

"C'mon, Coach!" Gary shouted. "Motivation!"

They chanted the entire final half-mile, drowning me out, until we arrived at the gym.

chapter

TWENTY-FIVE

The great Russian writer, Alexander Pushkin, once remarked that all of man's efforts are aimed at gaining the attention of women.

I pulled the white university van onto the 280 freeway as we headed to Crystal Springs, the site of league finals. The early morning was overcast and chilly. My team rode in silence, all of them looking fine, strapping, and sparkling in their bright green meet sweats with the school logo emblazoned in white block letters, front and back. On the desperate pretext that I needed every possible edge, Joy sat to my immediate right as I drove the van. What could it hurt? Coaches often brought spouses or significant others. This was a natural, perhaps even a healthy addition.

Alex sat shotgun and the rest of my sparse crew was settled behind us in silent, pre-race contemplation. Gary fiddled with his racing flats. Steve read a book by Nietzsche and nibbled a Power Bar. The twins studied chemistry texts.

Well, I had done what I could: aerobic training, anaerobic, hill work, pep talks, and now, the small, inconsequential addition of Joy, as Gary had suggested, for motivation. We cruised among the light Saturday morning traffic of the 280. I could only try to relax.

A large truck passed us, and just then, Alex began to fidget.

He gazed out at the traffic, pushed his brown hair off his forehead, shifted in his seat. He narrowed his eyes, pressed his lips philosophically, and it didn't take Nostradamus to predict: a speech was coming. Alex glanced once at Joy, then returned his attention to the middle-distance of the road ahead. "People ask me..." he said, "'*Why do you do it?*'"

I looked in the rearview. Gary stared inquisitively at Alex, then nudged Steve. Steve looked up from his book.

"Why... put in all that work?" Alex continued. "All that hard running... day after day." He shook his head and smiled, as if to marvel at his own, baffling peculiarity.

Steve appeared amused. Both he and Gary watched Alex in silence, waiting for more. Joy waited blankly. Though Alex spoke only to Joy, he had everyone's attention. He didn't seem to know or care.

"I tell them," Alex continued, "it's because of something... in *here*." He tapped his own chest. He looked at Joy, nodded, then he leaned back and continued to gaze at the traffic.

The effect of Alex's self-assessment was this: a polite smile from Joy and a restrained explosion of giggling in the back seat.

Moments later, Steve burst into laughter and said, "Stop it!"

I looked in the rearview. Gary was leaning toward Steve, tapping his chest and saying, "*In here*."

"I said *stop!*" Steve said, tears running from his eyes.

Alex was oblivious; Joy, distant and uninterested.

Gary caught my glance and stopped, but I felt briefly liberated from a growing inner terror that I did not wish to reveal to my team. Though my life was on the line, I knew that team confidence began with the coach. We had a shot at some kind of success, and if Pushkin was correct, Joy was a performance enhancer if ever there was one.

We arrived at the Crystal Springs Cross Country Course in plenty of time and I gave my guys their instructions:

Pee.

Jog three miles.

Meet me for stretching.

Runners from other schools arrived, looking slick and athletic in their colorful spandex and nylon meet attire. They exited their vans and milled about, bearing racing flats, water bottles, power bars, energy drinks, yawning away pre-race jitters in the cold morning air.

The Crystal Springs Cross Country Course is a challenging 3.1 miles with several hills, long and steep. Today, the runners would cover the course twice so spectators could see them at the beginning, middle, and end. The other teams began to stretch, jog, and run warm-up sprints. Sweat tops were discarded, revealing colorful singlets in green, red, yellow and blue. The league encompassed teams from much of Northern California, including one consistently tough group of runners from Oregon, and another, nearly as tough, from Reno. We'd never raced either of them, but the Oregon coach diligently sent us weekly newsletters, boasting of his team's prowess. No team besides mine had less than seven runners - each group was the cream of the crop skimmed off from a much larger squad, some with as many as sixty runners. At least I was spared the coach's headache of deciding who could compete on race day. Because the league was so geographically spread out, we actually hadn't seen many of these teams until today, and I knew there was serious talent among them. Gary and Steve had made impressive gains in the past few weeks, but in truth, I had no idea how we might fare.

An official blew a whistle, signaling the approaching start.

Coaches with clipboards and stopwatches gathered their teams. I did the same. I tried to look composed, confident. The six of us stood in a comparatively tiny circle. I looked them over. Their numbers were affixed to their singlets, a safety pin at each corner. I asked them to check their shoelaces, make sure the knots were tight.

"This is it," I said. "This is what all the hard work is for. Go out strong, but not too strong. Keep contact. Work the uphills, fly the downhills. Gentlemen," I looked at each of them. "We're ready!"

We put our hands in the center of the circle, shouted our school name. Other teams around us did the same. My five runners removed their sweats and headed downhill to the starting line with nine other teams.

My brief show of composure evaporated. For a moment, I shook like a newborn colt. Joy appeared at my side, as the non-competitors - coaches, officials and spectators - gathered at the top of the first hill. She wore jeans, and though my dark gray sweat top was large and baggy on her, Joy's lovely, dreadlock-framed face elicited the usual amount of attention. A tall trainer, with an armload of tape and plastic water bottles watched her for an extended moment, as if suddenly lost in a daydream. An elderly, gray-haired coach did a double take, then focused on his clipboard.

The clouds parted. The sun broke through.

I hoped this was a good sign.

I stood with Joy, the coaches and a smattering of spectators. Our sport, tragically, was never overrun by a rabid press of fans. I remembered two cheerleaders in my high school algebra class, complaining because they had to cheer at a cross-country race that afternoon. Other sports were infinitely sexier and beautiful women swarmed their stars. Running offered little in the way of prestige or feminine attention. The challenge was simply an intense, private battle with pain. The rewards: a possible personal best. A sweet endorphin rush. License to eat continuously. A dignity understood only by other runners. I could hardly blame Joy for appearing bored.

The athletes stood colorfully and nervously at the bottom of the hill, engaged in a stay-loose, starting-line dance, shaking their arms and legs. The perennial first place team from Portland was here in force, with seven fit looking runners. Even St. Mary's fielded seven athletes.

All I could do now was pray for my five runners who stood with the other teams at the starting line. I wondered if I should have rested them more. No, they were rested enough. More hill work? Maybe, but I didn't think so.

The starter raised his pistol.

The runners leaned forward, reached for buttons on digital wristwatches.

The gun went off, followed by a shout from the athletes.

A stampede of ectomorphs with fabulously efficient cardiovascular systems moved swiftly up the hill. In a race that required a careful, controlled meting out of precious energy over an intense thirty to forty minutes, at the hundred-meter point, one runner was sprinting madly in the lead.

No, I thought. Please God, no.

Alex Granger bolted up the hill and passed us at full tilt, ahead of everyone else, with a look of pure agony on his face.

I felt the blood sucked, vampire-style, from my body. My legs turned to water. *Alex*, I thought: *Don't do this to me*.

"That's your guy!" Joy said. "He's pretty good!" But I could not explain the disaster that was unfolding. I couldn't talk at all. I watched the other athletes run past.

At the halfway point, the first group, lead by a young, slight, Latino man of ungodly talent, flew by us. Then came the second pack; the more terrestrial athletes, including Steve, then Gary several strides back. They were just where I wanted them, both relaxed, running valiantly. The thoroughbred I knew Steve could be was finally asserting itself. His stride was long but efficient, his blond hair trailed like fire. Gary ran within himself, but he was keying off Steve and, if he kept it up, was running the race of his life. Nick and Peter were somewhere in the strung-out middle, just behind midpack and holding their own.

Where the hell was Alex?

Then I saw him, dead last, grimacing dramatically.

I calculated instantly that if all five completed the race at their present place, we'd finish around seventh at best, probably worse. Maybe we could still beat St. Mary's.

Regardless, in fifteen minutes, it would be over.

The first runners crossed the line, one leaning dangerously and dripping a huge, unsightly goober from his mouth. Joy winced.

Steve finished in a solid eighth place. Gary came in fifteenth. Nick and Peter arrived at twenty-nine and thirty. They had actually moved up about ten places each. We were in decent shape... but where was Alex? Had I missed his finish? He could be anywhere and we'd beat St. Mary's. The two top St. Mary's runners finished midpack, and the rest ran as a group among the stragglers.

Then every last runner had crossed the line, including a few smiling, overweight young men from St. Mary's who looked like they took up the sport as a lark to lose a few pounds. I looked everywhere but couldn't find my fifth runner. My four finishers were catching their breath, walking around, sipping from plastic bottles of donated Gator Aid.

Just then, a whoop went up behind me. I turned and saw the St. Mary's team. They were gathered around their coach, near a water fountain. They gave each other high fives, slaps on the back.

I asked an elderly official standing near me what the fuss was about.

"They didn't take last," the man said with a chuckle. "Guess that was their goal."

"And who took last?" I asked, dreading but knowing the answer. He checked his clipboard, pointed silently to our school. "Only four finishers," he said.

I went over to Steve, who held a water bottle in one hand. I told him he ran a great race, told the same to them all, then asked, "Where's Alex?"

Steve shrugged.

Gary, sweating and still breathing hard, pointed. "Over there, coach."

I saw him, sitting alone beneath a tree. His face was dirt-smudged and he held a bottle of Gatorade. I felt anger welling dangerously in my chest. Had Alex walked the course, we would still have beaten St. Mary's.

"What happened?" I asked.

"Dropped out," he said without looking at me.

I stared at him. “You *dropped out*?”

He nodded.

“Why?”

“Laces were too tight. You told us to tighten our laces. Foot cramped.”

As if to hear it myself, to aid comprehension, my voice came slowly. “Your laces were tight… so you… dropped out?”

Alex took what appeared to be the deep, noble breath of a fallen warrior. He squinted ruggedly into the distance and spoke solemnly, “It goes against everything I stand for.”

And just then I had in a vision. I saw Alex, a chronic TV watcher, sitting in the blue-gray glow, staring blank and zombie-like, at handsome, square-jawed, platitude-spewing men of mettle. Then I walked. Quickly. I did not wish to react in a way I would later regret.

My dream cracked, crumbled, fell before my eyes.

I found Joy, standing by the van. She asked if we were ready to go, she had Jeremy’s party to get ready for. I stared at her briefly, wondered at her impatience, and I never felt so alone in my life.

chapter

TWENTY-SIX

I cruised by Jeremy's house - a two-story, pricey walk-up in Pacific Heights - and continued on to find parking. I dreaded this event, but the day, I thought, could not get much worse. There would be no job for me as a coach in the spring or next year. Of this I was certain. Perhaps I screwed up; perhaps it was fate. But I was breathing, still alive and on this earth. I had survived a thrashing this morning and I could survive this party. After a third small check from coaching, the money would be gone. Maybe I could go into the Athletic Director's office Monday morning and explain about the improvement of four of my runners.

But no.

Tomorrow's sports page in the Chronicle would show us taking last.

Last.

The very sound of it would be blasphemous to Father Damian. I imagined him receiving the news as he sat in his huge red leather chair, backed by the picture of Jesus and flanked by the walls of trophies, each bathed in a golden, heavenly light of victory. Nowhere in his office were artifacts of significant improvement, near misses, or appalling self-delusion.

This was pure, unholy disaster.

I found a parking space blocks away near a grassy park and killed the engine. My Honda Civic grumbled in protest then died. Perhaps it wanted me to keep driving, to avoid this party. I hated to be around people when I felt like this. I could probably have excused myself with an illness or something, but that would be a coward's way out. I had no desire, after my catastrophe this morning, to further the insult by indulging such behavior. In the grand scheme, what was athletic defeat? A speck of a concern and nothing more. Without any decent writing to justify the life I wanted so desperately, what did it matter? Who really gets the life they want? Who's to say it's the best life for them anyway? "I'm sorry, Dad," I said aloud, for some reason. I only knew one thing; I would not return to teaching. There were other jobs in the world; I just wanted this one so badly.

On the seat beside me was a brown bag with a carton of ice cream.

Even now, I could hardly believe how silly I must have looked, standing in the frozen food section at Safeway, peering through the frosted glass doors. I considered Joy's friends, and wondered which brand and flavor carried the appropriate cachet. I could see it already; bring the wrong ice cream, and suddenly everyone's staring me, holding up their hands and saying, "*Whoa!*" Well, I could sweat this potluck. I would remain silent, off to the side, invisible. I would survive. I probably shouldn't have gone to Safeway in the first place, but Earthly Edibles was hopelessly beyond my budget.

I took the bag in my hand and exited the Honda.

Joy had gone to Jeremy's house early to help Marsha prepare. Joy loved parties, it seemed, as much as they loved her. I stepped up the short walk to the brick porch, and there, perched alongside the path, I noticed a small, stone Buddha. As I rang the doorbell, I tried to comfort myself with the not-so-small consolation that when this was over I would be in bed with my beloved woman.

The door opened. Joy's smile was radiant.

"Tim! Oh, thank you," she said as she took the bag.

Here was the woman I loved to distraction, who had witnessed my failure with little understanding or interest, but here she was nonetheless. Tonight she wore a short, black dress and looked downright mythic. I experienced an instant vertigo. Her hair was re-done with colorful African beads at the ends of each braid. Awful as I felt, she still had the power to set me reeling.

As I entered, I took in the alcove and the living room beyond. And I saw instantly that Jeremy was loaded. The decor of his house was expensive bohemian. Buddhist paraphernalia graced one wall, African another. Here and there were icons of nonconformity; among them, a picture of Jeremy wearing a headband, blond dreadlocks, and a tie-dye shirt in a forest. I followed Joy into the kitchen. "What does your friend Jeremy do for a living?" I asked.

"He's an inheritor," she said, spoken in the same tone one might say an engineer, or a baker. So, there it was: a trust fund brat. I guessed Joy lived here for a while, loved romping among the affluence, and probably, the endless flow of gifts, of dining out in restaurants. So why did she leave? The reasons could be endless, but shouldn't she have the decency to avoid subjecting me to previous lovers? Of course, it was an 'open relationship' she had told me once. 'No one can own anyone.' Perhaps this was the ethos of the commune; everyone fucks everyone, all remain friends. My own guess, unhip as it might be, was that she simply loved to be in a room where everyone desired her. I wondered how this felt; to be at the receiving end of intense desire, and if the feeling was palpable, like heat or cold.

I only knew with certainty that this would soon be over. In the meantime, I would force a smile and make polite, forgettable noises. And I saw them now, over the bar that separated the kitchen from the living room; Greg, Roshaldemond, Jeremy, Marcia, and a few others I'd never met.

"Let me get you a drink," Joy said, with a formality that unnerved me.

She placed the ice cream in the freezer, removed a Corona from the fridge, popped it open and handed it to me. She brought two tall, elegant crystal bottles down from a shelf and set them beside a large, colorful salad, then reached into a drawer and removed a wooden spoon and fork. She was far too familiar with Jeremy's kitchen for my taste.

Jeremy's kitchen. On one wall was a picture of reggae band. On another, an elaborate beaded necklace.

"What's this?" I asked.

"An African necklace," Joy said. "When Jeremy stayed a month with the Massai."

"And this?"

She looked. "From when he went to Jamaica."

I leaned against the sink, watched her for a moment, and said, "Just one cool thing after another?"

"Huh?" Joy said.

"Does he ever, I don't know... just change his oil or anything?"

Joy made a face of confusion, and I was glad she missed my sarcasm. She began to drizzle olive oil and vinegar over the salad and then I saw it. Joy's cloth black purse lay on the kitchen counter, and a familiar red book peaked out of it. A chill went through me. I set the beer down.

"Joy," I said. "What's that?"

My question was unnecessary. The book was Jonah Woods' short story collection, Quantum Theory.

"Oh," Joy said. "That's for you."

"For me?" I stared at her. "What do you mean?"

"Your friend gave it to me," she said. She lifted the wooden utensils and tossed the salad. "I don't want it."

I felt a dagger, invisible, painless until now, twist one quarter turn in my chest. "He *gave* it to you?" I watched her; measured her expression, which was now, a slight tightening of her lips. "Joy? What are you saying?"

She was silent.

"When did he give it to you?"

"After lunch. That day."

"After lunch?" I said. "Joy. What happened after you left?"

"Tim. Stop."

"Answer me."

She continued tossing the salad.

"Joy. I read that book. I have it. It's in my bookshelf at home. I don't need another copy. Why did he give you a book?"

She was silent.

"Joy?" I trembled.

She remained silent.

And then I knew.

"Oh my God."

My breath left me. I began to shake.

I watched her, and felt suddenly lost in this kitchen. How to comprehend this?

"Oh my God," I said again.

Joy paused with the salad, gazed abstractedly. She spoke with a strange, airy lilt. "There are... so many... who need me."

I grabbed the book, opened the cover. The inscription was in large, blocky handwriting: '*A lamentably paltry gift... for an afternoon in heaven*.'

"Oh," Joy said. "Did he write-"

My look silenced her. I wondered how to assimilate this; my worst nightmare. The kitchen was suddenly, excruciatingly airless. I grabbed my Corona, and for some reason, the salad, and exited the swinging doors to the living room. My shoe hooked on the thick carpet, and I stumbled. The salad bowl upended, much of it landing on Jeremy's Birkenstocks.

Jeremy, his hair now in dreadlocks like the picture on the wall, shook his foot clean, and said, "Mr. Coordination makes his entrance."

"I'm... sorry," I said. "It was an accident."

"There *are* no accidents," Roshaldemond said.

I looked at the young man, standing with Marcia, watching me through his spectacles with his practiced, penetrating stare. No one offered to help me, and then Joy appeared in the doorway. She watched for a moment, then said, "It's okay, I got it," and returned with a sponge and a towel.

"Excuse me," I said. Jeremy looked at Greg and released a mocking, nasal expulsion of air.

My Corona had not spilled. Somehow, I'd hung onto it. I stood. And I wanted desperately to disappear. I tried to focus on something: the room, the decor. A meditation bowl sat on an end table. A round-headed African carving perched on a shelf. A batik from Asia hung on the far wall. A Nepalese drum was in a corner, a Moroccan carpet covered a space before a Chinese gong. Jeremy's living room was a multi-cultural frappe - except for the people. Other than Joy's light brown skin, everyone was white. They continued to watch me. I excused myself.

The bathroom was of a similar motif - meditation and yoga magazines in an African basket, soap from Asia. I looked in the mirror.

I said aloud: *Joy fucked Jonah Woods*

The harsh sound of it - *fucked* - sickened me. It suggested something fast and vulgar, disgusting fluids flying everywhere. I was muddled and spent. I loved her - this didn't stop - but... what was it she said?

So many who need me?

My God.

I couldn't think.

I only knew this: I didn't want to leave, not yet. I couldn't simply walk out. Of all the options - from the thrill of mass murder to the utter humiliation of begging Joy's forgiveness for God knows what - the choice of leaving was not on the list. I couldn't even explain why.

For lack of anything else to do, with shaking hands, I washed my face.

I exited the bathroom, wondered who else Joy had fucked, and wandered down the hall, opening doors. I found a bedroom which had more Buddhist items: a prayer wheel, another zafu, a picture of the Dali Lama.

As I returned to the party I felt my perception retreating, and the wet cement of depression filling my head as I approached the table. Jeremy put on a Ladysmith Black Mombasa cd, and Marcia shouted, "I love this kind of music!" They were all sitting down to dinner, and though the chatter was audible, I could only discern bits of it, as if listening through a curtain of mud.

Marcia said she was searching for a sense of community.

Greg said he wanted more ritual in his life.

A woman said she used to drink a diet coke everyday, and then realized: "Why do I need all those chemicals in my body?"

Someone found a drumming workshop empowering.

Someone felt invaded.

"I'm in denial," Roshaldemond said. Everyone laughed. I had no idea why.

A woman found something highly offensive.

Another woman said her friend Ananda, was "... so grounded, so centered. But really intense."

I tried to tune in to their conversation but could find no foothold. I wondered what it meant to be really intense. No one asked.

A movie, Marcia said, was off-putting.

Roshaldemond said, "Who absconded my drink?"

Absconded *with,* I thought.

Garlic, someone said, is very healthy.

"A good relationship? When two people meet each other's needs on different levels."

"A part of me agrees with you," Roshaldemond said.

I should make an effort, I thought, as if nothing had happened. As if Joy's blithely uttered revelation meant less to me than a declaration of athlete's foot. This was the way to go.

I took an empty seat beside her. *Joy who fucked Jonah Woods.* A woman to my immediate left with an African head scarf and a German accent announced that she ran three miles a day. I perked up slightly. Her voice rose musically and she moved her hands like a conjurer as she spoke. "It makes me feel... wonderful. It... clears my mind. It... energizes me."

I willed casualness into my voice, and turned to her. "I been running for fifteen years. I coach runners at the university, hey, not even a few miles from here."

She continued as if I'd said nothing. "People ask, 'why do something that is so... painful?' They don't understand. It is pain, yes, but a *good* kind of pain."

Jeremy, sat on the other side of Joy, and related a brief tale about his mother, inspired I imagined, by the vegan fare before us. "Once, she made a bet with a man... that I could eat an entire steak dinner. So, I ate it. He said double or nothing. I ate the second one, too."

"All that meat," Marcia said.

"She sounds toxic," Roshaldemond said.

"Haven't spoken to her in years," Jeremy added with a flick of his dreadlocks. "I showed up at a family reunion a few years back. They couldn't handle how I looked."

Everyone at the table, dressed in various attitudes of bohemian, seemed suddenly, as a group, to pause, stare off and grin. I guessed they each imagined a similar hypothetical moment - shocking their own families. I thought about Jeremy eating two steak dinners, a topic lost instantly in a slipstream of unheeded, mindless chatter that seemed to strain for sameness. I guessed his mother was on a date, and that his father had died by then and left him a pile. After my failure with the German runner, I felt myself retreat further, and unable even to process simple phrases. I doubted my ability to talk, dreaded an inevitable halting quality in my voice. I knew what it invited.

Joy ate silently beside me as if nothing had occurred.

I watched platters of food move around the table.

"Pass the brown rice."

"Try the mu shu."

"Is that your famous tabouli?"

"Oh, *please*."

"I kill for pot stickers."

How I hate the person who says, "It's so quiet. Everyone's eating."

Roshaldemond said it.

"Ah, but you should hear the quiet of an African veldt at dusk..." Greg's huge frame occupied the head of the table. His plate was piled high, and he spoke in a ponderous baritone, apropos of nothing, as if awaiting his moment. He glanced off - a lost-in-thought stare - as if seeing it, as if reliving the event he was about to relate. Everyone at the table looked at Greg, and waited in expectation. He began as if the memory had just occurred to him. "One late afternoon, we were moving in the outback, on holiday in a jeep, when our path was blocked by a family of giraffes. Enormous, yet... graceful. Their feet were the size of dinner plates. They were five, perhaps a family. Wandering, nibbling the odd branch. They moved before us, majestic, slowly, then out of the road." Greg paused. He gathered himself, his great bearded head now barely a-tremble. His deep voice grew; and with his hand aloft, his spit Shakespearean, he said, "And... there... before us... *was Kilimanjaro!*"

"Mmm..." the women murmured around the table.

"How long were you in Africa?" Marsha asked.

"A year," he said, nodding once, grinning; then he added more quietly, "Well... almost a year."

"Live your dream," Roshaldemond said.

Joy smiled, wonderfully impressed.

I looked at Greg. He pushed food around on his plate, beaming amidst the sweet glow of feminine adoration. But his tale seemed odd. I wondered: could giraffes really block a view of Kilimanjaro? Wouldn't you see it for miles and miles as you drove? Well, I guess it wouldn't be the first memory retrofit for a dinner table full of attractive but gullible-

"What about you?" Greg said. He was looking directly at me.

"Me?" Had I smirked?

"What do you... *do?*"

"Tim's a writer," Marsha said.

Oh, God.

"A *writer?*" Greg said. "But what do you write *about?*"

I shrugged. "Just... stuff," I said intelligently.

Greg bore down on me. Joy, Jeremy, and everyone at the table stared in silence.

"But you must have experience if you want to write," Greg said. "What have you *done*?"

Why hadn't I left earlier? I could have begged off with a stomach complaint. My brain was empty. I repeated the question to myself. *What had I done?* The people around me all seemed to exist in some strange and distant place. I felt dizzy, my head stuffed with cotton.

"Tim is well-traveled, too," Joy said. I felt the intensity of their eyes increase.

"Oh, not much," I said.

They waited.

I took a breath. I spoke. "A few years ago... I took this... trip around the world." I looked upward, blinked, and rattled off a few of the countries I visited, starting in Tahiti and ending in England. I hoped this would wrap the discussion.

"But that kind of travel is so superficial," Greg said dismissively. "You must *live* in a foreign country to truly get to know it."

I had nothing in me to spar. I recalled a line from Anna Karenina. Levin said: 'Things work out best if you let people think you believe they are who they think they are.'

I heard myself say, "I... actually... wouldn't mind living in Africa someday." The wishy-washy sound of my voice sickened me.

"*Then what's stopping you?*" Greg boomed.

I'd stepped right into it.

Half-hidden, feminine smiles erupted around the table, followed by a sneer from the birthday boy. Greg was now Mr. Live-For-The-Moment; I, the wimpy writer. This assessment seemed confirmed on every face. Even Joy, beside me, stifled a smirk.

I stared numbly, mutely at the center of the table, any slick, ready answers wiped clean from the tabula rasa of my useless, mud-filled brain. The room tilted strangely.

I wanted nothing but escape. My team lost, the woman I loved was donating her cunt in gratuitous acts of mercy. I was whipped. Humiliated. A dishrag.

Greg, in good spirits now, launched into another story. "On a brief, return visit, I sat in the back of the village classroom where I once taught. One of my former students was now the teacher. As a student, he was quite difficult. Once, he got into some trouble, and... he... was dealt with... appropriately." The briefest shadow seemed to cross Greg's face, but he smiled instantly. "Now, as he taught, I sat in the back of the class and began... to cry. A student asked, 'teacher, why is that man crying?'" Greg paused thoughtfully. "And my former student pointed at me and said: 'Because he knows I want to be like *him*.'"

"Wow," the turbaned woman said.

"What an experience!" Marcia said. The others pressed their lips together, shook their heads in approval.

I glanced around. Such blatant self-congratulation; no one even raised an eyebrow. Even Joy shook her head in admiration, certain to gush later over what an amazing person Greg was.

Greg leaned back, once again staring down at the middle distance. "What I'd like to do next," he said, "is mine for gold in Arizona."

"Mmm..." came the feminine approval once again.

Horrible, unmoored as I felt, I wondered about this Greg. Something was fishy about him. Crying in the back of the classroom. I reached for my Corona, drank it quickly. After awhile, Marcia and Joy brought desserts from the kitchen. Protests of 'I'm stuffed,' erupted.

Marcia had baked a blueberry pie. "With whole wheat crust," she added.

"Tim brought ice cream," Joy said. She opened the bag.

"*Vanilla*?" Greg said, staring at me. "A guy who'd get vanilla," Greg said, "is the kind of guy who takes long walks in the fog."

Smiles, withheld laughter fluttered around the table. Joy, too, was openly grinning. My head was blank. The room seemed airless, stifling. I had actually picked *French* vanilla for it's cosmopolitan chic. A thousand slick answers would come to me over the next three years, but nothing now, when it mattered. Why was this happening? My ears, my entire face burned. My vision blurred.

Jeremy grinned.

"I gotta go to work," Roshaldemond said, checking his watch. He turned to Marcia. "Can you drop me?"

Marcia, his girlfriend, easily ten years his senior and who clearly a loved parties as much as Joy, frowned, then nodded reluctantly.

"I'll drive you," I said.

Everyone at the table stared at me.

chapter

TWENTY-SEVEN

"How long you had this thing?" Roshaldemond asked.

The evening was dark, but the traffic in this hilly, ritzy area was lighter now than when I arrived. My passenger sat beside me in his gauzy attire and a black trench coat, with the medallion around his neck. He looked over the worn interior of my Honda as we pulled into the street. His tone suggested he'd acquired a contact sneer at Jeremy's party, which he'd brought with him into my car. I turned off the residential street and into the heavier traffic on Park Presidio.

"A little while," I said. It was good to be out of there. My head still felt buried under a thousand feet of mud. I needed to breathe.

Roshaldemond glanced at the odometer and released a sharp burst of air. "I can see you don't care about the ozone layer."

I heard his voice as if from a vast, strange distance. I said, "Bought it used." He shook his head and looked out the passenger window. My woman had fucked Jonah Woods. I could hardly attend to anything else at the moment, least of all, the ozone layer. Joy had said I hated everyone. Was she correct? I was certainly beginning to hate this little bastard to my right. Was I supposed to like him? *Roshaldamonde.* He didn't have a car, mooched rides and sneered at odometers. Why was Marcia so enchanted with him?

"The *writer*," he said with a chuckle.

I worked diligently at politeness. "And what do you do?"

"Not a writer," he said. "Too much the perfectionist. But, who knows," he added dismissively. "Maybe I'll write a novel... get a Ph.D. Hard to tell at this point." He pressed his mouth into a half-smile and his eyes into slits, as if suddenly drunk on his own potential.

"So... what are you doing now?"

"*Me?*" He glanced over. "Just layin low for awhile. Turn here."

I turned onto Geary and he said, "So? How is going?"

"What's that?"

"The *writing*," he sang, like it was obvious.

I tried to focus. He had asked how the writing was going. I thought this over, and about the disaster of the cross-country race this morning. "Well, coming up with money to live is always difficult-"

My passenger laughed out loud. "Don't expect pity from *me*," he said. "You chose it."

I blinked hard. I imagined pulling to the curb. And I saw myself tear this snot-nosed, pajama-clad brat out of the car and stomp on his skull until his gray matter splattered across the pavement.

I took a breath. "You asked me how it was going. I answered you. I didn't ask for sympathy."

He said nothing.

I continued, and I heard my own voice rising. "If I'd said, 'it's miserable because there's no money when you're a beginner,' then you could have told me not to expect pity. But I didn't say that."

He must've heard something in my voice, because he glanced at me in silence. This lifted me somewhat, and for the first time that evening, I spoke with some volume, "Do you understand the difference, *Roshaldemond*?".

He shrugged, then said quietly, "Whatever. Um, turn here."

The place was a steak house called The Buckhorn. Every town and city in America seemed to have a restaurant called the Buckhorn. I pulled into the lot and cut the engine. The Honda rumbled a moment, then died.

"Thanks," he said, and got out of the car.

I unclasped my seat belt and exited.

"Where you going?" he said. The sneer was gone, and replaced, oddly, by concern.

I watched him for a moment and said, somewhat sharply, "Restroom. That okay?"

The young man, soon to write a novel or get a Ph.D., but watch out world because he's just laying low at the moment, turned uneasily and headed toward the glass doors of the Buckhorn. I followed a few steps behind.

The place was brightly lit. Roshaldamond headed with quick strides for a storeroom back near the kitchen while I glanced around for a men's room.

I stopped.

Off to my right, among the polished wooden decor of the Buckhorn, was a waitress; an attractive willowy woman, maybe thirty-five or even forty, taking orders at a table. Something about her... she seemed beautiful but weathered, perhaps at the end of a life as a head-turner, now entering her next womanly phase but not going gently. She wore a black mini-skirt and low-cut, bright red silk blouse.

I filled in the rest: Married as a young, starry-eyed knockout to some hot-headed, booze-swilling bastard, now divorced, and holding it together pouring coffee and taking orders while her looks held out. Because her legs were still gorgeous - everyone said they were - she wore an astonishingly short insinuation of a skirt. And men looked. (Why does the male eye, she wondered, study this terrain obsessively for a panty line?) And she would exploit the attention while it lasted. Her wisdom now, lay in firing this yearning to a ragged edge, to hold it there in a moment of power that first thrilled, then bored her. In another setting, she witnessed its fulfillment in the relinquishing of her greatest gift, saw the fire in her lover's eyes die, his interest wane, then listened to mumbled excuses about a busy morning, a need to get going. Thus, life taught her how far to go, when to stop and still hold the cards. This usually meant little more than chatting, smiling, fielding jokes, and a subtle sway back to the kitchen. She hated the game and only wanted a good man to love her and to hold her. Her face had lined and hardened over some ugly moments in her past - a violent divorce, abysmal dating, problems with money, with wine, and now, the first droopy intimations of middle age.

Here, among steaks and mounted deer heads, she poured coffee, inclining slightly from her hips in a fetching dance which increased desperately needed tips - she had a four-year-old at home whom she loved to distraction. She considered an affair with her boss – he'd certainly been flinging the double-entendres lately - and good god, who could support even a small family on what a waitress earned? But in her worst moments, she wondered how it had gotten like this; where was the innocent, hopeful, starry-eyed girl in her wedding pic-

Please.

I remembered why I came in and looked for the restroom.

And there, by the kitchen, was Roshaldemond, wearing a hair net, fiddling with his apron, looking like the little boy that he was, which was frankly a damn sight better than the way he looked earlier.

And I looked back at Cindy - this had to be her name - felt a saintly sadness for her and turned away, not wishing to claim kin to the hordes of lustful bastards who fucked her and fucked her endlessly in their prurient and wistful imaginations.

Suddenly, a group of grinning, brown, mustached Latino faces appeared at the metal door to the kitchen. They looked at Roshaldemond. One shouted, "*Doogie!*" They laughed.

The boy turned and saw me, his face red as Cindy's blouse.

I entered a bohemian coffee shop around the corner from Jeremy's house and ordered three double espressos. In my journal I jotted down everything I could remember about the waitress. I wrote about the boy exposed by kitchen doors, the now hideous thought of stomping on his skull, and the beautiful, grinning Latinos. I drank a double shot of bitter-tasting espresso. I wrote about my team's last place performance, Joy's transgression, and then the truly big subject. It was the thought I'd avoided and the only one that mattered. I was about to lose my father. The truth and finality of this caught in my throat. All else was nonsense before this single, horrific fact. He would be gone and this could happen within weeks.

I had yet to write something beautiful.

I honestly had nothing to lose now; a sad fact that was strangely, utterly delicious. And I could not leave the party as I had. This was suddenly and oddly of enormous importance. If nothing else went right, by God, this was one problem I would not leave unattended. I knew that if I did, I would relive it a thousand times in pure, debilitating anger.

I tossed down the second, then third espresso, winced at the taste, and wondered: Why *would* someone cry in the back of a village classroom?

No, I thought; Greg had missed it completely.

chapter

TWENTY-EIGHT

I stepped silently over the stone Buddha and onto the porch.

I opened the front door, entered, closed it behind me and stood quietly in the alcove. The birthday party had shifted to the living room, and its attendees lounged on sofas, chairs, and natural cotton pillows arranged around a coffee table. Dessert was finished; the organic blueberry pie with whole wheat crust, and yes, the entire carton of French vanilla ice cream. They had scoffed at its deplorable conventionality, yet ate it nonetheless. The empty carton sat beside the pie tin, along with dishes and coffee cups which were scattered about the table.

The glow of a joint moved from Jeremy to the German woman with the African head wrap.

Joy sat back, residing comfortably in herself. Her head inclined slightly, beautifully. Beauty was her ambassador. While some worked so hard to get noticed, she did nothing: no jokes, no clever commentary, no leaps or dives in the pitch of her voice, no explosions of expression. Just flat line nothing but pure beauty and it knocked everyone on their ass.

Marcia asked Jeremy how his novel was coming.

"I plan to write three hours a day," he said.

"What is it about?" Greg asked.

Oh, I thought; what impeccable timing.

Spill it.

Sing.

Food, alcohol, dope, his own birthday by God; all conspired to make Jeremy expansive. He dropped his head so his blond dreadlocks fell impressively around his face, then looked up. He nodded, then bit his lower lip to achieve a look of thoughtful sincerity.

And the trustafarian spoke: "Well actually, it's simmering."

Simmering. I nearly burst into laughter. I glanced about at the Buddhist and African decor, and imagined Jeremy shopping and arranging it all with such care as his novel simmered into completion.

The others listened; a near-devout audience.

"When I was young," Jeremy said, his voice now formal, literary, "my oldest sister bought our father a tree. It grew, blossoming with... little white flowers every spring. When my father died, this... water... actually... began to run from the tree." He glanced silently at his listeners, and then, "It was truly... as if... the tree... was *crying.*"

Murmurs of approval floated around the coffee table.

"Mmm," Joy said, "there's something to write about."

Jeremy pressed his lips together sadly, and nodded at the obvious success of his anecdote.

I waited a moment before I spoke.

"Sounds a little sappy to me," I said from the alcove.

A sea of heads - dreadlocked, pierced, pony-tailed and African-scarved - turned to look at me in silence; a very weird silence. It told me: *I'd been talked about.* Of this I was certain. Had they trashed me even more after I left? Had Joy commiserated? Or had she laughed with a reluctant hand to her mouth, which of course, would inspire more derision.

Were they certain I wouldn't return?

Did they place bets?

"Greg," I said. He looked at me intently. "I'm a bit confused. So I just came back to ask-" I pinched my chin to underscore my puzzlement. I spoke slowly, loudly. "Weren't you crying in the back of that African classroom because you felt guilty?"

"Guilty?" Greg stared.

I had his attention. I had the world's attention.

"You said the misbehaving boy was dealt with *appropriately*. You didn't cry because he wanted to be like you. You cried because you beat the poor, starving kid mercilessly when he was your student."

I kept it short, then waited. Everyone waited. It was a shot in the dark, but only somewhat. I knew that misbehaving students in much of Africa were caned, nearly always by their teacher. It was a practice left over from colonialism, and in the African context, quite common. I was certain Greg had caned the boy. His '*dealt with appropriately*' seemed far too halting and evasive, suggesting, like his giraffe story, a memory alteration, a bit of self-mythologizing. I wasn't sure about including 'starving' and 'mercilessly', but glad the sentence left my lips as it did. Regardless, the lovely, culturally sensitive women around the coffee table looked at Greg now with pinched eyebrows and mouths that might have recently sucked lemons.

Did Greg beat the African boy?

If he'd cried about it once, could he fake a reaction now?

The big, bearded man stared down at the white cloth on the coffee table, scratching what appeared to be a blueberry stain.

He scratched it for a long time.

He gave that blueberry stain much more attention than necessary, particularly for a world traveler like himself. He seemed suddenly lost in his leather jacket; a jacket, no doubt, full of maps of gold mines in Arizona.

Greg reddened behind his thick, black beard.

"How did you do it?" I asked, knowing now that I'd hit pay dirt. "With a whip? A stick? But here's what I'd really like to know big guy: *Did you enjoy it?*"

The man who had me ambling aimlessly in the fog a short while ago now looked up at me.

"Jesus," I said, "I'd cry too."

His look was murderous.

I turned to Joy. My date. I didn't bring her, but technically, etiquette deemed her my responsibility. Even my runner, Alex Granger, would understand this chivalric, if idiotic point of honor. "Joy," I said. "Would you like a ride home?"

Wrinkles of confusion formed between her eyebrows. She just stared, it seemed, utterly blank. She did not answer.

"I'll take that as a 'no'," I said like a man with an impossibly busy schedule.

I turned and headed for the door. I stepped off the porch, noticed how the sky had cleared, and the night was a cool, clean - when I felt a solid explosion in the center of my back. I flew onto the sidewalk, tumbled, and took a hard scrape on my elbow and shoulder. I raised myself, discovered a bloody elbow, then looked up.

Greg watched from the porch, said something like, 'fuckin' smart ass', and moved toward me.

From my supine position on the sidewalk, Greg looked far too large for a traditional square off and punch out. He had me by a good eighty pounds and the power in his shove told me it wasn't all fat. The fury on his face suggested that he probably did get a thrill out of beating that village boy. But I felt it clearly now: rage - for Jeremy, Roshaldemond, Jonah Woods, Mr. Mocha Java, and now, this Greg - and it had a will of it's own.

But a traditional square off and punch-out would be suicide.

I rolled into an off-balance sprinter's crouch. In four, quick, accelerating steps, my shoulder connected hard with his gut. I lifted his legs, turned him in the air.

It was a clean, sweet takedown.

I was instantly on top of him and about to let go a few sharp, satisfying jabs into his bearded face, but felt my leg yanked, my balance and advantage gone. I was dragged on my stomach. As I slid past his legs, a hard kick from Greg's boot connected with my cheekbone. Lightening flashed in my head, and I reached, gripped something hard, and swung it blindly into the air behind me.

A thunk was followed by Jeremy spilling onto the grass, a trail of blood running from beneath his blond dreadlocks. He was neither dead nor unconscious, and I felt a hard crack to my jaw, lost my balance, caught myself with a hand, then stumbled, half-blind, to my car.

I lay in my bed, retracing the events that lead to such a strange evening. I regretted none of it. Only one thought wouldn't let me alone: Jeremy had lost his father. It somehow made him real, and frankly, I hoped he was okay. I wondered if I should simply have gone home after dropping Roshaldemond off at the restaurant. Been above it all, dismissive. But we never quite buy that con. This felt different; not good, certainly, but complete, even though I had gotten my ass kicked.

Was this true? I made a quick tally.

Me: A tackle counted for little. Nailing Jeremy in the head was something.

Them: I had been shoved, bloodied, dragged, kicked hard in the face, and punched, again in the face.

An ass kicking, no question.

And if life is truly a system of karmic checks and balances, perhaps I deserved it. I deserved it for parading Joy like some trophy in front of my brother, and in front of Jonah Woods. Perhaps I deserved it for the sin of lust, or of ambition untempered. Well, either the universe was now in balance, or life was simply a random, undeserved hailstorm of blessings and shit.

Regardless, it was done. Over and in the past, which, in fact, was probably the best place for it. At the end of War and Peace, Leo Tolstoy says that the more a decision recedes into the past, the more correct it becomes. So this would all feel better tomorrow, and even better next week. My one, admittedly sick thought was this: I hoped, in the interests of tacky symbolism, that I had nailed Jeremy with the stone Buddha. I grew tired, very tired, and listened to the strange, incomprehensible voices at the edge of my consciousness before falling asleep.

I awoke aching.

My shoulder had some kind of deep-in-the joint, immobilizing pain. My elbow was blood-glued to the sheets. In the bathroom mirror, I saw that a nice purple bruise graced my left cheek.

Slipping on my thick gray sweats, I stumbled over shoes and clothes I had left lying in the hall the night before, and made my way to the kitchen. I boiled some water, took the Mocha Java from the cupboard, spooned some into an unbleached paper filter. I placed the filter in the plastic cone and set it over the cup. I heated some milk. The bag of brown sugar was empty, so I took a jar of honey from the cupboard. What possible difference could it make, I wondered, and unscrewed the lid. Of course, Mr. Mocha Java would gag, then share a good sneer with Ms. Henna Head right before my eyes. I poured the water, then the heated milk into the cup. I dipped the spoon into the honey. I held it high over the steaming cup and watched the honey drip in a long, slow amber string. I watched it fall... slowly... so slowly... just... like... the sap from Jeremy's tree. Jeremy, who, as a boy, on a bet, had eaten two entire - '*whoa!*'

And then, by God, I saw it.

All of it.

I was damn near shaking as I grabbed a yellow legal pad and a medium point Papermate. Soon, I was sipping sweetened Mocha Java and scribbling furiously because there it was, the entire thing; alive, beckoning and spewing forth in a thrilling, unfettered and spectacular vomit of words.

chapter

TWENTY-NINE

The Big Sky Appetite

"*Unconditional positive regard*? I only asked why you brought him? I don't need a lecture on Freudian-"

"Must you be so hostile? For Godsake, Frank, it's not like he's a problem or anything. We haven't even heard a peep out of him. In fact, he's been a perfect angel."

"Ever heard of babysitters, Margaret?"

Joey sat beneath the table and watched the heels of Frank Templin's tasseled, brown loafers tap hard as he pronounced this final word, Joey's mother's name. He returned his attention to thirty-five, square-jawed Heroic Army Figurines arranged before him on the low-pile carpet of the Buckhorn restaurant. To his immediate left were his mother's crossed, nylon stockinged legs, which ended sharply in sleek, tapered black high heels. In a gesture Joey recognized instantly as a prelude to asserting herself, his mother's foot began to bob.

Joey looked over his army. He chose a camouflaged captain, a sergeant, a bazooka man, a grenade launcher. He looked over the remaining infantry, tanks and jeeps, and after a thoughtful moment, divided them carefully into two, deadly, but evenly matched opposing forces.

"Babysitters," his mother said. "I just... I just don't trust... the last one had her boyfriend over the entire evening. When I got home, I told you-"

"I know, you found them doing the nasty-"

"*Frank.*"

Frank hesitated a moment, then placed a hand - arguably supportive - on Margaret's thigh.

"It happened *twice,*" she said, and Joey watched his mother squeeze Frank's hand in a vague display gratitude, then remove it from her leg.

Frank released a grumble of restrained annoyance. Joey bazookaed an enemy jeep, blowing it to kingdom come.

"I just haven't found one I can... I swear, girls today. The *passivity*!" She spat it with disgust; this word which had, quite recently, become a symbol of unconscionable disgrace for Margaret. Joey's father, roughly one year ago, had left her for a younger and prettier woman. Whatever it was - the self-help books, the support groups, the assertiveness tapes - that lifted his mother up from the silent, shell-shocked woman she'd become, well, Joey was grateful for it. The laundry no longer piled up ridiculously. She remembered to make his lunch in the morning, instead of mumbling a distracted, 'just take some money from my purse' before he went to school. But now, for her own sake, and for her son's moral edification, Joey watched with mild concern as she'd transformed into a spirited fount of gutsy parlance, aimed chiefly she claimed, at boldly guiding her young son to manhood. *Act, don't react. Be assertive, not aggressive. Stand your ground.* Life was harsh; passivity, disgusting.

What else could explain the deplorable meekness, the shocking docility, the nauseating *easiness* of an adolescent girl, stark naked on her employer's couch, availing herself to the vulgar needs of a pushy boyfriend?

Joey guessed he saw her point. Life *was* harsh, and you had to be ready to bust a few skulls when necessary. The minor obstacles weren't a problem. He got grades that pleased her, kept his room clean, ate his vegetables without complaint. But this intestinal firepower his mother suddenly worshipped seemed to elude him. Particularly with Jerry Hillis - the neighborhood malignancy, as Margaret called him - an older boy who ambushed Joey regularly and took what lunch money he had left over on his way home from school. But Joey saw the quality alive and potent in his mother, particularly now, since she'd begun dating. Take this Frank. That hand didn't last two seconds on her leg. It was his mother's third date with him, Joey's second time along, and one date beyond his own final attempt at conversation with the man. Frank Templin - tall, with a medium length, graying mustache - sat up straight now, in the upper realm of the Buckhorn restaurant, while Joey sat below, the best place, really, to wage a battle with his plastic army men.

"Know what you want?" Frank said, his voice resigned but touchy.

Two menus flopped open above Joey's head. An elderly woman one table over glanced down at him. She made a how-cute face, but this shifted instantly to something more serious, more investigative. She glanced at Margaret and Frank, then back down at Joey. Joey smiled to resurrect the earlier expression, and he thought, I'm fine down here; prefer it in fact. Initially, his descent beneath the table was amusing and boyish. Lately it seemed no novelty at all. He merely slid down to the floor and pulled out his toys. Some of his mother's dates didn't mind his presence. Others, like Frank, were openly annoyed.

"Joey want anything?" Frank asked.

"What?" Margaret said. "Joey? He ate at home. A beautiful pork chop. Right Joeman?" He felt his mother's hand on his shoulder.

"Mmm-hmm," Joey said. He picked up a cannon and placed it strategically, as a decoy, squarely in front of enemy lines.

"Know what you want?" Frank said.

"I don't know. The Shrimp Scampi looks kind of interes-"

"Why even bring him to a restaurant? I mean, if he's not even gonna eat, then why bother-"

"He *ate*," Margaret said. "He's not-"

"Hey, Joey!" Frank said, peering under the table. "You really not hungry?" He raised himself up again. "When I was a kid I was always hungry. Any minute of any day, I swear to God, I could eat. Christ, could I eat! Know why?" Frank spoke loudly now, as if pleading to the jury of diners in their immediate orbit. "*Because I was outside, that's why!* Shagging grounders! Going deep for the bomb! Roughhousing! Not like kids today. With their damn computers and TV sets in every room. Jesus, they don't even get up to change a channel. Just sit there crunching potato chips and flicking the damn-"

"Joey's not like that," Margaret said quietly.

"He's like every kid out there. All fat. No tone. I swear, this whole country's turning to flab. Or like your Joey down there. OK, fine, he's not fat. You're right. But he's *frail*. No meat on his bones."

Joey moved a tank stealthily to the left of his enemy. Margaret's foot twitched. Barely.

"Joey's the fastest boy in his grade. He just won two blue ribbons, for your information, at the Clover Elementary School track meet."

Joey winced. He'd won two ribbons all right, but they were white, not blue. Third place ribbons his mother had proudly magnetized to the fridge. It was a five person race, so third wasn't exactly bad. But why this sudden color change?

"*Him?*" said Frank with a laugh. "Please."

Joey's mother's legs uncrossed, then recrossed. Franks heels were pumping up and down, now - dancing, nearly - with the tassels flying. Clearly, these were the feet of a man who knew he'd just hit a nerve. Joey looked over his battalions. While the enemy foolishly went for the bait of the exposed cannon, Joey fired his tank and took out their grenade launchers. He released a deep, baritone explosive sound. The elderly woman glanced over with a seasoned busybody's expertise - that is, without moving her head - at Joey. She whispered to her husband, an elderly, dignified man who studied his menu and ignored her.

"Now me," Frank said. "I can eat all I want. Still can. Know why? Do you want to know why? Cause I burn it off, and boy, do I love to eat. Feel that." Frank lifted his shirt, offering Margaret his stomach.

"I'll take your word-"

"C'mon. Just a pinch."

Joey glanced up just in time to see his mother pinch Frank Templin's stomach.

"Eh? Like a rock. Not like most guys my age. Puffy cheeks. Guts blopping over their belts. But you know when it starts? Do you?" He paused. "This is the thing, Margaret. It starts when they're kids. Once you get the fat cells, you can't get rid of 'em. Fat for life. Tubbo for eternity. That's the tragedy of kids these days-"

"Joey's not fat."

"I know! But he's *frail!* He doesn't exercise *and* he doesn't eat. Not a good combo in my-"

"Oh, he can eat," Margaret said with a forced laugh. And Joey knew his mother must have heard the affect in her own voice and detested the weak sound of it. She calmed herself with a single, cleansing breath - a technique she'd practiced - then spoke from her center of equanimity. "He can eat as much as you." This, to her relief, sounded better. But Joey felt suddenly nervous.

"What? That little bird?"

"Absolutely," Margaret said.

Neither adult spoke for a moment.

Then Frank said, "Wanna bet?"

A silence reigned above Joey, and his ears reached up and into it. He admired this new aspect of his mother he guessed, but mostly, it embarrassed him. Last month, she bought him a pair of sneakers that he wore holes through within two weeks. They returned to the shoe store, found the salesman - a sad, bespectacled man - and

Joey's mother handed him the receipt and shoes. He vaguely and nervously explained the difference between factory damage and customer damage. She listened in silence, then stated calmly, just as her latest book had advised, "I hear what you're saying, but these shoes did not last nearly long enough for the money I spent." (She and Joey had practiced in the car on the way over.) And when this didn't work, she grew louder and louder, repeating herself, as people turned from their shopping to listen. Joey hid his face as the little man pleaded weakly with her to be reasonable, but she continued to repeat herself, diligently, over and over, until finally, they left the store with a full refund. That evening, Joey listened as his mother related the story over the phone to her best friend Sheila. She finished with, "I sure tore him a new asshole!"

"Bet?" Margaret said. "What could you possibly want to make a-"

"You said he can eat as much as me. I say he can't. I order whatever dinner I want, he has to eat the same and finish every bite. Loser pays the bill and tosses in... what? Say... twenty bucks."

Margaret's foot began to bob. The enemy forces shot down seven of Joey's infantry.

"But be warned," Frank said. "I hate to lose."

Joey considered this last utterance: *I hate to lose.* It sounded so cool, so rock-solid. You almost needed a mustache to make a statement like that. "I hate to lose," Joey said quietly. He smirked and tugged at a hypothetical mustache. He waited. He listened. He held his breath.

"Joey?" Margaret said, and he felt her hand on his shoulder. "C'mon up here."

Cindy, the waitress, brought her leggy, mini-skirted self to the steel, rotating wheel that sat at the window of the kitchen. She placed the check under the clip and spun it around. "I don't get it," she said to Rogelio, the cook. "I tell them about the child's portion, but they order him a Steak Deluxe. The sixteen ounce! I swear, he's no more than eight years old. Cute little guy."

"Where?" Rogelio said, as he peered over the customers. Cindy gestured with her head to the corner of the restaurant. He pulled the ticket. "Steak Deluxe? With a bake? No French fries?"

"I know!" she said. "He ordered exactly the same as the man."

"His father?"

She shook her head. "I doubt it. Nothing dad-like in that guy. What kid wants a baked potato when he can have fries?"

Just then, Mr. Hancock appeared. "I'm not paying you two to talk," he said as he headed to his office. "Lock up tonight, Rogelio. I need to leave early."

"Jes, sir."

Rogelio glanced across the room again, smiled, shrugged, and turned to his stove. To Rogelio, the man who Cindy thought was not the boy's father seemed oddly familiar. He looked, actually, like quite a few of the men who wandered into the Buckhorn. Mustached, middle-aged, graying curly hair. But to Rogelio, he was a man who in fact, bore a striking resemblance to Mr. Hancock, the boss and owner of the Buckhorn restaurant, who had just announced that he'd be leaving early. The resemblance was not in the fine, facial details. Cindy, for example, would not see a connection. But in the blunt, primary colors of perception that exist between races - inspiring such phrases as, 'they all look alike to me,' - well, to Rogelio and to the rest of the Latino kitchen staff, Frank Templin, the man who sat in the corner booth with the pretty, dark-haired woman and the small, frail-looking boy, could have been Mr. Hancock's twin.

The place was busy and getting busier, but tired as Rogelio was, he would make them a couple of nice steaks. Tired, because Mr. Hancock, the *pandejo*, kept him at work at least sixty hours a week. Still, this was fine. Rogelio liked to work. He was a hyper, wiry man and a fast, excellent cook. Even when the Buckhorn was a madhouse, the orders came up quickly, beautifully, and with a smile and a joke for the waitresses, who all loved Rogelio. The man was a find and Mr. Hancock worked him half to death.

Rogelio's younger brother Juan worked as a busboy. Julio, Arturo, Angel and Juan had been there a few months, while

Enrique, the youngest, had only arrived last week. All lived with Rogelio and got their start in America at the Buckhorn. All put up with Mr. Hancock. None had a green card. All but Rogelio received a sub-minimum wage, most of which was sent to struggling families back home. Rogelio's first goal was to buy his mother a small house in Mexico City. He didn't mind the hard work or the impossible hours. What he minded were the insults - the criticizing of every little thing from the fat pandejo. *The Handcock.* No one at home would dare treat him like this.

No, this was nothing like home, where men shouted in deep baritones, grinned broadly beneath thick mustaches and moved with grand, easy gestures. Home was nothing like here, where, after a time - after the bold dash across the border - a man found his true enemy. It wasn't the border patrol, or even Immigration, but something much deadlier. What was it this country did to his people? Broad grins turned sheepish. Men began to feel like boys. It wasn't the puny wages. It was seeing the huge shiny cars, the beautiful women with legs that extended forever. It was feeling ignored, and finally, invisible. And then, always, the tips. Tips, to which he would respond, "Gracias," with a slight bow of his head. Why did it come out sounding small? Where was the booming voice he had in his own country? How he hated this in himself! How he hated to see it in his friends and brothers. And then, there were cabbrones like the Handcock. You thanked him for your paycheck and he said, "Grassy ass to you too!" then laughed his fat belly off. Well, if he saw me in my own country, thought Rogelio as he placed the plates with care on the metal counter - two Steak Deluxes and one Shrimp Scampi - I would show him the sort of man that I am.

And he rang the bell.

Two dings, for Cindy.

"Ever had the Buckhorn Steak Deluxe before?" Frank grinned.

Joey shook his head.

"Just like the menu says. For the cowpoke with a big sky appetite! You got a big sky appetite, my man?"

The boy nodded. Frank laughed.

In truth, Joey wasn't at all hungry. The pork chop was down the gullet and he had no appetite. He was a light eater. And Frank, for all the rancor Joey felt for him, had Joey pegged. The ribbon was not blue, but white. That he'd won a ribbon at all surprised him and his classmates. And no question, he was lazy; glutted with computer games and cable TV. And now here he was, party to yet another mess-with-me-and-die enterprise of his mother's. He could not back out, not with this Jerry Hillis around the corner, whose apparition haunted him even at this table. The shame was not in the fighting. Joey fought valiantly as his little body was able, but Jerry was bigger and stronger. No, the shame occurred when he arrived home bruised and bloodied to a mother bent on cleaning people's clocks and tearing them new assholes. To enter the house with even a scratch that did not involve a tale of feisty triumph was pure mortification. When his mother coaxed the embarrassing truth out of him, she declared with venom that she, herself, would rip the lungs out of this older, bigger, ill-bred bastard who did this to her son, which only made Joey feel worse. Even that very evening, as she stood before the bathroom mirror putting on her lipstick, she seemed to be girding for battle. " '*Why yes,*' she said, mimicking her first phone call with Frank. '*I do happen to be a single mom.*'" Then she added sharply, "Probably thinks I'm dating above my weight class." She hooked on an earring. "Well, he'll find *this* girl's no easy take down, thank you very much!"

Joey looked at Frank and his mother and thought: no, to back out now was impossible.

Cindy set the huge dinners before them.

"Rub a dub dub!" Frank said.

"Thanks for the grub!" Joey said, ready now, to match anything that traveled in or out of Frank's mouth.

Joey rallied his courage. His mother would not see him fail this time.

Little bird, Frank had called him. *Frail.*

Well, he would show the man a thing or two about birds. He would teach the man about frailty.

"Enjoy!" Cindy said, then turned and headed back to the kitchen, where she met the cook and two other waitresses, Flo and Dee Dee.

Enjoy? Joey thought. Why did waitresses always say this? Didn't his teacher, Mrs. Marquis, just last week, tell them a sentence needed verb *and* a noun? Enjoy *what*? A good sneeze? The view? He looked across the room at the cook and thought: *stare*. He looked at the waitresses and thought: *gossip*. He saw a large man with a mustache man emerge from the back room. The women instantly separated. The cook ducked into the kitchen. He watched the man with the mustache exit through the front door.

Enjoy what? he thought as he looked, without the slightest bit of hunger at the huge steak before him.

He cut into it.

"Mmm," Frank said. "Nothing like a fat, juicy steak."

"Nothing like it," Joey said.

The elderly lady at the next table, peered, espionage-style, over her chef's salad. A couple in the far corner was in the midst of a passionate smooch. A woman to the right told her young son not to play with the ice in his water glass, and his older sister said, "He just does it to annoy me." A young couple to their immediate left finished a discussion about the tip and were sliding out of their booth. A female member of a large group across the room burst into wild laughter.

What could be so funny?

All Joey knew was that he had sixteen ounces of medium-rare steak before him. And one seriously fat baked potato. Frank blobbed on the sour cream. So did Joey. Frank mashed in two slabs of butter. Joey did the same. Frank sprinkled on the chives. As Joey reached for the dish of tiny green onions, he saw a busboy roll his cart over to the table that had just been vacated.

"Compadre!" Frank called. "Got some steak sauce?"

Juan stared at him, bewildered.

"Frank," Margaret said. "I don't think he speaks-"

"Steak sauce!" Frank said loudly. "S-T-E-A-K Sauce! No comprende?"

Juan looked around in confusion.

"What'sa matter, amigo? No speakada English?"

Juan turned crimson. He held up his hands, but in an instant, Cindy was there, placing a bottle of steak sauce in front of Frank.

Juan burned as he began to clear off the table but just then, he felt a light hand on his shoulder. "Reminds me of my ex," Cindy said as she passed, en route to the kitchen. And though Juan did not understand her, he felt warmth in her touch and in her voice. He continued to remove the dishes from the table and place them carefully in his cart.

Joey focused on his baked potato - this potato, that he had covered with sour cream, chives and butter to prevent any weaseling. 'Look there,' Frank would not be able to say, 'the boy didn't eat any sour cream. You said he could eat *as much as me.*' Joey had spent enough time on a schoolyard to know a weaseler when he saw one, and this Frank had possibilities. An aptitude, Mrs. Marquis might say. But there would be no weaseling tonight.

Joey ate.

And as he ate, he thought of Mr. Richards, his science teacher, a tall, slump-shouldered man who dropped in on his class once a week to teach a lesson. When you stretch a rubber band until it won't stretch anymore, Mr. Richards said, you've pulled it out to its elastic limit. Well, that's where Joey's stomach was now. Out, by God, to it's elastic limit. He looked at Frank, who ate with gusto, and, it seemed, with a slight grin. Joey glanced at his mother. She ate her scampi and watched, with guarded, then growing delight as Joey plowed through the steak, the baked potato, the sautéed broccoli.

The three ate in silence. The Steak Deluxe and all its trimmings moved into Joey's mouth with unflagging velocity. And he'd anticipated the other excuse - that the boy ate too slowly, that he'd dragged it out. Anyone could finish anything given enough time. Frank might say this but he could not say it tonight. Joey matched Frank bite for bite.

And he was two thirds there - most of a potato and some broccoli and carrots remained, the latter sautéed to perfection, staring up at him in defiance. Joey stabbed a last piece of steak with his fork. His stomach was packed and protruding. He could hardly lean forward now due to the girth of his mid-section. But he would not slow, pause, or give the slightest sign that he was struggling, or worse, that he was ready to toss his knife and fork on the table, push his plate away, lean back and announce that he was stuffed.

Because here it was, the home stretch.

Frank - the man who did not like to lose - watched and winced.

Wince away, Joey thought. Every weaseler's possibility was covered, and painful as it was, by God, Joey and his mother were about to win. He shoveled in a last mouthful of potatoes. He wiped his plate clean with some French bread - a touch unnecessary but added for panache - put it in his mouth and glanced around.

Several people watched: The wait staff. The busboys and cooks. The elderly lady across from him. In fact, a sea of mild, curious glances were aimed in Joey's direction. Restaurant work must be fascinating stuff, Joey thought. But his mother grinned. A tiny laugh escaped her lips. An airy melody. Didn't want to gloat but couldn't help herself. Frank tried a smile, but it seemed forced.

Forced, Joey thought, but then it turned malicious.

Why malicious? Joey had won, hadn't he? Certainly he had. He leaned back. He had no energy to contemplate the depths of a man's psychology as revealed in the sudden curl of his lip. Or a narrowing in his eyes.

What could this mean? Well, he didn't know or care. Just relax, Joey thought. I am a beached whale. A stuffed walrus. A pregnant Buddha.

"Guess I was wrong," Cindy said upon arrival. "The boy's got quite an appetite."

"He certainly does," Margaret said.

That's *pride*, Joey thought when his mother spoke. That's called *pride*. And it was the real thing. No color-changing ribbons. No threats to rip the lungs out of a bigger, nastier bully. This was victory, pure and sweet.

Joey slid down on the seat to accommodate the expanse of his gut. He gave it an affectionate pat, this gut that stood by him when his moment came. But now, its contents - the Steak Deluxe for the cowpoke with the big sky appetite - seemed to take on a life of its own. It seemed to shift, to alter, to mutate, requiring constant, squirmy adjustments in Joey's seating posture. Ah, well, so be it, Joey thought. A small price for so stunning a success.

"Will that be all?" the waitress said.

"I think so," Margaret said.

Cindy tore off the check, then reached out to place it upside down in front of Frank. And just as the check was mid-flip turn, Frank, in a move that struck Joey for its sheer theatricality, placed a strong, muscular hand around Cindy's narrow wrist. And his message was clear: the finality of this bet did not lay in Joey's last bite, but rather, in the bill hitting the table.

"Wait a sec," Frank said. His grin hardened. Joey, his mother, and Cindy stared at him. The bill in Cindy's hand hovered over the table. Joey caught the price of something - eighteen bucks. And it was the suddenness of this wrist hold, the utter audacity of it that revealed Frank as a man who could seize, if he so much as felt like it, the lion's share of power at this or any dinner table. Cindy relented, not due to the firmness of Frank's grip, but rather, because of an insatiable, innate curiosity. A mere wrist was easily relinquished as she waited - it's fair to say, quite breathlessly - to see what would happen next.

Frank held the grin; but his stare, and the deadly calm of his voice made his words all the more terrifying. "Double or nothing."

"*What?*" Margaret said. "Joey won. He won fair and-"

"Double or nothing."

Margaret was silent.

If Joey were older, he might have seen it: a war; violent, bloody, and, because of a gross mismatch, waged ever so briefly within his mother. The factions were these: a desire to kick some serious ass, to lay waste the opposition and gloat over the carnage, versus a simple impulse to be a good mom. If he were older, and he saw it, he would have prayed for the forces of the latter. But these were vague as of late. His mother turned toward him.

"Joey?" Margaret said, "It's up to you."

Up to me, Joey thought. The last words he wanted to hear. He was full; a bloated, stuffed cow. Pained, cramped and distended. Just to sit here was an act of misery. *Why up to me?*

But he forced a look of indifference, even nonchalance to his face. Nor would the sin of wishy-washiness be added to his faults, and to the long list of embarrassments his mother suffered because he was not the sort of kid Frank probably was. Frank, who Joey imagined as rugged, foul-mouthed, and strapping as a boy. The kind of boy who struck terror into the hearts of kids throughout his own neighborhood.

There was no decision here.

He shoved the pain in his gut aside. He willed mightily, an expression of pure, withering boredom to his face. He rolled his eyes, exhaled wearily. He glanced at his mother. "Bring it on," he said.

"You sure?" Margaret said.

Before Joey could answer, Frank released Cindy's wrist and said, "We'll have another Steak Deluxe."

The mere sound of it - *another Steak Deluxe* - sent a powerful wave of fear through Joey. Cindy saw the fear, shook her head, then turned in silence as she adjusted the check.

Cindy arrived at the waitress station, then leaned in conspiratorially with Flo and Dee Dee. The waitresses looked at Joey's table in shameless, maternal horror. Cindy then spoke through the window with Rogelio, who listened and stared across the restaurant at the party of three in the corner booth.

"He is a small boy!" Rogelio said. "Why do they do this to him?"

"Why does she *let him*?" Cindy said. "That woman-"

"It is *him*," Rogelio said. "The mustache pandejo who look like the Handcock."

"Mr. Han-" Cindy turned to look across the room. "Well, I guess, in a way, he does look a teeny bit like-"

"He force her. And she have too much pride. Aii. Such a small boy." Rogelio himself, had a nine-year-old son who lived with his mother in Mexico City, and a young daughter, the illegitimate result of a dalliance in Guadalajara. While many depended upon him, Rogelio thought of these two as Cindy showed him her wrist. And the cook looked again across the room, this time with venom. Then he turned. He spoke to Pablo, to the other cooks, and to his half-brother Hector. Hector told the busboys - Angel, Enrique, and Juan. Juan added his own story of the steak sauce, how the man mocked him and how he would've slit the *puto's* throat himself, had Cindy not intervened. All shot murderous glances at the man in the corner booth - *this other Handcock* - then instantly their brown faces shifted to sympathy for the small boy and his mother. And what about Cindy's wrist? How could he do such a thing to their Cindy? Cindy, who was always so generous with her tips. Even tries to pronounce a few Spanish words. "*Por favor, senor,*" she said in a way that tickled them. No, he should not touch their Cindy like this.

"In our own country such a man would not last two minutes," Juan said. "The way he treats women and children." Though Juan wasn't sure about this, he liked the sound of it. The others nodded their heads in agreement. In fact, none were sure of it's truth, but once it was spoken by Juan, they felt the gravity and power of it. No, they agreed, such behavior would not be tolerated. This other Handcock would not last two minutes.

Rogelio began to cook the second Steak Deluxe. The cooks and busboys gathered around the stove.

"Find a smaller piece of meat!"

"Fool! The pandejo would complain!"

"Trim it, just a bit!"

"No!"

"Spice! You must use spice!"

"Spice! Idiot! What are the merits of spice?"

"Why, to make it go down easier!"

"But would not salt make him thirsty?" Rogelio said. "Won't he then be forced to drink water, and thus, waste precious space in his stomach? Look at him, for God's sake! The boy is ready to burst!"

The group in the kitchen was instantly silenced. Seven heads turned to look at Joey, now managing the girth of his stomach and grimacing in the far, corner booth.

"He bears the pain manfully," Jose said.

"But the steak!" Hector said. "It should be tasty!"

"It will be tasty! Have you known me to cook a steak that was not tasty?"

Curses, threats and insults exploded from the kitchen. Open-handed gestures flew; aimed at the boy, the man, and then at the steak.

The men then watched quietly and intently as Rogelio turned the piece of meat on the grill.

"Cook it well," said Juan. "Then it will be smaller and easier on the boy's insides."

"Imbecile!" said Pablo. "It should be rare, so he can digest it!"

"Silence!" said Rogelio. "I am the head cook! I will decide how the meat is prepared! Now go! Everyone back to work back before the Handcock sends you back to Mexico!"

"I will send him to hell first," said Juan in a low, sinister voice.

And they dispersed.

With this explosion of voices and tempers from the kitchen, which Joey heard but could not understand, he felt emboldened. For pure bravado, and, because it cost him nothing, he said, "I could eat *ten* steaks!"

Frank snorted a laugh. Okay, so Frank knew a bluff when he heard one. Margaret looked anxiously and directly in front of her. Now that it was all decided and out of her hands, did the motherhood faction redouble its efforts? Was it guilt that silenced her now? Joey had seen this look many times before. She appeared muddled. And, despite her new found feistiness, whipped. Once, months ago, Joey found his mother in a similar state at the kitchen table. A mug of coffee cooled in her hand, and he decided, at that moment, to ask why his father had left. She looked at her son blankly, as if taking a moment to let the question settle. She shrugged and told him she couldn't really say. Then she added in a strange, weak voice, "I feel like I'm beginning to disappear."

Well, whatever it meant - this disappearing business - whatever his mother was trying to fix in herself, if Joey could help, he would. And if it took another Steak Deluxe, then by God, bring it on.

Bring the son of a bitch on.

Rogelio placed the plate on the counter. He tapped the bell twice. Cindy lifted the plate, and carried it across the room. Three other Latino cooks in tall white hats lined up at the kitchen window. Busboys pushed carts slowly, sneaking glances at the table in the corner.

Cindy set the steak carefully on the table before Joey. A Buckhorn Steak Deluxe. For the cowpoke with the big sky appetite.

Joey took a breath. He adjusted the massive protrusion of his mid-section.

"Joey," Margaret said. "Are you sure-"

"I'm starving, Mom," he lied. "I swear, I could eat a whole cow."

The words, drawn from nothing but pure brashness, suddenly found form and possibility in Joey's mind. *Eat a whole cow.* He had a quick vision of himself biting into the thigh of a live cow - a Holstein - and with this image, the contents of his stomach seemed to twist, expand, and head north.

But no.

He shifted his focus to the heads of deer mounted over the walls. All had horns. Those were the males. Males, yes, but what the hell was it? What was the word for a male-

Joey instantly noticed the sea of eyes watching him. Cooks, waitresses, busboys. A cashier, a hostess. The elderly woman stared openly.

Well, go ahead and watch, Joey thought. You wanna see a kid eat a steak? Feast your eyes!

Joey cut off a chunk and shoved it defiantly into his mouth. His mother's phrase, 'sit up and eat like a mensch,' came suddenly to mind. He sat up taller. This was as good a time as any to sit up taller. *Like a mensch.* The phrase resurrected an odd memory. He was younger, smaller, and his mother was home, mid-morning, watching a soap opera. Joey tore through the den, on the run to the kitchen, and he stopped. It was the end of a show she liked, and an attractive young couple was on the screen. "Well, I guess this is good-bye," the beautiful girl said sadly as she turned to leave. And the handsome boy said, "Wait. Wait a sec, Debbie. You know, I've done some thinking." She turned to him, and Joey watched his mother lean forward to listen more acutely. "These past few days, Debbie, we've been through a lot together-"

And Joey's mother, with tears in her eyes, shouted, "Now you're talkin like a mensch!"

Joey slammed in a second bite.

Was I a mench, Joey wondered? Was this Frank a mensch? Were there any menches in the world to inspire such emotion in my mother?

"The boy has cojones!" Rogelio said.

Juan nodded. "You made the steak well, my friend."

"In high school," Frank said. "I was bulking up to play tight end. Decided I'd eat twelve hardboiled eggs for breakfast one morning..."

Joey, the only one eating now, shoveled in a forkful of spuds, sour cream, and chives. A hunk of steak. Another hunk, then, a mouthful of carrots. Like pulling off a band-aid, he thought. Quick pain or slow misery. But despite his resolve, he began to slow down. He was full. Stuffed. Impacted. No amount of acting could alter this horrific fact.

"And, oh God," Frank said. "I can't forget the time in college I ate three bags of potato chips. Three huge bags, and a six pack of beer. I swear, did that room spin..."

But Frank's stories spurred Joey on. He wasn't taking punches now from a bigger and stronger Jerry Hillis. Jerry, who once took Joey's new mechanical pencil from his shirt pocket and tossed it over some houses. Joey instinctively tagged Jerry a good one - directly on the throat - which greatly angered the larger boy. Then the punches fell on Joey without mercy.

Well, this was food, not fists.

But Joey was full.

And the world watched. The restaurant staff was mesmerized. Flo and Dee Dee looked deeply concerned as they made their way to the other tables to take dinner orders. Worry creased Cindy's face as she stopped by to ask if everything was okay.

"Great," Frank said. "Couldn't be better."

The whole place slowed. Service halted.

All to watch Joey eat.

And he ate.

But differently now. The pretense of bravado was gone, packed and left with no calling card. And Joey was on the ropes and staggering. Each bite he pretended was his last. The steak was his enemy. It had arrived shaped like Africa. Joey worked his way around the edges, so that now, it had a shape vaguely, like California.

"And then there was the time I bought three frozen pizzas-"

"Frank," Margaret said. "Please."

"I'll say what I want," Frank said, and technically, Joey thought, they'd made no rule about talking. "And oh boy! Oh my god! I can't forget the time I ate – listen to this - an *entire gallon* of chocolate chip ice cream!"

The man's life, it seemed to Joey, moved from one gastronomic conquest to the next.

Joey was now near to bursting.

Cindy leaned in to Rogelio. "This is barbaric. It's child abuse. I can't watch."

And Joey looked bad; ill. He could only breathe lightly, because air space, well, was becoming food space. *A cowpoke with a big sky appetite*. That's what he needed to be. The steak was now an island before him. A Galapagos, defying him to finish it off.

Enrique, the youngest and newest arrival, cruised his cart into the kitchen. He whispered something to Hector in Spanish. Then Enrique performed a dramatic and violent rendition of throwing up. The kitchen staff stared at him in horror, and Juan instantly slapped him hard behind the head. Enrique winced, holding his head in pain. The busboys and cooks told him to be silent. And with this slap on the head, the gravity of the boy in the corner booth doing battle with his second Steak Deluxe fell hard upon them all.

And Joey heard it, the mock retching in the kitchen. This he didn't need. He could listen to Frank's stories all night, but the mere hint of release, of an end to the hideous pain in his gut was too much to bear. To tear his mind away from his swollen belly Joey looked away, again, around the room. Deer heads were everywhere. A large one was mounted away from the others on the far wall before him. It had antlers. If you counted the ends - one two three four five six seven eight - you called it an eight pointer. Of course it was a male because it had the horns, but what did you call a male? He shoved a carrot into his mouth then another piece of meat. Then he noticed antlers all over the walls.

And it struck him.

Buckhorn? *Buck*horn!

Get it, fool?

Buck... horn! he lectured himself sarcastically in a forced, improvised game of distraction.

Still don't get it? Okay, take a look now, all over the goddam walls. And what's the name of the place? C'mon, genius! Put it together! Don't tax yourself. Don't strain that miracle of a brain-

"And once, I ate four microwave burritos!"

Well, good for you, Frank. You're one seriously accomplished son of a-

"Four! Followed that an entire carton of rocky road. But do I show it? Not an ounce! The reason? *Exercise!*"

And Joey ate.

He looked at the horrified woman sitting across from him.

And he ate.

Would this steak never end?

He thought of his army men below the table, and he wished they'd live and breathe and grow to their full height, then raise their guns and blow away everyone in the place; everyone but Joey and his mother. They'd load them in a tank, crash through a wall and drive them home, mowing down anything that got in their way. Why was he forced to come in the first place? So what if babysitters were doing it with boyfriends when he got up use the bathroom. Was this such a problem?

Who knew?

Who cared!

Joey knew only one thing. He had to finish this steak. This impossibly endless steak. But he couldn't. Was it that fake retching in the kitchen? He was unable to take another bite. The army would not save him. So this was it? Would he have to call it a wrap and face this grinning, gloating bastard at the other end of the table? But that sound from the kitchen kept resurrecting itself. No, by God, try as he wanted, he could not take another bite.

The cooks watched, a communal empathy silencing them.

Rogelio shook his head. "*Andale!*" he said. "Hurry!" It left his lips timidly, an anxious whisper to spur the boy on. And the cook's subdued voice hit Juan's ears. This was Juan's language. The music of his homeland. A cry for a man to summon his power. And it touched a place so endemic in Juan that he forgot for a brief moment that he worked in an American restaurant as a busboy. Juan filled his lungs. He shouted, "*Ai yi yi yi yi yi!*"

The restaurant patrons hushed. Forks halted, mid-air. Heads turned and faced the kitchen.

The shout ignited Juan's co-workers.

"*Arriba!*"

"*Echowee! Arriba!*"

"*Poquito Amigo!*"

"Comer! Echowee!"

"Ai yi yi yi yi!"

The elderly woman looked in the direction of the kitchen. Work had stopped. Customers glanced around in confusion.

The shouts grew louder: *"Ai yi yi yi yi yi!"*

And louder still: *"ECHOHWEE!"*

Joey listened to the emboldening alien sounds, heard his own name among them. He cut another bite. He ate it. Other diners looked about, bewildered. Joey rushed two more bites. He picked up the last piece of meat, held it aloft, then slammed it into his mouth.

He threw down his fork. It clattered onto his plate, bounced off his water glass.

"ARRIBA!" The shouts exploded from the kitchen.

Joey leaned back, in serious pain. But he had done it. Eaten two sixteen ounce Buckhorn Steak Deluxes, for the cowpoke, by God, with the big sky appetite.

He stared at Frank.

Frank stood. And Joey could see the truth of Frank's self-assessment: He was a man who hated to lose. His facial muscles worked violently to conceal, what? Anger? Frustration? Tears? *Tears!* He pulled out his wallet, produced several bills and flung them across the table.

"Find your own way home," he said, and made a bee-line for the door.

A torrent of jeers rained on him from the kitchen.

"Chingatha!"

"Pandejo!"

"Pinche cabron!"

Joey and his mother watched Frank leave. "What a baby," she said as she gathered up the bills, counted them, put a few on the table the rest in her purse. "That should cover it. Guess I better call us a cab."

Joey sat in the cab with his mother as they pulled away from the restaurant and cruised through the traffic. He was in serious pain.

"Your army men," she said suddenly, and it was true. He had forgotten them. It was enough to maneuver his bloated self out of that restaurant with everyone staring. Joey waved a dismissive hand; a hand that said he didn't care about them, that he was tired of them, had no need of them. He was now practically laying down in the back seat.

The car stopped at a light, then continued.

His mother gave him a hug. "You did it," she said. "For awhile there..."

Joey nodded. And an inhalation - a single, cleansing breath - necessary for clear and forthright speech was nearly impossible, but he had one thing to say.

One thing, so there was no mistake about what had occurred tonight.

He took a breath and he spoke. "We sure tore him a new asshole."

Joey's mother stared straight ahead, as if frozen, as if stunned, as if Joey's utterance had brought her to some strange place, vaguely remembered. She glanced around slightly, shook her head almost imperceptibly.

"What?" she said, "What did you say?"

He was about to repeat what he'd said. But just then, a wave of nausea pounded at the back of his throat, which took all of his effort to hold back. And who could tell? Frank, the weaseler, might drive by at any moment, look in the window, witness such a defeat and claim victory.

No, by God, Joey would hold it down.

He closed his eyes, hard.

And he thought: *Buck... horn! Get it? Is it so difficult?*

END

chapter

THIRTY

I sat in silence, certain my classmates would skewer me for something; probably the camera shifts, which Birnbaum had advised were dangerous in a short story. The desks were circled as usual. The students and instructor were silent, though a few flipped through the pages of my story. I waited. The lanky young man with the shaved head and yoga mat stole a look at me, then quickly lowered his eyes. I had read my story aloud, and now I doodled at the corners of a yellow legal pad. I looked up at the faded institution green of the ceiling. I looked at my classmates, in their denim and their black clothes. I could read nothing on their faces.

"I think the boy is too successful," Nancy began.

I took a breath. Then, Professor Birnbaum herself broke in with uncharacteristic prematurity and force, "What success!" she nearly shouted, "This family is a disaster!"

Nancy was silent. In fact, at Birnbaum's statement, I watched all eyes sheepishly look up at me, then return to the pages before them. And I had a sudden, perhaps clairvoyant inkling of the thought that occupied the minds of every enrollee in my 404, The Art of the Short Story Writing Seminar:

They thought *my* family was *also* a disaster.

All were silent for the poor, innocent child, at the merciless vortex of such malignant forces. Silent and contrite for the adult, the fellow scribbler, their colleague; a bumbling novice like themselves, who they hammered so mercilessly over his previous effort.

I glanced around, mutely, at sympathetic eyes, trained intermittently on me, then returning to the safety of the manuscript.

And I began to feel sorry for myself.

A sweet, indulgent self-pity.

But it struck me: *Jeremy ate the fucking steaks.*

"I like the ethnic diversity," Yvette said.

"I like the success of the woman," Cathy added, "And the final come-uppance of the male-chauvinist."

"I particularly enjoyed the rebellion of the marginalized culture."

"The whole thing gave me a stomach ache," said one young man, who then added, "Which is good."

They laughed, offered a few more benign comments, but then were subdued for the most part, again stealing looks at me.

"Well," Professor Birnbaum said as she fiddled with the stack of papers on the desk before her, "While this has tone problems, a few point of view issues, and frankly, a long way to go before it's ready to send anywhere... I've been teaching for over twenty years... it's not often a student improves this much in one semester."

At that moment, Tara Wolff gathered her cloth book bag and purse, then bolted for the door.

I watched her leave. We all did, respectfully imagining some private emergency. While I certainly hoped she was okay, I wanted her opinion.

When the door swung closed, our teacher cleared her throat. Prof. Birnbaum looked up at me. "Tell us Mr. Lewis. Where *have* you been honing these story telling skills?"

Our eyes met, teacher and pupil. Her comment was uttered like a playful accusation of cheating. I didn't know what made her so hard-edged, but she smiled, opening a tiny breach in the professional edifice she erected between herself and her students. I stared, wondering what honing she might be referring... *oh my.* I turned red, as if she saw my thoughts. As if somehow, she saw me cavorting in the buff, with a slim, brown, stark-naked beauty on a tropical beach. Of course this was impossible. She knew nothing. But her compliments were meaningless because I had a feeling no one here knew anything. And the only person who did had gathered her few items and left moments ago.

When I returned home from class, the message machine was blinking.

I pressed play.

"Hello... this is Joy," it said. "I wondered... how you were doing... and... I would like... to see you. Bye."

After all that occurred, her voice, even rendered over a cheap answering machine, was still a siren song. It had been three achingly long weeks since I'd seen Joy. Even through writing and rewriting, I missed her so much I could hardly think of anything else. I wrote page after angry page about her in my journal, and felt a heady self-righteousness when I put down the pen. This lasted less than a minute, and was replaced instantly by a memory of the pure, delicate ecstasy of holding her sweet body in my arms. Gazing into those crippling dark eyes. Kissing those soft, full-

I stared at the phone. I would only have to punch in her number, each digit bringing me a tiny increment closer to a moment I desired more than anything, and to which a rational voice advised me to avoid like poison.

Prefontaine, Borzov, and Vermeer's turbaned girl watched me. Gauguin's topless Tahitian women watched and waited.

She picked up the phone on the third ring.

"Hello?" Joy said.

"It's Tim."

"Tim," she said. "I've been thinking about you."

This news, good or bad, inspired a blood rush that left me dizzy. It had been three weeks of fending off thoughts about Joy, three weeks of indulging them. A few tears.

I asked about Jeremy.

"What about him?" she asked.

"His head."

"Oh... I don't know," Joy said vaguely. It took me a moment to get past my shock over the odd fact that so much fell beneath her radar. Jeremy's head, and probably even Jonah Woods, occupied little space in her thoughts. Strangely, she remembered me enough to call, and I couldn't figure out why. I had to decide if this mattered. Every cell in my body said, don't sweat it, don't think too much.

I asked what she'd been doing.

"The usual," she said. "You?"

I told her I finished a story, the class seemed to like it.

"I'd like to see you," Joy said.

I decided this: I would see her, if only to find out what I truly felt; to suss out the situation. To get my final bearings on this woman. We hadn't technically broken up. I had never quite cozied up to the horrific notion that it was over. "Well, I've been thinking about you, too."

"Let's go to-"

"There's a restaurant I'd like to try," I interrupted. "This pizza place on Clement my runners have been yammering about."

"Pizza?"

"Pizza," I said, and waited.

After a brief silence, Joy said, "What time?"

I told her I'd pick her up at seven. I didn't tell her my car had starter trouble and what cash I had left after collecting my last paycheck was not enough to cover repairs. I just hoped the Honda would get me through the evening. Before hanging up she added, "Bring your story."

Of course I hadn't stopped loving her. That she had asked to see the story seemed wonderfully out of character, and while I had no idea why she made such a request, I decided that it was hopeful.

chapter

THIRTY-ONE

Joy exited her apartment. She wore her flowered skirt, her black Danskin top and, despite everything that had occurred, I was once again staggered by the impossible notion that this exquisite creature was my date. She locked the door behind her, turned to me and said, "I don't have any money. Are you treating?"

I studied her face.

Was this some joke?

But here it was: The same grin. The same teeth, plentiful and white, the same eyebrows, raised in expectation. The lovely bohemian, asking for the help of those more fortunate. When Joy said she missed me and wanted to see me, I assumed this implied a hand-wringing soul-search, an agonizing period of painful self-assessment, a tearful vow of self-improvement.

It meant only that she wanted to see me.

Are you treating?

Hadn't we discussed this? Did my words vaporize when they hit the air? Had I said them at all?

Of course she had no money; she'd just locked it up in her apartment.

I had two twenties in my wallet, all that was left of my savings. I'd cashed out my bank account, stretched what was left as long as possible. But I felt a love that would grace me only three times in a hundred years. For this, I would humiliate myself one final time.

"I'm happy to treat," I said without happiness.

She handed me a small coin purse. "Will you hold this for me?"

I dropped it into my pocket.

We arrived at Georgio's and took a booth. Chianti bottles hung overhead and Joy glanced around, assessing the crowd and decor.

"This place is... okay," she said with an appraising, connoisseur's nod.

I handed her a menu.

'Okay' was approval for this restaurant I had chosen, and it made me chuckle, not at Joy, but at the world of men who twisted themselves into pretzels for Joy's approval. So she bequeathed it like a queen. And her approval was *grudging*, I knew, because there were no vegans, dreadlocks, or free spirits anywhere. There were one or two ponytails but this was a pleated, pressed, oxford wearing, nine-to-five crowd.

I placed the story in front of her then ordered red wine and a large veggie.

Joy read.

And I watched her. At various times, her eyes widened, her mouth opened and closed. When the wine arrived, I filled her glass. She held it in one hand, the manuscript in the other. And as she read, errant bits of restaurant chatter fell upon my ears.

"... but it's the *good* kind of cholesterol!"

"I finally joined a gym."

"Stay hydrated."

Joy flipped a page.

"I don't eat red meat," said a woman behind me. "Just chicken and fish."

A balding man said he had a ton of frequent flyer miles and was heading to Rio.

A young, bearded man told his date about his balloon ride over the Rift Valley. "I work hard, I play hard," he told her.

A middle-aged woman spoke of her divorce, then said, "I looked everywhere for my anger... and... I couldn't find it."

"It's gone," her friend said, smiling sagely.

Joy looked up at me, her lovely eyes taking me in, oddly, as if for the first time, and she said with some surprise, "You have so much to *say*."

The pizza arrived and she continued to read. "*You have so much to say,*" she said again, flipping a page with astonishment on her face.

When she repeated it a third time, I thought it strange.

Hadn't I been yacking non-stop since we met? Why did she keep saying this, and looking at me? Across the terrain of a large vegetarian pizza, was the vapor that was me, shimmering, finally, into solid form before her eyes?

Joy asked, "Am I the waitress?"

I stared her for a long moment. I shook my head.

She finished, closed the manuscript, then gazed off among the patrons of Georgio's. She blinked slowly and said, "There is so much sadness in the world."

I felt light pass through me once again.

When the bill came I lay down my last two twenties.

I left an embarrassingly pathetic tip, pocketed the rest, and as we left, Joy took my elbow. Her touch was still incendiary, and my forearm warmed as if by a blissful infection.

Joy wanted to go dancing.

She also wanted to invite Marcia. As she dialed at a pay phone my enthusiasm for the evening faded. I felt my energy turn inward, gloom encroaching. Who cared if we went dancing? Who cared if Marcia came along?

It was already dark when we met her somewhere below Market at a place called The Stud. Colored lights flashed to the beat of unfamiliar music. Like Marcia, the patrons wore black; many had spiked, brightly colored hair, and some wore leather and chains. Nearly all were pierced. Joy pulled me among them onto the dance floor, and she was a wild, flamboyant dancer, at one moment, staring at me, spreading her fingers catwoman-style over her eyes. She threw out her arms and spun to painfully loud, pounding rhythms, while the more subdued dancers edged aside to give her space. I wondered how people leapt instantly into such baseless reveling.

Joy had no trouble making such a leap; nor did Marcia, who danced almost invisibly in the blinding light of Joy's beauty. I wasn't up for dancing. As I left the dance floor, two spike-haired, leather clad women moved in to dance with Joy. I retired to a bar stool, fell into a gloom, and watched. The women danced with Joy - one in front, one behind - and traced the outline of her slim and perfect shape with fluttering fingertips. And Joy's dance became a subdued, undulating seduction.

The dream had crashed. The coaching was finished, I had one story and no idea if it - or I - was any good. I had an impossible woman who I loved to a point of madness. And I just watched her, there on the dance floor, unleashing now what must have been the absolute full extent of her power. She moved slowly, like some lust-goddess, igniting libidos, inflaming passions around her. Enraptured dancers of all sexes - gay, lesbian, hetero, trans, cross-dressers, and bi, - were riveted, communicating in silent unison through the din: *oh yes, you are fabulously desirable.* Joy glanced over at me. A small greeting? To flirt? To show me who held the power on this dance floor? I didn't know, but there beside me, also watching Joy, was the ghost of Mr. Albert Camus. Placing a hand on my shoulder, he took a long, thoughtful drag on his cigarette. He exhaled and said: *It will be a long, lonely time ahead, mon ami; you'd best ready yourself.*

A short while later, Joy, Marcia and I exited The Stud and walked into a dark, cold, misty night. The attention on the dance floor seemed to affect Joy like a double martini. She seemed giddy. Her eyes were dreamy half-slits, her smile blissful, her walk, a near-drunken stumble. She alternately leaned into me, then Marcia.

And there, standing beneath a streetlight was a homeless man.

Mist formed a luminous halo around the globe above his head. He was short, filthy, unshaven, with the stare of the mentally unbalanced. Joy stood before him. She gazed at him angelically.

She reached out her arms in an unmistakable gesture of grace. A pious smile alighted upon her lips.

She closed her eyes slowly.

She opened them.

The homeless man held out a hand and said, "Can you help me?"

I watched Joy and thought: *Here go the contractions.*

She spoke slowly, devoutly. "I am sorry," she said, "But I do not have any money."

I shoved a hand into my pocket, pulled out Joy's change purse. Dear God in Heaven, *let it be a twenty.*

I opened the clasp. Inside was a single dollar bill.

Good enough.

I held it aloft.

"Joy!" I shouted. "Yes you do!"

Joy looked at me.

Marcia looked at me.

The homeless man looked at me.

There I stood, holding Joy's single dollar bill, high in the air.

She'd forgotten about this dollar.

Must have slipped her mind.

Of course, money was a nuisance. If you have it, get rid of it.

And I saw it: the tiniest wince on Joy's face.

She reached out, took the dollar - her very own - and handed it to the homeless man.

And in this single act, I saw truth, like Kilimanjaro when the giraffes finally clear the road. But giraffes can't block a mountain of that size. Certainly I'd seen it all along. I felt embarrassed; a revulsion for my own stupidity, and I couldn't stand it another minute.

"Joy," I said. "Please... just... go."

Joy looked at me for a moment.

Marcia tugged her arm.

Then she was gone and I never saw her again.

chapter

THIRTY-TWO

My car was dead.

Threatening for weeks, the starter now elicited a mocking click-click when I turned the key. I had twelve dollars and some change. Not enough for cab fare and it was late; too late for the Muni bus system.

I locked the car and wandered. Past Slim's, among the spike-haired, the ring-nosed. I walked among the homeless. Hookers were about but they ignored me. I'd only known Joy a few weeks but still, I couldn't stop the tears. Mr. Push-through-the-pain. *Make friends with it. Shake hands, get acquainted. It won't kill you.*

What a hypocrite.

A homeless man made his bed on cardboard and newspapers. He glanced up at me in silence.

On a corner was a phone booth. I felt horribly, absurdly alone and I wanted to talk to someone. But who? In my wallet was Tara's number, the only number I had. Besides Joy, Tara was the only other person I knew in this entire city.

I dialed.

In two rings, she answered.

"Tara."

"Tim?" she said in a groggy voice.

Jesus. She was asleep.

"I'm sorry. It's late-"

"Tim," she said. "Wow. Tim. I'm just-" She whispered something to someone. I heard the rustling of sheets, the whisper of another sleepy female voice, the creek of bedsprings.

"Hey, I'm sorry," I said. "I'll call another-"

"No. It's okay," she said. "You alright?"

"It's... um... Joy. We just-" My voice cracked. God, I hate when that happens. "It's nothing... really... I mean... I knew it was..." My voice betrayed me again.

"You broke up?"

"Mmm."

"Oh, God," she said.

A bit of actual empathy and I was over the edge, sobbing and embarrassed.

"Tara, really, I'm sorry," I said. "I mean, I hardly even know you. Listen, I'll call another-"

"It's *okay*," she said. "Really. Where are you?"

"I don't know," I said. "Some, stupid-"

"Just look around. Look at a sign."

I looked across the street. "There's something called the Dappled... pump, or something."

"*The Dappled Pony?* What in God's name are you doing down *there*?"

It was good to hear her voice.

"Jesus," I said. "She never even *noticed* me."

"She couldn't," Tara said. "Anyone could see that a mile-"

"Really?"

"Just let her go."

"Let her go. Let her go," I chuckled slightly, regaining some composure. "It'll be a long wait for another, according to Albert."

"*Camus?*"

"Three times in a hundred years."

"Tim," she said. "*Fuck Albert Camus.*"

I stood there, shocked, in silence.

"Do me a favor," she said. "Don't read anymore Camus."

"I only read one," I said, rubbing my eyes. "Didn't actually... finish it. Tara... I hate to ask. I mean... it's not like we're old friends or-"

"What?"

"My car's sort of-"

"You need a ride?"

"I hate to ask, listen, it's late-"

"Tim. Is there someplace you can just sit for a bit. I'll need a moment but I can be there in about twenty... thirty minutes."

"Tara, please, I don't want to put you to any-"

"Just shut up and wait for me," she said. "Is there a place-"

I looked around. "Well, that bar, I guess... the Dappled-"

"Okay," she said. "Wait there."

"Just a sec," I said. "Tara. Can I ask you something?"

"Ask away."

I glanced around, swallowed and said, "Why did you leave class early today?"

She was silent.

"I... um... just had to go."

"You had to go? Well, Tara, Jesus, I know it isn't the time... this is really stupid... but what did you think of my story?"

"Your *story*?"

"I mean, you left. In that room full of fools, you're the only one who's opinion-"

"Don't worry about what I think. Now's hardly the-"

"*Why?*" I was getting a bit hysterical. What a thing to ask at this moment, but everything else seemed gone, incinerated, up in smoke but one story and Tara's opinion was all I wanted.

"Tim. Can we please discuss this later?"

"Just tell me."

She was silent for a moment. A car passed.

"Tara, you there?"

"I'm here."

"You hated it."

"I didn't say that."

"You don't have to say it. I can tell by your-"

"Tim. You heard them. They all liked it. Birnbaum... everyone liked it."

"And then you walked out."

She was silent again.

After a moment, she said, "Tim?"

"What?"

"I think you were bullied into writing that story."

Bullied? I considered her words without comprehension.

"Tim?"

"What?"

"You asked."

"Tara. I'm... not sure I get you."

She took a breath. "You give us a victimy woman. All those chauvinistic men. A crew of multi-culturals so we can compliment your affirmative action. You're pandering to the lowest, easiest... *Tim?*"

"I'm here."

"I'm sorry," she said. "It's just my opinion."

"I know. I hear you. But... chauvinistic *men*?"

"Well, let's see. There's Frank. Mr. Hancock. Cindy's ex. Joey's father."

"Jesus." She read the damn story all right.

"You know, there are nice men in the world. Lots of them."

I was silent.

"But listen. I liked the little boy. The way he cared about his mother. And Cindy. The Mexicans... the little rebellion in the kitchen? That was cool."

I sat with this for a moment. Across the street, a sheet of newsprint lifted in a swirling breeze, then settled. "So... why did you leave?"

"Why did I leave? I don't know. I just had to get out of there. That or say something I'd regret. I don't like the way they treated you. I don't like the way it affected your writing. I'm a damn *dyke*, okay? It's like they expect every one of us to be just like - Jesus," she said. "You're depressed and I'm screaming at you."

"You're not screaming, Tara. In fact... it feels... really good talking to you."

"You sure?" she said.

"Absolutely."

After a brief moment, "Tim?"

"What?"

Tara hesitated, then spoke quietly. "Did my brother-in-law fuck your friend?"

Tara's simple query jettisoned a flood of cancer-causing chemicals into my stomach. "How did you know? Did he tell you-"

"Oh, God. Just the way they left the restaurant. I'm so sorry. That's how he is. I could kick myself for asking you to bring her. I'm so, so sor-"

"You were being polite," I said. I watched a light in an empty intersection change from red to green. "That was only part of it. Just a tiny, inconsequential... Tara?"

"What?"

"You sure this is okay?" I said. "I mean, you really don't mind picking me up?"

"Tim," she said. "I like talking to you, too, okay?" Then, after a moment, she added, "I... *like* you."

"You *like* me? I thought you said you were a damn-"

"I am," she said with a laugh. "But you're... a good guy."

"I'm not," I said.

"Shut up. You are too. Listen. Birnbaum was right... about your story. It was an improvement. A definite improvement. Just cross the street and wait for me."

A few days, despite Tara's assessment, I brought the story down to my father. I sat beside his hospital bed and personally read it aloud to him. It was early December and my father's time and health had nearly run its course. He looked weak, thin and gray. I sat in a chair beside his hospital bed. He clutched his liver-spotted hands before him on the white sheet, and as I read, he closed his eyes as if to rally all of his faculties in order to take in every word. And though he listened to the story, and I read it with as much energy as I could, I now wonder if he was not so much interested in the particulars of the tale, but rather, in what the story revealed as to whether his son had it: the stuff to make it in this world.

His response?

"The poor woman is *meshugana*."

But that was it, the best I could do in answer to his request for something beautiful. I could not say whether I had delivered on my end of this crazy bedside bargain. I could only say that I did my best to keep it. And I understood something else. My father's request, with it's unthinkable deadline, was not the frivolous notion of a dying old man, but rather, a clever, calculated effort to get his son serious and focused. Before I left, he patted my head, then pulled me against his chest - for the story or a final good-bye, I couldn't say.

Regardless, my father would die a few days later, and I would feel unmoored and adrift in ways I'd never imagined. Whether the story allowed him to go in some kind of peace is probably asking far too much of a few pages of scribbling. But I did sense, for the first time in my life, what it must be like for a father to truly love a son; to watch him grow up, do what he does, and to encourage him even when you think he's delusional and heedless your hard-earned, sound advice. I know this: I had a father's love, and for that, I was very lucky.

I felt a strong apprehension of this coming inevitability the instant I hung up the phone in that obscure area below Market. I crossed the street and entered the Dappled Pony to wait for Tara. The place had a seedy aspect I didn't mind and a few late-night, creepy-looking souls at the bar who ignored me. Given the hour, the establishment was oddly well attended. A picture of Joe Montana hung on one wall, and several neon beer signs completed the decor. I removed the last few bills from my wallet and counted them. I felt alone in this bar, in this strange, beautiful city, but happy that Tara was on her way. And I decided, just then, that tomorrow morning

I would phone my brother. I'd get the time and date of his barbecue. He had reached out, invited me. I'd hang out with his family, watch him wolf down red meat, and we'd chat - about women, about life. Once you got past the smug veneer, Robert was okay. And perhaps he'd see that his little brother wasn't a complete screw-up, but this was probably asking a bit much of an East Bay, afternoon barbecue. My thoughts then drifted to Joy, to the delicate contours of her abdomen; to a tiny mole just above a mystical forest where I once dallied in paradise - a fabulous moment of ecstasy I would undoubtedly return to, again and again in private, agonizing-

Just then, two elderly African American women entered the bar. They seemed lost and tired. Perhaps on vacation. I wondered how they happened to wander into this god-forsaken area, and into this bar. They sat at a table near me and removed their woolen coats. One wore a flowered dress; blessed relief from the drab, monochromatic idiocy that filled these barstools, the streets beyond, and probably, closets for miles.

Both women appeared to be in their sixties, with faces of beautiful, weathered brown skin. Two old friends, I guessed, on a wild, madcap adventure in The City. They eyed me warily, probably having been apprised of the number of weirdoes about. They sat nervously, as any out-of-towner would, upon entering a place like the Dappled Pony.

And I wanted to talk to them, to anyone.

"I like your dress," I said to the taller woman.

She eyed me suspiciously. "You like mah dress?"

I nodded.

"See girl!" the shorter woman said, suddenly animated. "I told you it don't make you look pregnant." She turned to me. "She step out the hotel shower this morning, sits on the bed and says, 'Ah'm wearin mah sun dress today. An if anyone says Ah look pregnant they can kiss mah-' *Excuse me.*" She turned to her friend. "An right there, you got you a nice compliment!" She laughed and looked at me once again. "Believe that? Sixty-five and worried about lookin pregnant."

Both women laughed, then stared at me.

Feeling a rush of success, I said. "You're shoes are nice, too."

The taller woman gasped. "*Mah sparkle shoes?*"

I nodded.

"Dat too!" Her friend whooped and slapped the table. "She said, 'Anyone make fun a mah sparkle shoes, Ah'm gonna pop 'em!' Didn't you say you gone pop em?"

"Ah done said it."

After a moment, I asked, "Did anyone, actually... *make* fun of them?"

Both women shook their heads.

No one had made fun of her sparkle shoes. But something had necessitated the swearing of an oath over every article of clothing she placed upon her body. I wondered if she dressed this way each morning.

I looked at them for a moment and said, "May I buy you beautiful ladies a drink?"

"No you may not!" the flowered dress lady said in a display of mock formality. "Das cause we gonna buy *you* one! Will you be kind enough to join us?"

I said I'd be honored and moved to their table. The woman with the flowered dress was LaWanda. Her more talkative friend was Rose. They were from Fresno, on a three-day holiday. "We was just comin from church and got all turned around," LaWanda said. "The rent-a-car's somewhere up one-a these streets. Thought we'd stop in here and rest a minute. Red wine okay? Or maybe you feel like coffee or something?"

"Coffee?" I said.

"They sure do love it around here."

"Coffee?" I considered this: did I want coffee? "You know... I'm really... not all that crazy..." I drummed my fingers on the table. Then, for some reason I blurted, "I hate coffee!" Why had this just dawned on me? I sat, perplexed at this sudden revelation, but the ladies watched me, their eyebrows raised and expectant. I'd known these gentle, spirited women barely a minute but trusted them completely. With their tacit encouragement a floodgate seemed to crack and breach: "I hate coffee," I said, "and dream catchers, and bores who think they're shocking, and fools looking to be offended every minute of their lives. And I like the color blue, and I'm Jewish, by God, and proud of it, unhip as that may-"

I stopped. Had I raised my voice? I wondered if I sounded like some rambling lunatic, but both women grinned openly, a tiny fire sparked behind their wide-open eyes.

Two men turned in their barstools. One was Asian, the other, a portly, good-natured looking Caucasian. Both stared. I thought, *an if anyone don't like it* - but they smiled. The Asian hoisted his beer mug. I smiled back, at the men, and at how strange and wonderful it felt to say these simple things. I looked Rose and LaWanda in the eye. "And I will *not... be... bullied*."

Rose filled her lungs and threw a tiny fist in the air. "An Ah'm a *black African American*!"

"*I'm Italian!*" came a shout from somewhere along the bar.

When the red wine arrived, Rose said, "Lots in common, Blacks and Jews. Ah been readin."

"Scattered and oppressed," I said, filling the glasses.

"Hallelujah!"

"Loud dinner tables and loud weddings," I said.

"Ain't that true!" Rose said. The women laughed and bumped shoulders - the unconscious gesture of a deep, enduring friendship.

"And lactose intolerance," I said.

"What's that?"

"Milk gives us gas."

"Jews get that, too?"

"Everyone I know," I said.

"Damn!" Rose said.

"And this is how we toast."

"Listen up, LaWanda," Rose said, "We gonna learn something."

Rose and LaWanda watched me carefully.

"We say, *L'chaim*. It means, *to life*."

"La haim," LaWanda said. "I like that."

"But you gotta say it right. Listen. L' *chchchaim*. " I said. "Like you're about to spit."

Rose let out a whoop. “Say it, LaWanda! Say it like you be draggin dat stuff up from yo toes!”

“L’*chchchchaim!* LaWanda said, sending both women into a fit of giggles.

And perhaps LaWanda nailed it; the gritty, onomatopoetic truth of this ancient and beautiful word. It was a toast to life in all of its odd, scruffy wonder, and frankly, I wouldn’t trade the last few weeks of mine for anything. Well, soon Tara would arrive. I would pour her a glass of red wine, and watch Rose and LaWanda speculate secretly and erroneously upon our relationship. Tara, I knew, would offer to help them find their car. Then, with Chekhovian sadness, I would step out of this bar and into the mystery of the next thirty-three point three years of my life.

I looked at LaWanda, I looked at Rose, two lovely women containing their laughter, drying their tears, and reaching now for appropriate solemnity.

“L’chaim,” I said.

“L’chaim,” they repeated a beat behind me.

And we raised our glasses.

END